RAVE REVIEWS FOR PENELOPE NERI!

"Penelope Neri always brings fascinating characters and a lively story to readers. You'll find all that and a colorful backdrop, sensuality and quite a bit of interesting historical detail in this memorable, fast-paced tale."

—*Romantic Times* on *Keeper of My Heart*

"This entertaining, sensual story . . . [will] satisfy readers."

—*Romantic Times* on *Stolen*

"Ms. Neri's romance with Gothic overtones is fast-paced and sprinkled with wonderful characters . . . a really good read."

—*Romantic Times* on *Scandals*

"Neri is a genius at creating characters that readers will love, and for spinning a magical tale that will leave readers longing for more."

—*Writers Write* on *Scandals*

"Penelope Neri proves again that she is a splendid writer of historical romances."

—Phoebe Conn on *Enchanted Bride*

ANYTHING FOR LOVE

Her lips parted eagerly for their first kiss. Just the touch of his hands upon her made her shiver with pleasure.

"Oh, Graham," she whispered when he took his mouth from hers.

There was a rosy blush on her features; a stunned expression in her shining gray eyes. A look that Graham—no stranger to women—recognized as desire. "Hold me. Hold me fast! Never—ever—let me go. . . ."

He slipped his arms about her, resting his chin on the crown of her head. "Skyla. My love. My heart," he whispered. "It willna be easy, ye know that. They'll no' give us their blessing so readily. We must fight them."

"Nothing worth having comes easily, McKenzie. You know that."

"Aye," he agreed. "But whatever it takes, I'll do it, if it means ye'll be my bride. I'd give my right arm for ye, love. Anything—!"

"Keep your arm McKenzie," she said huskily. "I'll settle for your heart."

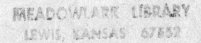

HIGHLAND LOVESONG

PENELOPE NERI

LEISURE BOOKS NEW YORK CITY

A LEISURE BOOK®

June 2000

Published by

Dorchester Publishing Co., Inc.
276 Fifth Avenue
New York, NY 10001

ISBN 0-8439-4724-1

For
Wilda Gray,
Special lady, special friend,
With love

One

The stag stepped hesitantly into the wooded glen, its nostrils flared to catch the scents on the summer wind.

Suddenly, it halted, its lofty rack of antlers invisible against the tracery of branches, its dark red coat blending with the dappling shadows.

A thrill ran through Graham MacKenzie, standing as still as the stag in a thicket of leafy saplings.

Penelope Neri

A buck in its prime meant fresh venison for Glenrowan's spit, he thought, drawing an arrow from the quiver at his back. The Mac-Kenzie—his laird and father—would be proud of such a kill.

Dropping soundlessly to one knee, Graham nocked his arrow. Sighting down the feathered shaft as Alistair had taught him, he drew back the bowstring.

Pale green spring leaves and mossy tree trunks framed the red stag's head, neck, and powerful chest. If true, his aim would sink the arrowhead just above the deer's shoulder and strike deep into its heart. Death would be quick and merciful for the proud creature.

"Fortune, guide my arrow," Graham prayed silently.

He was about to let fly when Skyla MacLeod stepped in front of him.

Gray eyes brimming with tears, she pressed her small palm so firmly against the point of his arrowhead, a trickle of blood welled instantly on her hand.

"Dinna kill him, Graham. I beg ye. Spare the bonny stag!" she pleaded.

"Whist, Skyla. Step aside, will ye no'? I almost killed ye, ye daft wee besom!" Graham flared.

Deep blue eyes blazed as he scowled down at the girl.

12

Did she know how close she'd come to being run through by his arrow? He thought not. Her fears were all for the stag, not for herself. He shook his dark head. Though only six years her senior, he felt a lifetime older.

"Why did ye stop me, Skyla?" he asked gently. "My clansmen are many. We have need of fresh meat, lassie, even if the MacLeods do not."

"Look!" she implored him by way of answer.

Following her pointing finger, Graham saw the doe and the brace of spotted fawns that trotted from the bushes in the stag's wake.

The fawns' little tails whisked about, showing the white of their scutts as, on spindly stilt legs, they frolicked after their dam, who lowered her dainty head to drink from the rushing burn.

Relief that he had not released the arrow flooded through him, though he made sure the girl did not see it.

At sixteen, Graham was a fine hunter with a keen eye, and justly proud that he could put game on his clan's spit like the older men. Yet he had no desire to rob any family of its father—not even a family of deer. The woods of the great glen abounded with game. He'd find meat for Glenrowan's spits elsewhere.

"Och. All right," he agreed gruffly, pretending to be vexed. Slinging the bow over his shoulder, he returned the feathered shafts to his quiver. "I'll not shoot it this time."

"Oh, thank ye, Graham." Skyla smiled up at him through her tears. "For a MacKenzie, you're no' so bad."

Her smile, he noticed, was like the sun shining through a rain shower.

Looking down into her tear-streaked, grubby face, Graham felt his heart skip a beat. His mouth was as dry as feathers.

She would be bonny when she came to womanhood, with long curly hair the color of dark fire, and eyes gray as the Highland mists that drifted over the moors with the gloaming. Aye, and the way she eyed him was that of a maid far older than her years!

He swallowed. The wee minx somehow made him feel important—brave as the MacKenzie himself!

" 'Tis welcome you are, Skyla MacLeod," he murmured huskily. "But there's a price ye must pay for the stag's life."

"Oh?" Her smile of joy became an uncertain, wary frown. "And what price is that?" she demanded, wrinkling her forehead.

"Ye must join your blood wi' mine. Swear a blood oath that we'll always be friends."

She did not hesitate by so much as a heartbeat.

"All right. I'll do it. But not for the stag. For *me*. Because *I* want to," she replied pertly. Tossing long auburn plaits with chewed ends over bony shoulders, she thrust out her wrist.

14

Although she was but ten or so winters, she had a queenly air about her, Graham noted, hiding a grin. But then, it came as no surprise that she had.

Skyla's clan—the Clan MacLeod—were Lords of the Isle of Skye. Her people claimed their descent from Conn of the Hundred Battles and, like kings, ruled their sea-girt kingdom from Dunvegan, the clan's ancestral keep.

Aye, and if the MacLeod menfolk were the lords of Skye, then surely Skyla—the MacLeod's eldest daughter and the apple of his eye—was its lady!

He grinned. If he'd ever doubted MacLeod blood ran in her veins, he did not now, not with her chin jutting so obstinately, and her head tilted so regally.

"As ye will, my lady," he murmured, bending a leg and making her a gallant bow just as his friend Will—who had been to court in Italy and met the Holy Father himself—had taught him.

Drawing a dirk with the MacKenzie's badge—a stag's head—carved into the hilt, he touched the sharp point to his palm.

When blood welled, he took Skyla's hand and pressed their palms together, binding a leather cord about both hands to keep them joined. "Now, brat. Repeat after me: *'Now joined by blood are we—'*"

15

" 'Now joined by blood are we....' " she echoed dutifully.

"—so joined forevermore shall be!' "

He had invented the oath himself on the spur of the moment, yet liked the way it sounded. His tutor, Father Andrew, would have approved, too. The words had a solemn, weighty ring, and would have been as binding as marriage vows or a holy oath, had they been sworn before a priest.

More official, perhaps, than the oaths of Edward Longshanks, God rot him, whose armies now occupied Scotland's noblest castles.

Clarty parasites! Filthy Sassenach leeches! Like fat yellow ticks, over the years Longshanks and his constables had gorged themselves on the lifeblood of the Highlands, drop by precious drop. They'd also drained Scotland of her considerable wealth and grown sleek and fat-bellied on Scottish misery.

The blood of more of Scotland's sons would water the Highlands before Scotland became free. Aye, and she would be free someday—or so his friend, Will Wallace, swore. *"Pro Libertate!"* was the Wallaces' family motto, after all. "For Freedom!"

"... *so joined forevermore shall be,*" Skyla repeated a second time, far more loudly. She was scowling up at him, her gray eyes no longer gentle or misty, but dark as fog in her impatience.

"Hmm? Och, aye! I heard ye the first time, lassie. Dinna glower at me, aye? *In nomine patris, et filii, et spiritus sancti, Amen,*" Graham finished crossing himself. Perhaps he should have made the vow in Latin, too? Solemn oaths called for a solemn tongue, to his way of thinking. Besides, he was proud of his education, and eager to show off his knowledge.

"Amen," Skyla echoed dutifully. She gazed up at Graham with innocent trust and—or so he fancied—no little adoration.

As their eyes met, he felt a peculiar tingling sensation in his chest. An awareness and warmth that swelled and filled his heart to bursting.

Could it be love? he wondered, confused. Was it possible to fall in love so quickly? If so, it was like being taken by the spring fever. He felt light-headed, and weak in the knees. Even, he admitted reluctantly, a mite daft in the head!

"Now we—er—now we must seal the oath wi' a wee kiss," he added impulsively. The blood pounded in his ears as he waited for Skyla to comply.

He could almost taste her soft lips on his. Could well imagine how her small hands would feel, pressed shyly to his still-hairless chest. His nostrils flared. The scent of her was wild and sweet as heather.

"*What?*" she exploded, gray eyes smoldering. "Ye took my blood, and that I didna mind, but *kiss* ye, ye great lummox? That *I will not!* Devil take ye, MacKenzie! What do ye think I am, ye clarty dog?"

Her cheeks pink, she drew back her small fist and punched him squarely on the nose with enough force to draw a great spurt of blood. Then, gray eyes blazing, she turned and ran from him, dark auburn plaits flying as she twisted in and out of the trees.

In seconds, she had vanished, headed back to the MacLeods' camp at the head of the Great Glen, no doubt.

"Damn and blast ye, Skyla, ye bluidy shrew!" Graham cursed under his breath as he nursed his bleeding nose.

He was furious at himself for teasing her so. He should have expected as much from a fey wee lassie who'd been raised on Skye, isolated from all but her kinsmen. Still, he'd not intended to frighten her off—nor rile her to the point of punching his nose.

"I'll kiss ye, Graham MacKenzie. I'm no' afraid," piped a voice at his back.

Whirling in surprise, Graham saw Fionna MacRae standing in a thicket of white-flowering hawthorn behind him.

She was his own age, sixteen, and a daughter of the MacRae bodyguard clan that had attached its numbers to the MacKenzie clan long before Graham was born.

Graham scowled at her.

Although they were practically kin, and although Fionna was bonny enough, with her tumbling dark hair and dark eyes, he couldn't stomach the sly wench.

She was forever following him about, snooping, spying on him, just as she was spying today. She also had the unsettling habit of showing up where he least wanted or expected her, stepping silently, stealthily, eager as an unwanted pup to catch his eye or win a kind word

And in the past, when she did not get her way, she'd proven to be a vicious, lying bitch! More than once, he'd felt the weight of the MacKenzie's belt, thanks to Fionna MacRae's tittle-tattling to his father, the laird.

"Aye, I warrant ye would, Fiona—for me, or any other man. But I didna ask ye, did I?" he shot back, his jaw jutting stubbornly as he glared at her.

Still scowling, he stomped past Fionna MacRae, not caring that her face crumpled with hurt, or that her dark eyes had filled with tears.

"I'll tell the MacKenzie ye wanted t'kiss a MacLeod!" Fionna threatened, throwing the

19

words after him. "I shall, I swear it! Someday, you'll be sorry ye scorned me, Graham MacKenzie! Aye, that ye will!"

"Go ahead. Tell him what ye will, ye bluidy tattletale. I care not!" he crowed.

The way he'd felt when Skyla thanked him was worth any number of wallopings from Father, by God. Aye, and worth a bloody nose, too, he thought, wiping the blood on his sleeve.

He was whistling jauntily as he strode back to camp.

It was summer, the Year of Our Lord 1287. He was sixteen, in love for the very first time, and life was sweet. . . .

Two

He'd been right, Graham remembered, grinning as his memories of that August day in the Great Glen flooded back.

Fionna *had* run to his father after he'd spurned her kisses. And sure enough, she'd told the Mackenzie all about his meeting with Skyla MacLeod, too!

After the lecture and walloping that had followed as surely as day followed night, he'd run down to the burn and lowered his throbbing posterior into its icy flow.

But, although hurting, he'd been fiercely proud that he'd admitted nothing that day, despite the sting of the laird's broad belt across his backside.

Ten years had flown since then. He was a grown man now. A man who, since the murder of his father a year ago, had become laird of the MacKenzies of Glenrowan in his own right.

It was a grown man who shaded his eyes against the sunlight as he stood among the shaggy, long-horned cattle that were scattered across the hillside of Lochalsh.

A grown man, not a green boy, who gazed seaward, waiting for the woman he loved.

Waiting for Skyla . . .

The isle for which his love had been named rose from the silvery sea veiled in mist, and crowned by the jagged black Cuillins.

From the highest point soared Dunvegan, the Clan MacLeod's ancestral keep, a forbidding fortress of gray stone built upon a craggy mount of solid rock. The crenellated towers were etched in daunting charcoal against a sky of robin's-egg blue, while seawater lapped at the foundations.

Gulls nested on the rocky mount on which the fortress stood, and seals sunned themselves in the warm sunlight. The smaller cows fiercely guarded their round-eyed babies from the rutting bulls, whose bellows drowned out the screams of the gulls.

"Halloo, the shore!"

Graham glanced up. While he had stood there, wool-gathering, Skyla had rowed herself across the Strait of Sleat from Skye to Lochalsh. Her dory glided out of the golden mist and hazy sunlight like something from a dream.

She waved gaily as she shipped her oars.

Sweet lord. She had grown to beauty, and no mistake!

His heart lifted at the sight of her, dressed in a forest-green kirtle, an arisaid of fringed plain pinned at her right shoulder by a silver brooch that was the badge of the MacLeods.

She wore her dark red hair flowing loose about her shoulders, as befitted an unmarried maid. Its long, fiery tresses twisted like flames on the breeze as the boat cleaved the water below him.

As ever, there was a welcoming smile on Skyla's sweet lips—one he knew was for him alone—as she scrambled into the prow and waved.

He waved back just as vigorously, then ran down the hillside to meet her, leaping tussocks and rocks, splashing through the shallows to grab the mooring line she tossed him, and loop it about a handy rock.

He gave no thought to the seawater lapping at the hem of the faded plain he wore belted about his waist, nor to the heavy leather boots upon his feet that were now soaked.

His thoughts were all for Skyla as he swung her up, into his arms, and carried her ashore like an armful of feathers.

"So, lassie. You came, aye?" he said unnecessarily when she stood, breathless, upon the shingle before him.

She brushed a strand of windblown red hair from her eyes and cocked her head to one side.

"Aye," she agreed, fondly amused. Her gray eyes sparkled as they searched his rugged, handsome face. "That I did."

He grinned. "And I'm right glad of it, Mistress MacLeod," he added, smiling broadly.

"Oh, are ye, now? And why would that be, my laird MacKenzie?" she asked with teasing courtesy.

Carefully avoiding her eyes, he flung the smooth, round pebble he'd picked up seaward. He watched it skim the tops of several waves in the narrow channel before he answered. "Och, it's hard t'say."

"Och, is it, now? Then happen I shan't come again till ye've found the words to explain yoursel'," she teased, pretending to turn back to the boat.

"Dinna say that," he ordered harshly, his dark head snapping around. He took her by the upper arms and shook her gently. "Dinna tempt the Fates, not even in jest, lassie!"

The teasing sparkle in her eyes softened.

She'd forgotten how superstitious he had grown since his father's death. It would pass, she was certain, once his grief had eased. But meanwhile, the wounds were raw, and still sensitive to the slightest touch.

Gently touching his forearm, she murmured, "Forgive me, Gray. I didna mean it, love. Ye know I'll always come to ye, so long as I draw breath."

"Come what may?"

"Aye," she promised softly. "Come what may. Now. Did ye bring the horses?"

He shook his head, shamefaced by his outburst now. "Nooo. I thought we'd walk for a wee bit, instead."

He'd left his own mount at a crofter's hut, just over the hill, while his kinsmen awaited him in the village of Lochalsh— his cousin and best friend, Alistair, and his younger brothers, Jamie and Ian among them. These were not times when a Scot dared ride abroad alone, unless he had little care for his life.

The English constables who now occupied the keeps and castles that had once belonged to Scottish lairds were always eager to pick a fight. A man riding alone was easy prey, as his own father had discovered, to his peril . . .

Besides, what he wanted to ask Skyla could not be asked from astride a horse. It was better asked upon one knee.

25

"A walk, is it? Aye. I'd like that," she agreed softly.

He offered her his arm. Smiling, she took it.

They set off along the shingled sands, the fringed ends of her arisaid flapping around them.

Seagulls wheeled and screamed overhead, their white wings carving bright arcs across the pale blue sky. At times, Graham and Skyla had to clamber over rugged outcroppings of black rock that jutted into their path, or evade the waves that broke in bursts of salty spray against them, before surging up the sandy shore.

The blustery breeze was laden with the scents of brine and kelp. And despite the season, it had a chill edge that whipped ruddy color into Graham's cheeks, and painted roses in Skyla's.

Beyond the narrow beach, the hills of Lochalsh collided, their slopes cloaked in golden broom, emerald turf, and dark green gorse.

For now, summer ruled as king, and the Highlands dreamed under hazy robes of purple heather. But in just weeks, the leaves would turn russet, gold, scarlet, and brown. Then Jack Frost would etch each leaf and blade with silver, and winter would be queen, mantling the glens in her furs of snow, and rendering them impassable.

"Summer's almost gone," Skyla observed sadly, as if reading his thoughts.

Her wistful tone mourned the swift passing of the season, and he knew why. It would be difficult—perhaps impossible—for them to meet in autumn and winter. Far less easy to slip out from under the watchful eyes of their respective families. Absences were noticed when bitter weather forced everyone inside, to congregate about the roaring hearths in the great halls.

When they had first met again by accident last summer, after ten years without ever setting eyes upon each other, Skyla had enlisted the help of the MacLeod's gillie, Auld Hamish, to keep her trysts with him, Graham recalled.

Hamish had doted upon the MacLeod's eldest daughter, cosseting her like any grandfather. The old fellow had been easily persuaded to keep their meetings a secret.

Once a week—sometimes more often when the weather was fine and warm, like today—Hamish rowed the Lady Skyla from the isle to Lochalsh to meet with the Mackenzie, on the pretext that she wanted to gather fresh herbs, berries, and roots from Lochalsh for her Granny Elspeth's healing simples or wool dyes.

Penelope Neri

Hamish had tactfully mended nets or whittled away at some piece of wood or other while the sweethearts talked, walked, or rode.

The faithful gillie waited until the sun dipped low in the sky and stained the sea gold, before returning Skyla to Dunvegan and the watchful eye of her mother, the Lady Shona.

Auld Hamish had continued to aid and abet their meetings all last summer until Skyla had learned how to navigate the strong rip currents and could row to and from the isle herself.

"The wind has teeth to it today, does it not?" she observed, breaking into his thoughts.

"Aye. Summer's waning." He flashed her a quick glance, then took her arm, brusquely turning her to face him. "Skyla. There's something I must ask ye. It canna bear waiting any longer."

"I thought as much. Ye have a look about ye. Well? What is it? Ask it quickly and be done, Gray. Your face! It's so verra stern, it scares me!" She searched his eyes, her own now dark with worry.

"My uncles are after me t'marry, Skyla. But as well ye know—or should, by now—there's no maid I'll wed but yoursel'. So, I'm asking."

He dropped down onto one knee and knelt at her feet on the sand. Taking her right hand in his, he drew it to his lips and kissed it tenderly. "I love ye with all my heart and body, Skyla

MacLeod. Och, wi' my very soul! Will ye wed me, sweetheart? Shall ye be my bonny bride?"

His eyes—the vivid blue of harebells—shone with love in his handsome, wind-browned face.

Looking down at him, Skyla felt her heart swell. Her throat ached. Tears stung behind her eyes. In answer, she slipped both hands in his, joy filling her when his large fingers curled about her own and squeezed.

"Aye, MacKenzie. I'd be honored," she whispered, raising him to stand before her. Her lilting voice was husky as she smiled up at him. "I'll be your bride, and no other mon's."

He released the breath he'd been holding, wanting to whoop and leap about like a—a lunatic with joy—and relief.

"Och, lassie. Och, ma sonsy lass," he murmured. "Ye've made me a verra happy man." Of a sudden, he pulled her close.

He tilted her head back, letting silken strands of dark red hair spill like fiery water through his fingers.

Her lips parted eagerly for their first kiss. Just the touch of his hands upon her made her shiver with pleasure.

"Oh, Graham," she whispered when he took his mouth from hers.

There was a rosy blush on her features; a stunned expression in her shining gray eyes. A look that Graham—no stranger to women—

recognized as desire. "Hold, me. Hold me fast! Never—ever—let me go. . . ."

He slipped his arms about her, resting his chin on the crown of her head. "Skyla. My love. My heart," he whispered. "It willna be easy, ye know that. They'll no' give us their blessing so readily. We must fight them."

"Nothing worth having comes easily, MacKenzie. You know that."

"Aye," he agreed. "But whatever it takes, I'll do it, if it means ye'll be my bride. I'd give my right arm for ye, love. Anything—!"

"Keep your arm, MacKenzie," she said huskily. "I'll settle for your heart."

He laughed. "Aye, and ye might get it, too—served up on the point o' your father's dirk!"

She poked him in the ribs. "You! Have your uncles named a bride for ye, then?"

He shook his dark head, still stern despite her teasing tone. "Not yet, no. But I warrant they'll be naming names before long, if I don't. They're wanting an heir for Glenrowan, aye?" His expression was gloomy now. "I canna wait any longer, Skyla! I shall tell them tonight. That 'tis you I'll wed, or no lass."

"So ye say. But I'm thinking 'twill be the MacRae lass they've chosen for ye. Fionna—your own true love," she teased, needling him in an effort to lift up his dour mood. She was not disappointed by his reaction.

He scowled blackly. *"Fionna?* The devil ye say! Bite your tongue, lassie! I'll have none of her!" He spat in disgust. "The wee whore was lifting her skirts for the English constable. A Scottish lass, sleeping with the enemy! When her father learned of it, he whipped her and sent her forth from Glenrowan, forbidding her to return. Nay, lass. 'Tis you I'll take for my bride, sweet Skyla—and well you know it!"

Laughing, they strolled along the shingled beach, arm in arm. Skyla's head rested upon Graham's shoulder. Her fingers were linked through his.

Despite all the times they'd met since last summer, this was the first time either had confessed what lay in their hearts. It was also the very first time they'd touched, except by accident, let alone embraced or kissed.

Now that they had, they knew. Nothing had ever felt so *right*.

The knowledge that Graham loved her as deeply as she loved him made the wondrous moment doubly sweet.

"Look," Graham murmured, nodding at some rocks that rose from the pale sands ahead of them.

Caught between the black outcroppings were branches of bleached driftwood, like deer antlers, along with other flotsam and jetsam that had washed ashore.

"The sea has given up her treasures," he said.

"What's that?" Skyla asked curiously, crouching down as Graham raked through kelp and shells with a stick of driftwood. "Why, 'tis a unicorn's horn!" she exclaimed, gray eyes shining in wonder.

"No unicorn, lass. This horn once belonged to a narwhal."

The long, twisted horn lay amidst a tangle of seaweed and shells, its point caught in a scrap of torn fishing net.

Crouching down, Graham pulled it free, brushed the sand off it, and handed it to Skyla.

"Here. Take it. 'Tis said the narwhal's horn has magical powers. 'Twill bring ye good fortune, my lady Skyla," he teased, brushing a tendril of auburn hair from her cheek.

"It already has," she said solemnly, yet with a naughty twinkle in her eyes. "I have you, Mac-Kenzie. And I have your heart, too, do I no'?"

Her lips were still faintly swollen from his kisses, as red and ripe as cherries. Her face glowed, as if lit by a rosy candle from within. She had never looked more lovely, Graham thought, his heart full of love.

"Aye," he breathed. "And ye'll have it forever, come what may." Gently, he caressed her cheek with his knuckles, then—unable to stop himself—took her in his arms again and kissed her, this time with even greater ardor.

Jesu! The feel of her small, round breasts flattened against her chest, her auburn head cradled by his hand, her soft lips parting beneath his, surrendering their honeyed secrets, was more than he could bear—!

Desire had kindled a burning hunger within him—a lusty need he could not slake, lest he dishonor her. And that he'd never do, he swore. He loved her too much to lie with her before the handfasting. First, his ring must be on her finger and their marriage vows exchanged. . . .

"The light's fading," Skyla murmured later, peering up over the rocky shelf they were using for a windbreak. "And the wind's changed. I'd best be getting home, before I'm missed."

Despite what she said, she made no move to escape Graham's embrace. Rather, she sighed and snuggled deeper into the crook of his arm, wanting—as did he—to prolong the moment, to postpone the inevitable storm that lay on their horizon.

The prospect of confronting her father, the MacLeod, was not one she relished. Questions would be asked. Father would be furious. He would demand to know exactly how and when she had become so well acquainted with a MacKenzie. And when she told him, all her small—and not so small—deceptions would be exposed. They would never trust her again.

Her family loved her, she knew that. But

their love would not silence their anger, nor their fierce objections to the man her heart had chosen ten years past, in a leafy glen.

The MacLeods of Skye and the MacKenzies of Glenrowan had been at odds for as long as Skyla's grandmother and Elspeth's grandmother could recall. No one could say exactly what the old quarrel had been about, except that it had ended in bloodshed on both sides.

She could only pray that, God willing, her parents' love for her would persuade them to cast old enmities aside, and give their blessing on her marriage to a hated MacKenzie. . . .

Taking her slender hand in his, Graham turned it over and kissed the tiny white scar in the well of her palm. It was the one she'd made herself all those years ago, by pressing her hand against his arrow to keep him from shooting the stag.

Finding the matching scar upon his own hand, he pressed the two together and said softly, " *'So joined forevermore shall be!'* Aye, my sweeting? First as friends . . . then as man and wife . . . then as lovers. . . ."

"Aye," she whispered fervently, blushing. Her lower lip trembled. But, though her eyes brimmed with tears, she did not cry.

Slowly, they made the walk back along the beach to where she'd left the dory. They walked arm in arm, silently, each contemplating the lonely hours that lay ahead. Each dreading the storm of contention that would break when their respective families learned of their intentions.

"When will ye come? You know, to ask my father for my hand?" Skyla asked.

He thought for a moment. "Next Sabbath. Look for me in the morning, after matins, aye? God willing, your father willna kill me on the Lord's own day!"

"I hope not. But there's still my Uncle Douglas MacLeod to watch out for. He's no' half as religious as Father, mind. . . ."

Her twinkling eyes belied her words. Laughing, she gently cupped his scowling face in her cool hand. It was no soft hand, Gray noted absently, but one that was strong and capable, firm with hard work.

"Lucky for you, I happen to know my uncle will be away that day. He left last night for Kyle of Lochalsh. Och, I'll miss ye sorely until then, my love," she said shyly. "I pray you, stand firm in the certainty that our love shall conquer all."

Scrambling into the small boat, she stowed the narwhal's tusk carefully in the bottom and took up the oars.

Graham freed the mooring line from about the rock.

Shoving the small craft out into deeper water, he held onto the dory's side and waded after it, murmuring huskily, "I shall miss you, too, my sweet and only love."

They touched lips in a farewell kiss; then with a wave, Skyla began to row. Slowly, surely, steadily, her small, fragile craft pulled away from the shore. It was soon swallowed up by the glittery golden haze of the setting sun.

"Farewell, my heart," he murmured softly, lifting his hand in salute. "Farewell, my bride."

He stood there, staring out at the Isle of Skye, until the fiery red sun dropped over the rim of the world, and the amethyst of the gloaming became true dark.

Only when moonlight silvered the lapping waves did he trudge back up the Lochalsh hills, through the herd of shaggy, lowing cattle, to the crofter's hut where he'd left his horse and companions.

The Sabbath seemed a lifetime away, he thought as he went. Aye, and as distant as the evening star . . .

She lay on her belly in the heather, watching as he gazed after the small boat.

He was gazing after *her*. . . .

His precious Lady Skyla MacLeod.

And Fionna did not need the Sight to guess what he was thinking. A blind woman could tell he loved her. Her—a *MacLeod*. A sworn enemy of his clan!

36

Highland Lovesong

Seeing them together—watching him hold her, kiss her, knowing he loved her—was bitter as gall. The taste was as sour as bile in her throat.

She felt nothing but hatred for him now. That, and a burning desire to hurt him as deeply and as utterly as he had hurt her.

For far worse than the knowledge that he had hurt her was the certainty that he had done so without *ever knowing*, because to him, she didn't exist. Or if, by some miracle, he remembered her at all, it was as "another of the MacRae lassies." A maid his own age who, imagining herself in love with the lanky lad he'd been, had become his faithful shadow years ago.

Seeing him and the MacLeod bitch together last summer had curdled the last drops of her love for Graham. Soured it as surely as vinegar sours milk until all that remained was this need for revenge that gnawed at her innards.

The MacKenzie must pay for scorning her! For not even knowing she existed! Aye, she thought as she slithered backwards over the brow of the hill. He *would* pay!

Brushing sprigs of heather from her skirts, she sped down the hillside to the village of Lochalsh.

The wind dried the tears on her cheeks as she went.

Three

"I know you!" the old woman hissed.

Skyla sighed. "Of course you know me, Granny. I'm Skyla, your granddaughter. Don't ye remember?" Skyla arched her aching back. Flexed fingers grown stiff from holding her spindle.

"Granddaughter? Dinna try t'confuse me, lassie. I know who you are! You're my wee Moira," Elspeth MacLeod declared, her own murky gray eyes now bright with triumph as she patted Skyla's cheek.

"Nay, Gran. I'm *Shona's* daughter. Your John's first child. He named me Skyla, remember?"

The old woman snorted, shoulders bristling. "Ye think I've forgotten my own flesh and blood? Whist! Twelve bairns I birthed, and all but one survived its infancy!" she said proudly. Her knobbly fingers stilled on the lamb's wool in her lap. "You, Moira, were my first lass. Aye, and what a bonny lamb ye were, too! Those in Lochalsh say they heard your father crowing like a cock from the top o' the Cuillins the morning ye were born. '*Tis a lassie for the MacLeod,*' he was after roaring."

"That's a fine tale, Granny," Skyla murmured, smiling now, and resigned to the fact that her father's mother was having one of her bad days, and had confused her with her aunt. "Tell me how ye met my grand—my father?"

Granny Elspeth MacLeod chuckled. "Why, he was a braw, handsome lad, that one. Aye, and he had himself an eye for the lassies, too! My father said if I so much as glanced his way, he'd wallop my arse till I couldna sit for a week! But then he came to the Gathering, and . . . well, I glanced his way, all right! And *he* glanced my way, too—! Hee! Hee!" The old woman chuckled, slapping her bony shanks. "Och, what a handsome devil he was, my Lachlann!" Her eyes took on a crafty gleam. "Nearly as bonny as *your* sweetheart . . ."

"*My* sweetheart?" Seated at her spinning

stool, Skyla suddenly grew still. "I have no sweetheart. My betrothed, Robert de Mornay, drowned the spring I became fourteen, remember, Granny? Before I ever met him."

"Not Mornay. The new one," the old woman insisted triumphantly. "The handsome one."

"My 'new one'! And who is he, Grandmama?"

"A MacKenzie whelp, I'd say," Elspeth said with a sly grin. "From the height and breadth of him. Aye, and from all that bonny black hair—! Tell me. Has your sweetheart the MacKenzie eyes, too, Skyla? Are they the bonny blue of harebells?"

The spindle fell from Skyla's grasp with a loud clatter, and drew a rolling circle on the flagstones.

"How should I know? I have no sweetheart!" she insisted. She hated having to deny Graham's existence, but now was not the hour for their secret to be known. "Come, dinna speak so foolish, Gran. The carding, remember?"

Elspeth MacLeod chuckled. Setting aside the fluffy mass of raw wool and her deer-horn carding comb, she rose stiffly to her feet and tottered over to Skyla, who sat at her spinning wheel, close to the hearth.

Framing her granddaughter's lovely face between her spotted hands, she murmured, "Not just a sweetheart, mayhap, but a future

41

husband. A man who'll love ye true, through all adversity. Aye, and there's plenty of that ahead for ye, my poor wee lass!

"I see a time coming when your man will stand at the Hammer's right hand, and spit in England's eyes!" She shuddered bony shoulders. "When that day dawns, God bless and keep ye both, I say, and strengthen your love for each other. 'Tis high time the feud between our two clans ended. The MacKenzies and the MacLeods were as brothers once. They shall be close again. God knows, we Scots have enemies aplenty, wi'out squabbling amongst ourselves! Ye make a bonny pair, you and him. Ye'll breed bonny bairns, too, I'm thinking."

"Grandmother!"

Elspeth chucked Skyla beneath the chin. "Hee! Hee! Never fear, my lovie. Your secret is safe with Granny MacLeod."

But was it? Skyla wondered, gnawing at her lower lip as the dear old lady hobbled away.

Truth was, she could not depend on Granny to keep her secret, not if the old lady slipped into one of her rambling spells. And what had Granny meant when she'd said that Graham would one day "stand by the Hammer's side, and spit in England's eye?" Had it been nothing more than rambling nonsense? The wishful thinking of a senile old woman? Or one of

Granny's rare prophecies? Proof that the Sight was still strong within her?

Skyla sighed. Only time could answer that question.

Torn between joy that the Sabbath—but two days hence now—would bring Gray to the isle to seek her hand, and dread of how that day would end, she resumed her spinning, outwardly calm, deeply troubled within. A tranquil well that hid a whirlpool at its heart . . .

She and her serving maids had been in the woods of Lochalsh, gathering berries and roots for wool-dyeing, when she'd met Graham again last year. It had been the first time since the great gathering of the clans, ten years earlier, that she'd seen him, she remembered.

She'd heard a low voice calling her name, but could see no one amongst the trees and bushes when she looked up. And then, just seconds later, the calling had come again.

"Sky-laa! Over here! Sky-laaa!"

She was about to flee in the other direction, certain the hidden caller was up to no good—perhaps an English soldier, out for sport—when Graham stepped from the cover of the trees before her, large as life.

She had recognized him instantly, and her jaw had dropped. He had been tall the last time they'd met, but his height back then had been the lanky-limbed, gangly, awkward height of a boy.

The man who stood before her towered head and shoulders above ordinary men—as tall as Longshanks, the Plantaganet king himself, she'd wager. Or the Scots' champion, Will Wallace of Elerslie. And, no longer awkward, he carried himself with a warrior's easy masculine grace.

He was broad-shouldered, well muscled, with hair that fell to his shoulders in unruly midnight waves. The inky slashes of his brows were just as black, his nose long an nobly shaped, his mouth generous and made for kisses, she had thought wickedly.

The eyes hadn't changed, though. *MacKenzie eyes*, her grandmother had called them. They were the vivid lavender blue of harebells, just as she'd remembered—no, *dreamed* of—set like gems in a square-jawed, handsome face!

Sunlight falling through the leafy canopy overhead had dappled that face with shadows. And for a second, some trick of light and shade had lent him an almost frightening cast. . . .

He had looked, she thought with a shudder, like a warrior in the heat of battle, blood smeared over his face.

The image, although quickly come and gone, had made her shudder with foreboding. A premonition? Nay, surely not. She had nothing of her Granddam's gift . . . had she?

But her misgivings had been quickly dispelled by Graham's teasing smile—and just as quickly forgotten.

"Well, now! Don't ye remember me, Skyla MacLeod? I would have known *you* anywhere," he declared, grinning down at her. "We met at the gathering in the great glen, ten long years ago. I'm Graham. The MacKenzie of the MacKenzies of Glenrowan," he added proudly.

"Remember ye?" She shook her head, stirring the long ringlets of dark red hair that spilled down her back, splashing vibrant color over the coarse homespun of the worn kirtle she'd donned for her herb-gathering. "Whist, that face is hard to forget!" she shot back, responding like a ten-year-old, instead of the gracious, poised young gentlewoman she had tried so hard to become—and dearly wanted him to see.

But to her annoyance, instead of being affronted, he snorted with laughter, apparently delighted.

"Ugly, am I? Well, by all that's holy, *you're* not, praise the Lord. In fact, my beauty, you're about the farthest creature from ugly I've ever seen!"

His compliment, though clumsily worded,

45

brought a delighted smile to her lips—one she quickly dimmed.

"Thank you for your compliments, sir," she said demurely, inclining her head as her mother would have wished. "But now, by your leave, I really must go back to my maids. They will be wondering what has become of me."

"All right. If ye must go, I suppose I canna make ye stay. So. Tell me! When may we meet again?"

"Meet again? Sir, we cannot! 'Tis impossible," she protested. "Where is your head? You are the MacKenzie of the MacKenzies! I'm the daughter of the MacLeod of Skye! Our families are sworn enemies! My father would never permit it—and neither would yours!"

"My father's dead. Didn't ye hear what I said, lass? *I'm* the MacKenzie now. I decide what is permitted and what is not! *Hallooo!*" he suddenly bellowed, cupping his mouth with his hands to amplify his voice. "This way, lads and lassies! Your wee mistress is here, flirting wi' a MacKenzie—"

"Hush!" Skyla hissed, face flaming. "I am not! Stop that shouting this instant, you rogue!" she urged in a hoarse voice. "My maids. Our escorts. They'll hear you, you great dolt!"

"Aye, I warrant they will," he agreed, laughter dancing in his blue eyes. "In fact, I guarantee it." His voice was every bit as loud as before. Maybe louder. "So, if it's my silence ye want, lovely lady, promise ye'll meet me again. That you'll come here, to Lochalsh.

"I dinna ken what draws me. But I must see you again, my lass. And I swear," he added in a stern tone, waggling a callused finger at her, "if you willna come here t'me, then by all that is holy, I'll swim the strait to your fairy isle like a kelpie, be damned if I willna!"

She had the sudden, horrifying image of a huge, dripping-wet MacKenzie bursting into the great hall of her father's keep, looking like the sea serpent that lived in Loch Ness. Of him standing there, demanding to see her, with seaweed tangled in his black hair and water streaming from his plaid to puddle amongst the rushes strewn over the flagstones.

In fact, the image was so very powerful, she hastily agreed.

"Oh, very well, then! I—I'll meet you. Somehow," she promised quickly, rashly—anything to silence him.

"When?" he demanded straightway.

"A week from today?" she suggested uncertainly. "I—I shall use the excuse that I need more berries for Grandmother's wool dyes."

His broad, conspiratorial grin was contagious. And, despite herself, she smiled back.

"Use any excuse ye choose, my lady Skyla—

so long as ye come. I shall count the days. The hours. The very moments," he declared, pressing his feathered bonnet to his heart and rolling his eyes. "God be with you, till we meet again, ma bonny sweetheart."

And—despite her promises to herself to be demure and poised, the perfect lady—she giggled.

"Ye'd best count your fingers and toes instead of moments, ye great lout," she suggested with twinkling eyes, not entirely jesting. "For if my kinsmen catch us, *I'll* be sent to a nunnery—and you, sir, will have no toes or fingers t'count!"

And so it had begun for the two of them. With just a few teasing words that had quickly deepened into a true and lasting love.

A love that would, God willing, she prayed silently, endure forever.

Four

Fionna MacRae grimaced as she sponged the Englishman's seed from her thighs.

She had been Hartford's whore for four years now, but her time was running out.

The sheriff had grown tired of her. Her spies told her he bedded younger maids when he left Fort Edward, the gray stone keep he and his garrison occupied in its rightful owner's stead.

It came as no surprise. At six-and-twenty years, she was no longer young. Her beauty had faded. Her glossy black hair was threaded with silver now, her body no longer firm. Only her skills remained.

It was time to carry out the plan she'd come up with last summer. A plan that, properly carried out, would bring enough gold to live in comfort to a ripe old age, for she had no man to provide for her, nor any clan to take her in.

The MacRaes, a sept of the MacKenzies, had cast her out years ago, just as the MacKenzie himself had denied her his bed, God rot him, all because she had played the whore for the English constable. . . .

She had nowhere left to turn now. Of a certainty, no decent Scot would have her.

And so, desperate, she forced herself to smile as Roger returned from the adjoining chamber, where he'd gone to pass water.

Hartford was her own age, of average height and stocky build. He had dull fair hair, blunt features, and a ruddy complexion that was coarsened by pox scars. His pallid blue eyes could shift from wintry to pitiless in a heartbeat.

Aye, he was terrible cruel, was Hartford. She had heard him order a man murdered while, his hand spitefully knotted in her dark hair, he forced her down onto her knees and made her pleasure him with her mouth.

And, since the constable was a dangerous man, she would have to be doubly careful.

His lust spent, Hartford eyed her with contempt as he stretched out on the bed they'd recently shared.

"What? Still here, slut? Be gone with you, I say!" he snarled. "This night, I sleep alone."

"Weary, my lusty stallion?" Fionna purred, making her tone as bold and saucy as when she had first caught his eye. Palm pressed to his hairy chest, she smiled to hide her loathing. "I'm not surprised! But, dinna toss me out just yet, sir. I—well, after what ye did to me wi' that great staff, I can hardly walk." She pouted and Roger Hartford smiled.

Gullible fool! He thought a woman's pain after coupling was proof of his sexual prowess. A testament to the size of his male rod!

Nonetheless, the slap he dealt her was a hard one. Hefty enough to make the blood drain from her face.

"Up! Up, you lazy slut! Up off your scrawny arse, and out of here! Go sleep in the hall, with my men."

He laughed spitefully, knowing there would be precious little sleep for her there, amongst that randy lot!

"As ye will, then, sir," Fionna said demurely, dressing herself. As she laced her kirtle, she turned away to hide the fury that seethed inside her like scorched porridge. "It's just that . . . well, I had something t'tell ye, sir. A wee scrap of gossip about the MacKenzie, it was. But it can wait, aye? Sleep well, mi'lord."

Tying her shawl over her breasts, she went to

the door, knowing he would call her back before she went through it. At least, he always had in the past.

Over the years, she'd learned that Roger Hartford was as curious as any cat by nature. He would be especially curious when it came to the doings of the rebellious Scots like Will Wallace of Elerslie, and his good friend the MacKenzie of Glenrowan.

Graham. Neither man made any secret of his hatred for the English. Wallace's young wife, Marron, had been slain by the English sheriff of Lanark in retaliation for her husband's open defiance of the English. And, like Wallace's father, Graham's father, Adam MacKenzie, had likewise run afoul of Hartford and his men while out hunting. He had not lived to tell of it.

Aye, now that she had baited her trap, Hartford would not be satisfied until he ferreted out her secret. For all he knew, she could be hugging the plans of a Scottish ambush to her bosom!

England's bitter failure to subdue the Scots, whom they considered a band of ragtag outlaws and barbarians, rankled in the hearts of all the Sassenachs. . . .

"Wait!" Hartford barked, right on cue. "Not so fast."

One hand on the door latch, she froze. Careful to keep the triumph from her tone, she asked, "Aye, milord?"

"What was it you had to tell me?"

"Och, that! Whist, it was nothing, sir. Nothing at all. Just a wee bit o'gossip about the MacLeod of Skye's oldest daughter, ye ken? She has taken the MacKenzie of Glenrowan as her sweetheart, wi'out her father's ken."

"Glenrowan, ye say?" Hartford's pale brows lifted. The wintry blue eyes ignited with interest. "What about him?"

The MacLeods of Skye and the MacKenzies of Glenrowan were two of the most powerful families in the Highlands. Like the Wallaces of Elerslie and other rebellious clans, ever since John Balliol had relinquished his kingship of Scotland, the two clans had openly defied the constables the English King Edward had appointed in order to keep the peace and squelch any uprisings.

Constables such as Hartford.

Still, this was the first time Hartford had heard the two clans linked in the same breath. . . .

According to his informants, a long-standing feud existed between them, although they had been joined by bonds of blood and tradition until some forgotten slight several decades ago had torn them asunder.

His Majesty had expressed his wish that all such feuds be encouraged to continue, Hartford recalled. For, when the Scots were busy squabbling amongst themselves, the clans were unable to unite in significant numbers to rise up against their English masters.

In fact, fanning such petty squabbles into blazing feuds was one of Hartford's more agreeable duties as constable of the area.

A smile bared his teeth as he recalled the death of Adam MacKenzie the year before.

Despite being cut off from the rest of his hunting party and outnumbered more than six to one, Glenrowan's laird had put up a fiercely valiant fight before he'd met his bloody—and inevitable—end. The Scot had taken more than one Englishman to hell with him that day.

"And? What about them?" Hartford demanded irritably. There was a chance the whore could yet serve some purpose, before he rid himself of her. "Tell me what you know!"

"Nooo, nooo, sleep, good sir. Sleep! My poor bit o'gossip can wait till morning, aye?"

Hartford lunged across the room. In less than a heartbeat, he had his fist twisted in her long black hair.

"*Now*, bitch!" he rasped, his spittle spraying her face. He cruelly yanked her hair to give weight to his words, startled to find himself growing hard as he bent her against him. Her

54

breasts strained against the lacing of her kirtle. "No more games, slut! Tell me what you know!"

"Please, sir! You're hurting me," she whimpered. "Please, let go, I b-beg ye!"

Slowly, he released her.

Fiona hid a smile as she smoothed down her hair and garments, and rubbed her bruised, reddened wrists. The Englishman was so predictable. She knew what he was thinking as surely as if she had the Sight: *That he'd find out what she knew, then get rid of her, once and for all.*

Her jaw hardened. *Not bluidy likely! By the time that day dawns, I'll be long gone from here, God willing.*

"Thank ye, milord. Now. Back to bed with ye, where it's warm, sir." The flagstones were cold as ice beneath her bare feet, which had turned blue. The fire on the hearth was dying, and needed another log. "I'll tell ye over a drop o'whiskey, aye? A wee dram will warm ye and help ye t'sleep, sir," she cooed, well aware that her pain had stirred his lust.

Before she told the Sassenach anything, he must first agree to her price, she promised herself. And he was more likely to do that if a little drunk.

Accordingly, she splashed aged malt whiskey into golden goblets encrusted with jewels.

Both the water-of-life and the goblets had

belonged to the Scottish earl who once owned this fine keep. Like many other Scottish nobles before him, his lordship had been hanged from his own battlements for refusing to pay homage to the English king, Edward Longshanks.

Loving relatives had quickly spirited the dead earl's lady and children away to the Highlands, before Hartford could have them murdered, too.

Fools! Fionna thought. *Her fellow Scots were all fools!*

What did it matter who was king and who was not? Scottish or English, such great men cared naught for the common people who were their subjects. Who knew if Fionna MacRae went hungry or cold to her bed? Or cared if a man's children were fed or clothed or cared for?

Nobody, that's who.

Nor would Robert the Bruce prove any different, should he and Will Wallace succeed in ousting the English from Scottish soil, and winning freedom for Scotland!

Nay. Every man had to look out for himself in this life. To live off his wits. To cheat, lie, beg, borrow, or steal—do whatever it took to survive, even if survival meant taking another's life or, in the case of a woman, whoring for the enemy.

Love, loyalty, trust, honesty had no place in her existence. In truth, only once in her score-and-six years had she ever truly loved another.

And to what end? The object of her affection had spurned her, cast her aside for a mere child. A child who was, moreover, the daughter of a rival clan . . .

Skyla MacLeod had been that child, God rot her! Fionna scrubbed the tears from her eyes.

For that slight, her sweetheart would pay tenfold—but not with his life. Nay, death was far too quick, too easy for him.

First, she would bring him to his knees.

Very soon, Graham MacKenzie, the MacKenzie of the Glenrowan MacKenzies, would wish to God he had never been born!

"Ye come so rarely t'see me, dear sir," Fionna purred as, taking the big, bearded Scot's hand, she led him inside her little cottage the following Saturday.

The man had to duck his head to clear the lintel of her little peat-roofed cottage, for he was almost as tall as Will Wallace, who stood head and shoulders above other men.

He chuckled. "Not by choice, my lassie. Not by choice! Now, then. What are ye waiting for? Must I beg your kisses?"

Laughing, Fionna went willingly into his arms, her conscience pricking as his brawny arms wrapped her in a fond hug.

Whiskery lips smacked against hers. "There, lassie. Aaah. That's better."

For all that she was his sometime-whore, she felt a fondness for this bearlike man that she'd never felt for Hartford or the others. He was fond of her, too.

Which made what she had to do even harder, she thought with a heavy sigh, touching the stolen dirk she wore, strapped to her leg.

It was still there, its hilt pressed cold and heavy against her bare shin.

"Och, ye feel so good in my arms, my wee bannock!" he purred, nuzzling her neck. "Aye, and ye taste sweet as honey to the bee! Hmmm." He nuzzled her again. "Nectar, lassie. Like the honey ye have here for me." He felt between her legs, laughing when she pretended to be shocked.

"Flatterer," she accused, twisting free of his arms. "Come. Sit ye down, sir. Let me take off those shoes for ye, unless"—she eyed him coyly from beneath her thick dark lashes—"ye've a mind t'wear them t'bed?"

"It wouldna be the first time, eh, lass?" He chuckled, rubbing his whiskery chin against her cheek. "Remember?"

"You!"

A hearty chortle of laughter burst from him as she squealed and squirmed away, playfully pushing him down onto the narrow cot.

Working slowly, seductively now, she undid the broad band of studded leather that belted his woolen breachan of dark green-and-blue plaid over his impressive belly. That done, she unlaced his cambric shirt, its seams closed with stitches so fine and small, they were all but invisible.

His precious, delicate wife's fine work, no doubt, she thought jealously as she stroked the hairy chest she'd bared. But the lady's fine way with a needle had not given her husband bairns to dandle upon his knees. . . .

Lastly, she tugged off his shoes, his sporran, his dirk.

"Your turn now, lassie," he urged, his gray eyes lambent as, naked and unarmed now, he leaned on one elbow to watch her, chewing on a small, frayed twig.

His voice was thick with lust. "Make haste and undress, Fee. I'm starved for the sight o'yer plump teats and bonny quim!"

She felt a moment's twinge of regret as she turned away. She liked him more than the rest. He was generous with his coin, and kind to her, besides, always wanting her to take pleasure in their couplings, too.

But, pretending to lift her skirts, she hardened her heart and palmed the hidden dagger, nonetheless.

She *had* to. There was no other way.

His eyes widened in shock when he saw what she brandished above her head.

Its fancy hilt and blade winked slyly in the murky light. The green-jewel eyes of the stag seemed alive. Alive, and glittering.

"Fee? For the love o' God! Whatever are ye doing, lassie?" he asked hoarsely.

"Forgive me, Dougie," she whispered.

And showed him.

Five

"Well? How do I look?"

Jamie MacKenzie grinned. "Like a damned peacock, brother. That feather in yer bonnet is awful big! Is it no', Ian?"

"Aye," Ian, the youngest of the three, agreed. "Ye all but poked out my blasted eye wi' it a moment ago, Gray. I canna help but wonder, brother. Which part o' ye is so lacking in size, ye must make up for it wi' such a big plume in your cap?"

"Lacking? I think not, laddie," Graham insisted with a grin. "Everything I own is five times what my brothers together can lay claim to."

Snorting with laughter, the MacKenzies, along with a half dozen of their clansmen, spilled from the laird's chamber, jostling and elbowing each other as they clattered noisily down the spiral staircase to the great hall below.

"My laird! I gathered these for yer sweetheart!" a serving woman offered shyly, bobbing Gray a curtsy as she offered him a posy of late wildflowers, bound together by a riband.

"A bonny posy, in truth, Maid Mary. My thanks for your kindness. I shall be sure the Lady Skyla receives it," Graham promised. "And, once we are wed, mayhap you could attend her at Glenrowan, if it please her?"

The girl beamed and bobbed him another shy curtsy. "Thank ye, my laird! I would like that, verra much."

"Mayhap I spoke too soon of the Lady Skyla coming to Glenrowan? Do ye think her father will even consider my suit?" Graham wondered doubtfully as he mounted one of the saddled horses the stable boys led into the courtyard for him and his men. "He could as easily refuse it out of hand. Send me packing!"

"Why would he not consider it?" Ian said. "'Tis past time the feud between our two clans was mended. Our energies would be better turned t'ridding Scotland of the bluidy Sassenachs, instead of squabbling with each other. Besides, you are the Lady Skyla's equal in both breeding and rank, Graham. An obvious choice for a husband! 'Tis said the MacLeod is a just man, too—and the lady well past marriageable age. If she's willing t'admit she looks with fondness upon ye—"

"—which she does—"

"Then I'd wager the odds favor ye, brother!"

They had ridden halfway to Lochalsh when Ian spied the woman bathing in the icy burn.

He waved his brothers back into a spinney of pines they had just passed, silencing Graham's protests that they had no time to tarry.

"Would ye deny us unmarried fellows the bonny sight of a naked woman at her bath, brother?" Ian winked and grinned under his thatch of long dark hair in which the autumn sun danced with fiery red glints.

"Hmm. 'Tis a hardy wench that picks an icy stream for her bathing!" Graham observed, frowning.

"Holy Mother of God! Hardy, indeed. Look! 'Tis the Sassenachs' harlot, Fionna MacRae!" hissed Jamie, dropping down to one knee.

The woman was squatting in the burn's flow, scrubbing her kirtle between her hands. Her bare torso rose from the water like that of a kelpie, or water sprite. Her full breasts were puckered by the cold, while her black hair stirred, witchlike, on the wind.

She wore a faraway, dazed expression, and was muttering to herself as she scrubbed, but the men were too far away to hear what she said.

Graham shivered as a shrill cawing broke the hush. His head snapped up, in time to see two great black crows rise from their perch in the oak above him and take to the sky.

Squinting against the light, he watched with narrowed eyes as they and several of their fellows wheeled over a tumbledown cottage, roofed with peat, almost hidden by the brow of the hill.

So powerfully had the crows' wings flapped as they flew over him, a single ebony feather had escaped their plumage.

It spiraled down from the sky to land on Gray's chest, like a macabre flake of ebony snow. *A sign of some evil portent, surely!*

Taking the feather between his two fingers, he uttered a fervent prayer before he hurled it aside, his heart suddenly heavy, his belly churning with foreboding as the wind blew the feather back at him.

Sweet lord! he thought, trying to throw it away again. But for a second time, it blew back, clinging to his woolen breachan.

Sweat sprang out upon his brow. *He could not rid himself of it!*

Highland Lovesong

Ill fortune enough to see a single corbie—a crow—as one set out upon a journey. To see *two*, flying together, foretold death. Disaster—!

"Hold hard, brother. They are but birds, nothing more," came Jamie's deep voice to his right. Low. Calm. Reassuring.

So. Jamie also remembered the morning their father had been killed.

His brother plucked the feather from his chest and let it flutter to the turf. Their eyes met as Jamie's fingers bit into his shoulder. Their numbing pressure steadied him. Forced his thoughts away from the dark day he had found their father, and back to the present.

"It is only to old women that carrion crows are soothsayers of doom," Jamie murmured for Gray's ears alone. "In truth, they are but crows, whether in pairs, or in a great black flock. Nor is that quill there anything more than a fallen feather." He nodded at the turf where the feather now lay, crushed and broken by the horses' hooves.

Graham winced. For all that Jamie was the leanest of the three of them, he had the grip of a vise and nerves of steel.

An honorable man he was proud to call brother and friend, Jamie was worthy to take his place as laird, should the need someday arise, Gray thought absently. Aye, and better suited to the chieftain's place than me, he added. His own temper burned the hotter of the two, flaring easily into anger, whereas Jamie was more inclined to react coolly, with logic and reason and careful consideration.

"Aye," Graham agreed at length, again meeting Jamie's grave blue eyes. "You are right, as ever, brother. The corbies mean naught! All of you. Mount up. We ride on!"

And so, despite much grumbling and lewd glances at the nude woman splashing in the stream, they did so.

Never had any Sabbath come more swiftly—or more slowly! Skyla thought as she sat before her looking glass, fidgeting with excitement as Moira coaxed the snarls and tangles from her dark auburn hair.

The rose kirtle and plum-colored surcoat, bordered with silver-and-gold tablet embroidery, were becoming. But Skyla made a face at her reflection in the polished oval, nonetheless.

Now that the Sabbath was finally here, she did not know whether she was excited—or simply terrified!

Ever since she and Moira had returned from matins in the keep's chapel earlier that morning, she had run to the window slits numerous times to peer out. So many times, in fact, that Moira had asked what made her so restless. Needless to say, she had not told her.

Highland Lovesong

Gray eyes narrowed against the bright, almost wintry autumn light outside, she gazed eastward, across the gleaming Strait of Sleat, toward the distant, misty hills of Lochlash. It was from that direction that Graham would come.

Matins had already come and gone. Indeed, it had taken the utmost restraint for her to sit still during Father Anselm's long-winded sermon! But now—if Graham was true to his word—he would soon be here.

She *had* to take another look.

Evading Moira's comb, ignoring her protests, she ran to the window slit and drew aside the tapestry that hung there. And this time, as if her thoughts had conjured them, she spotted a small craft with several men inside it, bearing down upon the isle. The rowers were bending powerful backs to their oars.

At last! It was beginning! Although she could not make out their features at this distance, it had to be Graham and his escort.

Whirling about, she flew to the door. Moira trailed after her, comb still in hand, her plump face, framed by a wimple, confused. "My lady! Your hair!"

"Whist! 'Tis good enough as it is, Moira," Skyla flung over her shoulder. "Anon!"

At the foot of the steep, spiral staircase, she forced herself to pause and drew a deep, steadying breath.

Better. Much better.

Outwardly composed now, she entered the great hall at an unhurried pace, as befitted the eldest daughter of the household. Her kidskin shoes trod lightly over the rushes and dried lavender as she made her way between the lofty pillars of oak.

Dunvegan's ancient walls rose all around her, their cold stone warmed by vivid tapestries and by iron sconces in which torches of pitch burned brightly. The flaring golden light dispelled the gloom, and winked off the brass or silver candlesticks placed at intervals along the trestle tables.

Grandmother Elspeth dozed in a carved chair drawn up to one of the wide fireplaces in the hall, her feet resting on a footstool. She slept more and more often of late, her old bones cushioned by plump tapestry pillows fringed with tassels of gold thread. And, although a huge fire crackled on the hearthstone, she was swathed in fur pelts against the drafts.

Father's shaggy hunting hounds slept in a tangle of paws and tails about her feet.

A small round gaming table of inlaid wood had been drawn up to the hearth's warmth. On one side of it sat her mother, the Lady Shona. Her braided red hair formed a regal crown over which she'd draped a gauzy blue veil, held in place by a filet of silver.

Her father, Laird John, the MacLeod of the MacLeods of Skye, sat facing his lady, a tall, striking man in his Sabbath breachan of MacLeod plaid.

The lord and his lady were playing at chess, laughing like sweethearts over a board of ivory and ebony inlaid squares, with carved playing pieces of walrus ivory.

Skyla's younger sisters, Rowena and the baby of the family, little Catriona, along with her older brother, Alec, were looking on and offering advice as their parents made their moves.

From another chair, Aunt Alison, Uncle Douglas's lady, was also watching the players. Her face, though drawn and pale from burying so many babes, looked delicate and pretty by firelight.

In all, it was, Skyla thought with a pang, a leisurely domestic scene. One typical of Sabbath afternoons at Dunvegan when summer was waning and the winds of autumn blew chill across the Isle of Skye from the sea.

Watching her beloved family, Skyla felt a twinge of guilt and sorrow that the tranquil picture would soon be forever shattered by Graham's arrival and his request for her hand in marriage.

Penelope Neri

"Whist! There ye are, daughter!" her mother exclaimed, startling Skyla from her thoughts. Holding out a ringed, elegant hand to her, the Lady Shona smiled. "Come, sweet girl. Help your poor mother best your lord father at this wretched game!" She sniffed. "For I fancy *he* has counselors enough."

The Lady Shona cast a reproving eye upon the rest of her treacherous brood, who were either ranged staunchly behind her husband or peeping over his shoulder.

"'Tis only because Father needs us, Mother!" piped little Catriona, whose hair spilled down her back in carrot-colored curls. "You *always* win!"

"Cat's right, Mother. You do," Alexander agreed solemnly, although his lips twitched.

A tall, stocky young man at two-and-twenty years, Alec was handfasted to wed Flora, the MacDonald of Islay's daughter, come the spring.

"Poor Father needs all the wise counsel he can get!" he added with a wry grin.

His father scowled and playfully punched him in the arm. "Whist, mon! Ye dinna have to agree with the bairn," he grumbled.

All of them laughed.

Knowing what she knew, Skyla felt their laughter tug at her heart.

Leaning down, she dropped a nervous kiss

70

upon her father's brow, then impulsively embraced her mother, holding her far more tightly and for much longer than she would usually do.

"Why, dearling, what is it?" Shona asked, holding her at arm's length when she released her. Gentle eyes searched Skyla's face.

"My lady mother. A moment alone, I pray you," Skyla murmured in her mother's ear. "There is something I must tell you before you—"

But she had time for no more, because at that moment, the double doors at the far end of the hall flew inward.

Made of massive wooden boards, they crashed back against the stone walls with a thunderous boom that brought the inhabitants of the hall to their feet and froze servants in their tracks. Even the sleeping hounds sprang instantly awake, snarling deep in their throats.

Gil MacLeod spilled into the hall. He was so distraught, the torches guttered with the violence of his passage.

"My laird, I—we—!" he began, coming to a halt before John MacLeod. But his voice broke before he could say more, making Skyla's belly churn with apprehension.

So. It had begun—and promised to be worse than she had feared!

If Gil's solitary—and explosive—entry was

anything to judge by, Scottish hospitality had been cast to the four winds by the sudden arrival of her suitor and his escort!

At any moment, she expected to see her beloved marched into the hall under a close guard of angry MacLeods. Then Father would demand to know what a bluidy MacKenzie was doing on Skye, and the storm would break about their ears. . . .

"Well? What is it, mon?" she heard her father ask Gil in a loud voice. "For God's sake, get a grip on yoursel', and tell me—!"

But there was no need for poor Gil to answer—no need at all, for even as he opened his mouth, four men strode into the hall, hefting a wooden door between them.

And on it, a breachan of their clan tartan thrown over it, was a body.

Gil flung the plaid back, baring the dead man's bearded face for all to see.

Skyla shrank back in horror.

The kind gray eyes had already clouded over, so that the corpse seemed to stare blindly up at the rafters, or to eternity and beyond. But there was no mistaking the dead man's identity.

She tried to swallow over the great lump in her throat, her lips quivering. It was her father's brother, Uncle Douglas Alexander MacLeod. Her Aunt Alison's husband.

"Blessed Mother of God, nay, Douglas!" her father swore softly. "Not you, brother!"

"*Douglas!* Oh, dear God, noooo!" screamed Aunt Alison. Her sudden, anguished shriek shredded the air. Set everyone's teeth on edge.

Springing from her chair, the frail widow flung herself across the body the men had placed with such reverence on the laird's high table. Her embrace dislodged the plaid, revealing a burly body as naked as Adam's in Eden.

"Noooo!" Alison shrieked. "Not him! Not my mon! What befell ye, Dougie?" she beseeched the corpse, cupping the gray face between her palms. "Who did this to ye? *Who? Tell me!* Och, my puir, puir lovie, ye've grown so cold!" she sobbed.

Rivers of tears slipped down her cheeks to soak the hairy chest in which the great heart was now forever stilled.

"Jesu!" whispered her father, visibly shocked and pale at the sight of his younger but bigger brother, whom Skyla's brother, Alec, resembled.

The MacLeod's hands curled into huge fists at his sides. "Was it the English?" he demanded in a hoarse voice. He looked from man to man, searching their faces for his answer. "Well? Gil? Rory? Speak, damn ye!"

"I wish to God it had been the Sassenachs!" Rory growled, fixing the MacLeod with a long, meaningful look. Lifting a brow in the widow's direction, he nodded. "I'll tell ye all the . . . details . . . anon, milord. Meanwhile, take a look at this pretty bodkin. I plucked it from his belly. Do ye ken whose it is?"

His own features crumpling, Rory tossed a dirk to John MacLeod.

The laird caught the glittering weapon in midair, and raised it to the light.

From where she stood, frozen to the spot beside her mother's chair, Skyla recognized the small dagger, even if the others did not.

The last time she had seen the fancy piece with the stag's head hilt was ten years ago, in the Great Glen. Only then, it had been brandished in Graham's hand.

A stag's head was the MacKenzie's badge, after all.

And—unless one of a pair—this was the same pretty dirk Gray had used for their blood oath, all those years ago. . . .

"Now joined by blood are we. . . ."

". . . joined by blood . . ."

". . . by blood . . ."

". . . blood . . ."

BLOOOOD!

She shivered convulsively.

"We all know who it belongs to, man! A bluidy MacKenzie!" Gil growled. He spat upon the rushes. "The weapon that killed your brother bears their badge! Likewise, the sett o' the torn plaid in his fist."

"*Nooo!*" Like Alison's, Skyla's cry of denial was wrenched from deep inside her. It escaped as a choked scream.

"Noooo!" Whirling about, she fled the hall, running from it as if the hounds of hell snapped at her heels.

"Skyla!" little Catriona whimpered, her lower lip wobbling. "Come back! Don't go! What is happening, Mother? Why is everyone so sad?"

"Shoo, shoo, dearling," Lady Shona murmured, drawing the frightened little girl into her arms and stroking her bright hair. "Your sister grieves for your poor uncle, who is dead, aye? Let her go, sweeting. She'll return anon, when she's done wi' weeping. For now, go with your nurse, hinnie. Rowena, accompany them, if ye please. My ladies and I have much to do here."

"I am no' a child any longer, to be sent t'my chamber, Mother!" fourteen-year-old Rowena protested. "Please. Let me stay. I can help you."

"Not now, Rowena. And don't argue, pray. Just do as I ask."

Rowena scowled, but bowed her head. "Yes, Mother."

When both child and nurse had left the hall, Rowena trailing in their wake, the Lady Shona turned to her women.

"Moira, accompany the Lady Alison to her chamber. Have the cook prepare a posset of poppies t'soothe her. You, Betty, and you, Joanna, shall help me ready our kinsman's body for burial." She bit her lower lip, pale, yet composed, every inch her laird's most gracious lady.

"Aye, madam," the serving women murmured, bobbing curtsies. "We'll help ye."

"While we track down the cowardly bastard that killed him!" Alexander swore. The Adam's apple bobbed in his throat, his only outward sign of emotion. His eyes remained dry, although his handsome face was hard with grief.

"There is no place his murderer may hide, not from us!" Alexander added, his eyes meeting his father's. "Not even should he run t'the far ends o' the earth!"

He had used her, Skyla thought, her throat aching as she grabbed the narwhal's horn from its special place in her betrothal chest. Graham had used her—used her affections—to strike a blow at her family and further the feud between them.

Because of her naiveté, her gullibilty, her uncle was dead—and who knew how many others would fall to a MacKenzie blade before this day was done?

Her thoughts in chaos, she hurried back down the steep spiral staircase.

Her kinsmen were gathering in the great hall, summoned by runners and by horns from all corners of Skye, drawn by the loss of their great kinsman, Douglas MacLeod.

Their voices, some hoarse with tears, others shrill, all loud with anger, reached her as, breathing heavily and still trembling with shock, she scrambled down the black mount upon which Dunvegan stood.

She had headed instinctively for the water gate and the rowboat there that would carry her across the Strait of Sleat to Lochalsh, and thence to Graham, as it had so many times before.

She did not know what she intended to do when—if—she found him. Logic and reason had both fled when she saw his dagger in her father's hand. She knew only that grief and a deep sense of betrayal clouded her love for him now.

All she could think of was returning the narwhal's horn to him. For—at least in her heart— the wretched thing had become a symbol of their love, and of the magical future they'd dreamed of sharing.

A future that would never be. Not now . . .

A wave of grief, of loss—loss of Graham, God

help her, more than her uncle—swamped over her. The emotion was so raw and painful, she lost her footing and stumbled on the slimy wet rocks.

What sort of woman was she? she wondered as she pulled herself up right, breathing heavily through her sobs. A harlot, surely, for no decent woman could mourn the loss of a sweetheart who had almost certainly slain her uncle!

Douglas had been a second father to her, cosseting her and her brother and sisters in place of the children Aunt Alison had never been able to give him. He had deserved to die peacefully in his own bed at a great old age, surrounded by his nephews and nieces. Not to die naked, spitted on an assassin's blade.

Nevertheless, she knew a treacherous part of her loved Graham still. Would always love him. Because of her love, she would warn him away from Skye. She would send him safely out of reach of her kinsmen's vengeance, as she bade him farewell forever. . . .

Loosening the line that moored the rowboat to the iron rings of the water gate, she tumbled clumsily over its side.

Taking up the oars with a heavy heart and a desperate urgency, she began to row.

"Mother of God, what is it? What brings ye here? Whyever are ye so pale, my love?" Graham cried as he waded through the shallows to meet her.

This dark morning, he looked more handsome than she had ever seen him, dressed, she realized, her heart wrenching, like a proper Highland groom, come to claim his bride.

His bonnet sported a jaunty feather, while a fine lawn shirt with full sleeves set off his broad shoulders and powerful torso. A length of the MacKenzie tartan was kilted about his waist, pinned at the left shoulder by a huge round brooch, cast in silver.

A stag's head was etched upon its face, like the bloody dirk. . . .

The reminder served.

"Be gone from here!" she cried in a harsh, lifeless voice, shrugging off his hands when he would have lifted her ashore. She thrust the narwhal's horn at him. "Take this, and be gone with ye, damn ye! My kinsmen are hard behind me! If you would live another day, run! Run for your lives—all of you! Else stay, and pay, God rot ye all!"

"Pay? For what?"

"Ye ken verra well for what! Blessed Mary! Had I the spleen for it, I'd avenge his death mysel'. But I canna! God help me, I canna!" she sobbed, tears streaming down her cheeks.

"What blather are ye talking, lassie? Come here t'me, do! Ye're making no sense."

But when Graham tried to lift her, sobbing, over the side of the boat, which was rocking dangerously now, she beat at his chest with her fists.

"Why, Gray?" she demanded brokenly, searching his face with smoky eyes that were shadowed with pain. "Was your kin's hatred of mine so verra great? Your love for me so wee, so false, it paled beside some wretched feud?"

"What are ye saying? Have done wi' your riddles, woman!" Graham bellowed, trapping both her wrists in his hands. "You're making no sense. Tell me what happened. Did they find out about us? Is that what you're trying t'tell me?"

"If only it were!" she said bitterly. "But ye ken well enough that ye murdered my uncle, ye bastard!"

"Uncle? Douglas MacLeod is dead?" Graham demanded, his dark brows lifting. "When? How?"

"Later, mon. The lady's right. They come!" his brother Jamie cut in, nodding his chin toward the strait. "Come away wi' ye, Gray!"

"Not yet. Not when I have unfinished business here," he growled, nodding grimly at Skyla. "You go on. All of you, *go!*" he ordered his brothers and their clansmen. "I'll stay and face them. If the lady is ever to be my bride, I must clear our name, aye? Convince her kinsmen of our innocence!"

Alistair snorted. "You could sooner convince the stars not to shine than convince a MacLeod of anything, when his blood is hot and his eye red! Come on, Gray! They'll be ashore verra soon!"

Alistair was right, he saw. Other small boats had put off from Dunvegan's water gate between the rocks—the only access to the forbidding keep. Three small dark craft were inching toward the shore, all bristling with Skyla's kinsmen.

With anger fueling the oarsmen's backs, they would soon reach Lochalsh.

"He's right! Go on!" Skyla urged him. "Flee, while you still can!"

"Run like a whipped hound, when there's such terrible doubt in your eyes, ma sonsy?" he murmured bitterly, cupping her chin and tilting her tearful face up to his. "Run, knowing I'll never see ye again? You who are my heart, my love, my life?"

Slowly, he shook his head. "I canna leave ye, lassie. Not now. You and I, we belong together, aye? *'Now joined by blood are we, so joined forevermore shall be!'* Remember our vow? Mayhap the world has changed, but we havena. Our *hearts* havena. I love ye—and you love me. I know it! Why else would ye risk all to come here, if not to warn me? Here. Take my hand. Come wi' me, lassie!"

Penelope Neri

"No! I can't go with you. I won't!"

Something flickered in his turbulent blue eyes. His mouth compressed, then set in a stubborn, determined line. "I willna ask ye again, woman," he said softly. "Ye'll come away wi' me! *Now!*"

His voice was rough. Demanding. Urgent. Authoritative. Brutally insistent. The voice of a Graham she had never heard before.

Was it also the voice of a cold-blooded murderer? Was there another, darker side to his character she had yet to see?

After all, what did she know about him, really, beyond the fact that he was a braw, bonny man, and that she liked his kisses?

Precious little.

She glanced over her shoulder. The boats were no longer dark specks now. They had grown larger, taken on shape, form, and substance as they drew closer.

"I've done no man harm, Skyla. Nor have my kinsmen done murder in my name," he swore softly. "If ye truly love me, trust me. Come with me of your own free will."

"I—I—can't. Dinna ask it of me, Gray. What you—what your kinsmen did—!" She shook her head, closing her eyes as if to blot out reality. "My father would never forgive me! My family would disown me," she whispered. Her mouth worked uncontrollably.

"Then, so be it," he muttered in a tone that was ominously final.

Before she could twist aside, he jerked her into his arms, then flung her over his shoulder like a sack of barley.

"Fall back!" he roared, anchoring one arm about her knees and tucking the narwhal's horn under his arm. "T'the horses, lads!"

The boats were very close now. The men inside were close enough to witness Skyla's fierce struggle to escape him. The way she fought him, tooth and nail.

A murdered kinsmen. A kidnapped maiden. The MacLeods would be howling for blood when they came ashore! There would be no reasoning with them. Not now. Mayhap never.

Nothing to lose—and everything to gain . . .

And so, he carried Skyla, still screaming, still struggling wildly, up into the misty hills above Lochalsh, his breathing labored as he wove a path between shaggy, long-horned cattle to the crofter's hut.

There his mount waited, cropping the coarse turf.

Flinging Skyla over its back, he loosened its hobbles, then sprang up behind her, gathering the reins in his hand.

"Devil! Clarty bastard! Let me go, damn ye!" she shrieked as the horse, scenting danger, circled nervously about, snorting and tossing its silvery head. Her legs flailed. "Flee with your bloody kinsmen! I'll only slow you down. Let me—let me stay here. I'll explain everything to my father, I swear it."

She tried to push herself off his horse, but Graham planted his hand firmly across her backside so that she could not.

"Please, Graham!" she begged, her words muffled by her ignominious position, dangling over his horse's neck. "Don't make things worse! Leave me and go! Just—just go—! Flee for your life!"

The MacLeods had reached the shore, Graham saw, risking a glance over his shoulder, squinting against the harsh midday light. They swarmed up the hills behind him with claymores drawn, like angry bees swarming to a hive.

He smiled, grimly amused. Run for his life, when he could easily outdistance his pursuers on horseback? Not bloody likely! On foot, as they were, the MacLeods would never overtake him and his men, despite the angry threats they hurled after them.

"Ye shouldna have done it, Skyla," he said softly, scowling down at the back of her auburn head. "You shouldna have looked at me that way! Holy Mother of God, the *doubt* in your eyes, woman! I could have left ye behind, knowing ye believed in me. But leave, with ye thinking me guilty of murder?" He shuddered. "*Never!* Yeeaggh!"

Digging his heels into his mount's flanks, he set its head north, for the Highlands and Glenrowan.

As the first MacLeod arrows rained down, the other men spurred their horses after their laird and his stolen bride.

Six

They camped that evening in a hollow carved from the moors, close to a noisy burn. Although the site took them out of the wind, it offered little more than water by way of comforts for their camp.

Unaccustomed to spending long periods of time on horseback, Skyla was stiff and chafed by the time Gray lifted her down from his horse's back.

Shrugging off his helping hand, she tottered like an old woman to warm herself at the fire built by the one called Jamie.

She thought he might be Graham's younger

brother, for he had the MacKenzie features, though his eyes were not half as blue as Graham's and he was leaner.

Shivering, she stood before the fire, holding her chilled hands out to its poor heat in an effort to get warm. But, in her heart of hearts, she doubted she would ever feel truly warm again.

Since that morning, in Dunvegan's great hall, her heart had turned to stone.

"I know what ye're thinking, lassie, but you're wrong," Graham said quietly after he'd dismissed the other men.

He came to stand beside her.

"Like your father's clansmen, my men are bound by their oaths of fealty to do my bidding. When we met again last spring, I forbade my clansmen to raise arms against your own. Your uncle wasna killed by a MacKenzie. My oath on it!"

She shuddered. He sounded so sincere. And yet . . . she could not bear to look at him, let alone believe him. Loving him was so new, trust still so very fragile between them, while the enmity between their clans was old and deep.

So why—*why*, for the love of God!—did her treacherous heart still long for him to hold her, as he had held her that day on the shore? Why did she ache so for his kisses?

Confused and ashamed, she sank wearily to the coarse turf without answering him. Her knees folded, her chin propped on the heels of her hands, she stared into the smoky fire.

"Ye're shivering, lassie," Gray murmured. Draping his own heavy plaid about her, he cupped her shoulders, gently massaging. "Skyla? Talk t'me, lassie! Say something! Give me some hope. Tell me that by and by, ye'll believe in me? That ye'll trust me?"

"Trust ye, MacKenzie?" she said in a bitter, incredulous voice. "When all I can do is wonder how ye came to be there in the woods, the day we met again? When I wonder if it was truly by chance, as ye claim?"

He snorted. "Ye think your uncle's murder and our meeting part of some grand plot?" His anger was barely held in check now. "Then I confess, lassie. You're right! 'Twas not by chance we met," he growled.

"I'd seen you some days before, while hunting near Kyle of Lochalsh. You had gone there with your maids, to gather herbs, I suppose. There were daisies and thistles crowning your bonny hair and ye looked sae blessed fair, I . . . well, I had t'see you again.

"I went back there every day, until ye came again, although my companions believed I'd lost my wits. Aye, Skyla. I 'conspired' t'meet ye. But did I conspire t'murder your uncle? Never!"

"Well? What was I t'think?" she muttered in a

guilty tone. "Glenrowan is far from Lochalsh. And I—! Well, it was I who told you that my uncle would be gone from Skye!" she admitted, stricken by fresh guilt. "I remember it very clearly. It was the day we found the narwhal's horn. I gave away his whereabouts."

"You said you loved me that day, too, Skyla. If ye can recall the rest of it so bluidy well, remember ye love me, too!" he demanded, grasping her upper arms to pull her to her feet. "And while you're about it, tell me why ye rowed clear across the blasted strait t'warn me, if you truly believe I killed him?"

"Because I . . . because I . . . ! Och, I don't know," she cried. Shrugging off his hands, she sprang to her feet and began pacing the turf, back and forth.

Taking her elbow, he turned her to face him. "I know why. 'Tis because your heart remembers what your silly wee head forgot. That you love me, Skyla. That you love me, as I love you. And that ye want to be my bride!"

She struggled to find another answer. Any answer, rather than admit that he was right.

"I was wrong. Blinded," she whispered brokenly.

He shook his head. "Not so. You said what was in your heart. Your loyalties were not torn then. Your feelings were not compromised by guilt."

"Guilt!" Her knotted fist came out of nowhere and smashed into his nose, just as it had years ago in the Great Glen. *"No!"*

He yelped as he heard the delicate cartilage crunch. Pain filled his eyes with sudden tears. Warm blood splashed against his upper lip.

"You're wrong, damn you!" she hissed, her face stark and pale in the moonlight, her gray eyes dilated by grief. "I dinna love you! And I dinna want t'wed ye. Not now—not ever!"

Spinning around, she ran blindly away from him.

With a heavy sigh, he pinched strings of blood and snot from his nose and started after her, cursing under his breath.

He had little fear that Skyla would encounter her kinsmen nearby. They had ridden too far and too fast since leaving Lochalsh for the MacLeods to overtake them.

Furthermore, in the hour before the gloaming cloaked the moors, they had followed tracks through the heather known only to the Clan MacKenzie.

He did fear that she might hurt herself, however. Snap a slender ankle in a rabbit hole. Fall and shatter her collarbone.

And, obstinate though she might be, he could not bear to think of her suffering.

And so, he sprinted after her, bringing her down with a flying leap that drove her legs out from under her, but softening her fall with his own body.

Winded, he held her loosely against his hard frame, supporting her on his chest while he recovered his breath.

"I know it hurts t'lose someone ye love, lassie," he said between panting breaths. "But ye must trust me. Someday, you'll know the truth, and be verra glad I carried ye off."

"And someday, you'll have bitter reason to regret it, sir," she swore through clenched teeth, fighting his hold on her.

"Aye, aye. Ye've made your point. Now have done, lassie. Have done," he growled, rolling her off him, to the turf, and forcing her arms down to her sides.

His actions brought their faces only a hairs-breadth apart. Their breaths mingled. Their eyes locked and Graham knew, in that blinding instant, that he was lost, as surely as he knew his own name.

"Och, Christ!" he swore, then crushed his mouth down over hers in a kiss so fierce, so hard, it was almost brutal.

There was a brief stiffening of her body, a moment's recoil; then the fire between them exploded.

To his delight, she arched against him. Parted her lips beneath his. Feverishly touched her tongue to his.

"Oh, God, *Gray*—" she murmured thickly, shuddering when they broke apart. But what it was she meant to say, he did not know—and what's more, he did not care, so help him God!

Months—years!—of wanting her had taken their toll.

He knew only that her hands were framing his head, pulling it down to hers, and that she wanted to kiss him. That her breasts were pressed so fiercely to his broad chest, the hardened crests rubbed against him like small pebbles through the cloth of their garments. That his knee was thrown over her belly and thighs.

Easing himself onto her, he ground his pelvis against her own. Pressed his burning mouth to the hollow at the base of her throat. Nipped a pearly ear lobe between his teeth until she whimpered.

Slipping his hand up beneath her skirts, he stroked the long, lithe legs he had often imagined wrapped about his hips as he rode her. Touched the curls that crowned her womanhood.

At his intimate caress, her eyes flew open, reflecting the night sky that wheeled above them. Her lips parted on a breathless sob, and he knew.

She was his, if he so chose!

His to take, right here, right now.

His to claim on a bed of prickly furze like two wild things, mating under the moon and stars.

All he had to do was part her thighs. To kneel between them and take what she offered—and what he craved. To free his aching, eager shaft and drive it home, drive it deep. She would not resist. Nor could any honest man call it ravishment.

Except . . . they were not wild creatures, any more than they were husband and wife. To take her here, on the moors, without benefit of marriage, would be adultery in the eyes of the Church, and of her family. The act would dishonor her, pleasurable as it might be. . . .

And so, still shuddering with desire, he turned away from her, ashamed of how close he had come to dishonoring the lassie he cherished above all others.

He had come just a heartbeat from losing the hard-won self-control that he had practiced this past twelvemonth, every time they'd been together.

A hasty tumble on the grass was not what he wanted for his bride on their wedding night. Not for her first time, anyway. Time enough for such rough-and-ready bedsport when they were seasoned lovers, and the blood ran hot and quick between them!

These dew-damp moors were not the bower strewn with flowers he'd planned to give her. Nor this turf a feather bed with scented linens, nor the burn's dark waters the silver flagons of sweet wine and honeycakes he'd intended them to share, just as they shared their bodies and their hearts.

"What is it?" she whispered, gray eyes searching his face. "Did I do something wrong? Have I displeased you in some way? Why do you hesitate?"

"You, displease me?" Ruefully, he shook his head, smiling down at her. "On the contrary, madam. Ye please me far too well! Another moment, an' I would have dishonored ye."

Her mouth took on a bitter twist. "What of it? What do you care? In truth, what could you do to me, sir, that the world will not assume has passed between us?" she asked. "In the eyes of my family, I am already dishonored."

But the venom that should have loaded such a statement was gone. The sting was missing from her words. There was only exhaustion now, and a depth of pain in her eyes that tore at his heart.

"Aye? Then it willna hurt t'tell ye."

"Tell me what?"

"That Hell shall freeze before I dishonor you!" His voice was husky with emotion. His eyes blazed as he added, "And devil take those that say otherwise! All that matters is what *we* know, Skyla MacLeod."

So saying, he brought her chill hands to his lips and kissed her fingertips, then slid his hands down her arms to cup her elbows and raise her to her feet.

As he held her close, he could feel her heart against his own. Like wings, it beat against the cage of her ribs.

"You are my heart, lassie. My life. My dearest love. I want only what is right and good for ye, even if no one believes it but myself."

He kissed her brow—a chaste kiss that was almost brotherly, though God knows there was nothing brotherly about the way he felt when it came to Skyla MacLeod.

"Come back to the fire, lassie. Try t'sleep. At first light, we ride on to Glenrowan."

Seven

A drizzling rain was falling when Skyla awoke the following morn. Graham was crouched beside her, shaking her awake.

"A good day to ye, slugabed," he murmured. His smile was wary, as if afraid she might lash out at him again.

And why not? she thought with a twinge of shame. Both his eyes had turned black overnight, and his nose was still bloody.

Scowling up at him, she waved away his helping hand and struggled to sit up, rubbing gritty eyes. All around them, the others were

97

throwing off the plaids into which they had rolled themselves for the night.

While Skyla splashed icy water from the burn over her face, and stumbled behind a prickly gorze bush to relieve herself, Gray's companions quickly broke their makeshift camp, tossed saddles over their horses' backs, and mounted up, ready to ride on in a matter of moments.

She and Gray quickly followed suit.

What seemed only moments later, she was riding pillion behind Gray again, still only half awake despite the snap in the morning air.

The constant motion of the horse jarred joints that ached from sleeping on damp turf. Nor had stamping her feet banished her bone-deep chill.

She sighed and blinked back tears, heavy-hearted. Losing Uncle Dougie had been terrible, but so was her abrupt separation from her family, and the rift between her and Gray. Although not a physical parting, it was very real. A parting of the spirit. Of the heart. The death of love and trust.

For the past year, most of her waking hours had been consumed by pleasant contemplation of the life she and Gray would one day share as man and wife. Of the love that would deepen between them over the years, and the children they would raise within the circle of their love.

Now, having told herself she must smother her feelings for Graham, it was so hard to wrap her arms about his waist and keep her seat upon the horse's rump behind him. She found embracing that broad masculine body—for whatever purpose—pleasing, she discovered. Secretly, she mourned the growing intimacy they'd shared, now lost forever. . . .

At some point during the night, she remembered, resting her damp cheek against his broad back, she had woken, confused, to find a canopy of stars above her. A nighthawk's shrill shrieks had pierced the midnight hush as it glided over the moors on silent wings.

Graham's heavy woolen plaid was wrapped snugly around her—as was Graham's hard body. And she'd shrugged neither of them off, nor spoken of severances then. Far from it!

Her back had been shielded and kept warm by his broad chest. Her bottom had been snugly tucked into the cozy angle of his flanks and thighs. One of his arms had pillowed her head while trapping her hair beneath its weight, while the other was protectively flung over her, long fingers curled ever-so-gently over her breast.

For a while, she'd tried to squirm out from under that weighty arm. To lift his heavy hand from her breast. But in the end, she had not disturbed what had been, in all honesty, a most pleasurable arrangement.

And so, she'd drifted off to sleep again, acutely aware of her hardened nipple nudging his palm, and of the hot virile body pressed to her own.

Graham had surely passed a far less comfortable night, without the warmth of either breachan or mantle, yet he had not complained. Then again, why should he? She had not asked him to carry her off!

Besides, if he was stiff and chilled this morning, the wretch certainly didn't look it, despite the bruises that ringed his eyes. He seemed well rested, as if he'd slept on a down-filled pallet. He was trading good-natured insults and comments with his brothers and their fellows like a man without a care in the world!

Surely his ability to sleep like a babe, despite unpleasant circumstances, proved he was lacking in conscience? Or—a second, contrary voice insisted—did it mean instead that he was completely lacking in *guilt*?

"We'll be stopping soon. Ye can rest then. There's a village just over the brae." Gray's deep voice, soft with the lilting Highland burr, broke into her thoughts sometime later. " 'Tis no wealthy hamlet, ye ken, but its villagers will surely trade broth and bread for a coin or two."

Broth and bread? Hmmmm! She was so hungry, her mouth watered as if he'd promised her venison or fruit tartlets!

But the traditional welcome Scottish travelers had a right to expect was not forthcoming from this village.

Scrawny curs snapped at their horses' heels and barked furiously as they rode between the scattering of peat-thatched cottages. A small, ragged lad with a shock of red hair and a ferocious scowl hurled stones at them as their cavalcade rode by. The half-dozen sullen women gathered about the well spat in the dirt and cast them evil glances, like a coven of witches.

"A good day to ye, Grandfather," Graham called, reining in their horse.

A white-haired old man ducked under the lintel of one of the cottages. He remained in the doorway, leaning heavily upon a gnarled wooden staff. The way he carried his grizzled head lent him an air of authority.

"Ride on, my laird MacKenzie. There's naught for ye here." His tone was hostile. Although the faded blue eyes had swiftly recognized the sett of their tartans, they remained unfriendly.

"Ride on, ye say, Grandfather? Whist! 'Tis poor hospitality ye offer us weary travelers, sir! My companions and I will be happy t'pay for a bit of bread and a bowl of broth."

"Happen you would, but we've none t'spare. Not for the likes of you. My people work hard for what little they have. They dinna toil t'line the bellies of your ilk, MacKenzie."

101

Penelope Neri

"My ilk? How so? What manner of man d' ye take me for, sir?" Graham demanded. Though his voice was still low and cordial, his former good humor had fled. His blue eyes were glacial now, his jaw tight and hard.

"Not your father's, that's for sure, honorable man that he was. If ye must have an answer, ask Douglas MacLeod!" the old man suggested. As the village women had done, he spat in the dirt. "Or better yet, ask his grieving widow!" He shook his head, his expression contemptuous.

Gray's jaw hardened. Skyla felt him stiffen before her. His knuckles grew white on the reins.

"I have no need to ask, old man. I know full well what manner of man I am—as does Our Lord. A man of honor, wronged by the lies of others. A man accused of a crime he didna commit! One who shall, someday, prove that he is innocent."

Looking over his shoulder, Gray gestured to the others to follow him from the village.

"Who's the lassie with ye, MacKenzie? Another of your whores?" the old man hurled after them. "Another bone for guid Scots t'sniff after like dogs, before they die—?"

Graham ignored him and rode on, leading the way into the deep woods.

Yet the old man's insults continued to gnaw at him as he rode. . . .

* * *

Within moments, the forest enclosed them in heavy shadow, for the boughs of the trees above them were interlaced and, like a leafy canopy, kept out much of the light.

They rode through a tunnel of wavering sunshine that dappled their garments like golden coins. Thick mosses and turf muffled their horses' hooves.

Despite an abundance of foliage, no birds chirped or fluttered in the branches overhead. Nor had any of them spoken since entering the woods, Gray noticed suddenly. The only sounds were the dull thuds made by their horses—and the sudden racing of his heart.

The fine hairs prickled at his nape. The sixth sense that, in the past, had often warned him of danger was screaming through him now.

Reining in his horse at the edge of a small clearing, he stood in the stirrups and looked warily over his shoulder, first left, then right, then in all directions. His hand closed over the hilt of his dress sword in readiness as he held his breath and listened.

Not a twitter of birdsong, nor the rustle of wild things, reached his ears. Why not? he wondered. What—or who?—had passed this way, and frightened the wild creatures into stillness and silence? Were they watching him, even now—?

Penelope Neri

No sooner had the thought entered his head than his horse reared in sudden fright. Pirouetting on its hindquarters, it almost spilled them both to the ground.

Skyla's grip about Gray's middle tightened convulsively as a huge man dropped, feet first, from the oak before them.

Like a cat, despite his size, he landed nimbly on the balls of his feet, and stood there, fists on hips, laughing at them.

He was tall and broad-shouldered, and garbed in green from head to toe. Over his head he wore a loose, monklike hood that hid his eyes, yet left his lower face bare.

"Well, now! An outlaw, is it!" Gray exclaimed. He released the breath he'd been holding with a chuckle of relieved laughter. Swinging his leg over the horse's neck, he dropped to the ground. "And a hooded one, at that! Is it our purses ye're after, sir rogue?"

Sir rogue—! Here they were, being set upon by robbers and Gray was taunting the wretch, Skyla realized nervously. What was he thinking? Had he gone mad?

Deciding she must think for herself, she hitched forward, onto the saddle, an inch at a time. One eye still on the outlaw, she carefully gathered the reins into her hands, ready to flee.

"Shoo, shoo! Dinna bolt, my lady! 'Tis not what it seems!" Ian, the younger of Gray's two brothers, cautioned her, bringing his horse alongside her own. To make sure she heeded him, he reached down and caught her mount's bridle, preventing its flight. "He's a friend, aye?"

"What will you now, outlaw?" Gray was demanding. "Must I throw down my arms and beg for my worthless life? Or—shall I run ye through?"

"Run me through?" the outlaw echoed with a snort. Fists on hips, he roared with laughter, a giant of a man who stood two tailor's lengths in his booted feet. "With what, mon? Your razor wit? Or that pretty skewer strapped to your side? Go on then. Try it! Such a puny blade will but tickle my liver!"

Grinning scornfully, the outlaw shifted his attention to Skyla, still perched in the chestnut's saddle. He looked her up and down and something flickered in his eyes. Doffing his hood, he swept her a gallant bow.

"Forgive me if I frightened ye, lady. Allow me t'present mysel'. William of Elerslie, and your humble servant," he murmured gallantly as he straightened.

Skyla inclined her head, unable to hide her excitement. *William Wallace!*

"And yours, sir! In truth, 'tis an honor to meet you," she babbled, blushing scarlet to the roots of her hair. The words spilled from her in her eagerness.

The brightness of her smile, the self-conscious way she fussed with her hair—as a woman does when drawn to a man—drew a jealous scowl from Gray.

Skyla quickly looked down at her hands, embarrassed. She had never met the Wallace before, but there was not a freedom-loving Scot in all the Highlands who did not recognize his name!

William Wallace of Elerslie hailed from a village near Paisley, farther to the south. As the second of three sons, he had not been entitled to any of the lands and property his family owned, and so had been studying to enter the priesthood when his father, Sir Malcolm, had been murdered by the English, just like Graham's.

Malcolm's death, coupled with his family's refusal to swear fealty or pay homage to the English king, had transformed William from priest to outlaw-fugitive with a hefty price on his head.

In recent years, Wallace had turned his family's motto, *"Pro Libertate"*—"For Freedom!"— into a rallying cry as he fought to regain Scottish freedom from English rule. They said he never missed a chance to slay enemy English, wherever and whenever he found them. Once crossed, he took no prisoners. Wounded men were dead men.

As a result of his bloody exploits, now legendary on both sides of the Borders, the English feared and hated Wallace, whereas the Scots hailed him as a hero. Why, her own father toasted his health with drams of his finest whiskey!

But although the man's great height was made much of in tales of his exploits, no one had mentioned that William Wallace was also handsome, with the sad eyes and gentle smile of a carved stone angel.

"What brings ye so far from home, friend?" she heard Gray say. "I heard you were to be wed."

"So I was," Wallace said softly, but he added no other comment. He nodded toward Skyla. "And you?"

"Nay. Not yet, anyway," Graham explained with a rueful twist of his lips. "I was bound for Skye last Sabbath, when my lady here delivered unwelcome news."

"Douglas MacLeod's murder? Aye, I heard. They say ye killed him over a woman."

Gray's brows shot up. "Do they, by God?" The rumors had flown faster and farther than he and his men, Gray thought bitterly as Will's nod confirmed his question. "What woman? The lady with me?"

Wallace shook his head. "Fionna, of the Clan MacRae. 'Tis a sept o' your clan, is it no'?"

"Fionna MacRae!" Graham's jaw dropped. It had been months—years—since he'd even thought of her.

"Ye know the lassie, then? 'Tis said ye slew Dougie because she bedded wi' him behind yer back."

Gray snorted in disgust "If that were true, I'd have t'kill half o' Scotland. Aye, and England, too! The lassie's a whore, mon. She makes her living on her back."

Wallace nodded. "Does she now? Then a mon might wonder what purpose such a lie served her?"

Gray nodded grimly. "I dinna ken—but 'tis one that may yet cost me my life. It appears I must find her, aye? If anyone knows who killed Dougie MacLeod, 'tis Fio—"

"*Gray!*" Skyla's warning rang out.

Both men flung around as horses burst into the clearing, ridden by helmeted soldiers! Two of the Sassenachs led packhorses with wooden caskets lashed to their saddles. What did they hold? Skyla wondered fleetingly. Church treasures, stolen from Scottish cathedrals to swell England's treasury?

The English seemed as startled to see the Scots as the Scots were to see them.

"Scatter!" Gray roared.

In the same instant, Ian MacKenzie released

her horse's chin strap. He thwacked its rump. "Ride, lassie!" he rasped. "Ride for your life!"

But instead of fleeing, Skyla yanked her horse's head around and brought it alongside Gray.

Abandon him, horseless and armed with a sword no bigger than a bodkin? She couldn't do it, not to him—not to any man!

Their eyes met for an instant; then he grasped a handful of the horse's mane and vaulted up onto the saddle behind her. Taking the reins, he was about to dig booted heels into the horse's flanks when another rider appeared between the trees.

His mantle was trimmed in fur, and his mount finer than his fellows.

"Well, well, now. What have we here?" His voice rang out, nasal and hard, with none of the melodic burr of the Highlands. "Lady . . . MacLeod, is it not? Charming. Most charming! I wonder. What do you here, madam, so far from your island home, with this rebel band?"

"The lady's doings dinna concern ye, Constable," Graham growled back, glowering at him.

The constable smiled. "Aaah. You must be the murderer Glenrowan, must ye not? A good day to ye, MacKenzie. Although we've never met, I've been told we share the same well-plowed quim, do we not?"

Skyla gasped. Gray's neck darkened in fury. "Shut your clarty mouth, Hartford. I've shared naught with the likes of you—nor will I ever do so!"

The Sassenach smirked, catlike. Satisfied he'd achieved the reaction he wanted, he shifted his attention now to William Wallace. The pale blue eyes glittered like chips of ice. "You, by your oafish height and outlandish garb, can only be Wallace! Your reputation precedes you, outlaw!"

"As does yours, Hartford," Will retorted, sniffing the wind exaggeratedly. "But then, when the breeze is right, the stink of shit is carried in all directions, is it no'?"

For the second time, Skyla gasped. Both Gray's and Wallace's insults were calculated to provoke violence—and they were outnumbered, two to one, were they not?

But to her surprise, the constable merely inclined his dirty-blond head, as if acknowledging that Wallace had scored a point in their contest of words. Yet while his gesture said one thing, his eyes told a very different tale. So did his complexion, which had darkened to a livid plum.

"True," Hartford allowed mildly. "Not unlike your bride's favors, which were shared hither and yon, or so I've heard. Eh? What's that, Ralph?" he asked. He cocked his head, pretending to confer with one of his men-at-arms. "Ah, yes. So she is! I had forgotten. How very un-Christian of me, to speak ill of the fair Lady Marron, when she can no longer defend her honor for herself."

The constable's false smile made Skyla's flesh crawl. Graham's mouth opened, then snapped shut again. Confused, he shot William a questioning look, which his friend stoically ignored.

In fact, Wallace seemed unnaturally calm. He continued to stare at the constable, unblinking, silent, looking neither to right nor to left. Only the tic of a nerve at his temple betrayed the chaos of his innermost feelings.

"Your luckless lady is already worms' meat, is she not, Wallace?" Hartford taunted softly. "So, as a man of Christian forgiveness, I shall ignore your insults—*if* you beg my mercy on bended knee!"

"Go fuck yoursel', Hartford," Wallace said softly, yet crisply.

Without shifting his eyes from Hartford, William told Gray in Gaelic, "Ride, my friend! Take your lady and leave, All of ye, *ride*! Leave these bastards t'me and my merry men! We'll join ye later, at Glenrowan, Lord willing, and share a dram in celebration."

Gray answered with a curt, almost imperceptible nod.

At the touch of its master's heels, the horse

111

sprang forward. Its sudden powerful lunge tore an opening through the ranks of startled Englishmen.

Skyla clung to his belt for dear life as Gray unsheathed his weapon. He sent one English soldier flying with a blow from the flat of his blade, as the horse soared over their ranks.

Behind them, Will Wallace gave throat to a wolflike howl: a bloodcurdling, barbaric cry, born in a time when men worshipped the pagan gods of war.

All at once, the woods came alive! Outlaws in russet and green sprang up from the ground, dropped from the trees, or bristled from bushes and shrubs, almost invisible against bark and leaf.

Armed to the teeth with staff and bow, dirk and sword, cudgel and club, they set upon the English straightway as Graham and Skyla made good their escape.

Eight

A half league on, where a crumbling stone bridge spanned a rushing river, Gray reined in the lathered horse and sprang down from its back. He tugged Skyla down after him.

"If someone comes, hide under the bridge," he told her urgently. "You'll be safe there. I'll come for ye when I can."

"You're going back." It was a statement, not a question. No honorable man would desert a friend in need.

He nodded. "The Wallace willna thank me for it, but aye. I must." Grasping his horse's mane, he flung himself onto its back and gathered up the reins.

"Wait! What if ye—what if ye don't come back?" she cried, hanging on to his stirrup leather.

Reaching down, he plucked her hand from the leather and drew it to his lips. "With someone like yoursel' waitin', ma sonsy, how could ye doubt it?"

She snatched her hand away. "Damn ye, MacKenzie, that's no answer!"

"No?" His eyes were dazzling. "Then take this." He drew his dirk from his boot and handed it to her by the point of the blade. "If I dinna come for ye by morning, head southwest at first light. Use the dagger t'defend yoursel', if ye must. God willing, ye'll reach Lochalsh within two days. But more likely, your kin will find ye before then."

Leaning down from the saddle, he cupped her face in his hand. "God be wi' ye, my heart."

"Don't you dare ride off, MacKenzie!!" she yelled. "Ye canna do this t'me! You *kidnapped* me! Ye canna abandon me now!"

But apparently, he could, for after he wheeled the horse about, he spurred it back the way they'd come, giving her not so much as a backwards glance.

"Ye bluidy bastard!" she screamed after him,

hurling a rock in his horse's wake. "Damn ye t'hell!"

But the rock missed, and Graham—if he'd heard her—gave no indication.

Within moments, the galloping horse and its rider had vanished into the distance.

Would she ever see him again? she wondered. Or would the English murder him?

Weepy and exhausted, she sank down onto the rocky bank of the river, and lobbed pebbles into its foaming current, consigning Gray to a deeper and hotter hell with every stone she tossed . . .

. . . while trying desperately to squelch the ache in her breast that was fear for his safety.

Nine

She was deep in the arms of Morpheus, dozing in a hidden hollow beneath the bridge, when she heard a voice calling her name. It sounded like Gray, yet was different, somehow. Far away. Disembodied

'Tis a dream, she told herself, reluctant to wake up. Or Gray's ghost, come back to haunt ye! Dinna answer, and 'twill go away!

The past twenty-four hours had taught her that sleep was less painful than being awake.

It was unlikely Gray had survived the skirmish in the woods, she thought, a catch in her throat and an ache in her heart, even as she drifted between sleeping and waking. He and the Wallace had been outnumbered two to one by the Sassenachs. The Scots had also been far less heavily armed than the bluidy English.

They were armed for courting, not feuding or murder, a tiny, nagging voice reminded her.

Surely Gray would never have come to Skye so poorly armed if he meant to do other than court her, she thought guiltily. That fact, more than any other, screamed that he was innocent of everything she'd accused him of.

His heavy claymore had been left behind at Glenrowan. His companions, like their laird, had also been unarmed, as custom demanded. Guests arrived without weaponry to demonstrate their trust that their host and his clansmen would do them no harm while they were guests of the household.

It was a custom as old as Scotland herself.

As a result, except for a handful of dirks and a few ornate dress swords, Gray and his followers had been virtually unarmed. Hardly the mark of murderers! That very fact might well have cost them all their lives, she thought. She stirred fitfully in her sleep as the disembodied voice called her name again:

"Skyyyylaaa! Skyyyylaaa!"

Whist. It doesna sound human at all! 'Tis far too hollow and too deep, like a ghost's.

It was a ghost—it had to be!

Granny Elspeth had spoken often of—and to—ghosts as she grew older. She'd told Skyla that not all ghosts were the same. Some were the ghosts of the living—what she termed a "fetch," a spirit that left its sick or sleeping body to wander abroad.

Others were true ghosts, the spirits of those whose earthly lives had ended. After they cast off their mortal bodies, they returned as phantoms to visit their loved ones, not knowing that they were dead, and could be seen only by those with the Gift. And so, instead of flying up to heaven—or tumbling down into fiery hell, as the case might be—they remained earthbound, haunting the places where they'd lived while alive.

Did that explain the voice she could hear, calling her name? she wondered. Had Gray's spirit returned to haunt her, not knowing he had been killed by the Sassenach constable and his men?

Terrified of what she might see, she forced her eyes to open.

But instead of a misty wraith hovering over her, as she half expected, there was only Graham: solid, sweaty, his handsome face streaked with blood and dirt. Undeniably—disgustingly—alive! His voice was amplified in some mysterious way by the belly of the stone bridge that arched over them.

"It is you!" Her own voice echoed as she pushed herself up from the scrap of gloomy riverbank where she'd hidden to wait for him.

"Aye. Were ye expecting a kelpie, ma sonsy?" he demanded, grinning. "Or auld Longshanks himsel', mayhap?"

She clicked her teeth with annoyance as she scrambled to her knees. "Never mind your nonsense. What happened with the English? Did you—?" She left the rest of her question to hover in the air, but he knew what she meant.

His grin vanished. He shook his head as he crouched beside her.

When he'd returned to the forest, he'd heard the metallic clang of blade on blade ringing through the hushed woods. The grunts and screams as men on both sides fell dead or dying. Human screams had mingled with the terrified screams of the horses as they scented fresh blood.

In the few moments he'd been gone, Wallace and his men had felled a half dozen of the English. The rest, Hartford among them, had abandoned their pack animals and hastily fled.

They had left their dead and dying to the hungry ravens and crows that waited in the treetops, and to William Wallace, bane of the English who, like the carrion-eaters, took no prisoners.

"Nay, lassie," Graham said in answer to her

question. "We didna kill them all, more's the pity. Hartford and some of his men escaped, God rot 'em! But . . ." Here his engaging grin resurfaced, shining from his dirty face. "They left wi'out their coin, thanks t'the Wallace and his men. Hartford will not be happy about that. Nor will he soon forget, I'm thinking! The caskets held silver chalices and gold platters, stolen from Scottish kirks and cathedrals. It will be put t'good use in the fight for Scotland's freedom! Every army needs a full purse, for it canna fight on an empty belly, nor wi' an empty hand."

"And where—er—where is the Wallace now?" Did she sound a little too eager? Too interested? She hoped the shadows under the bridge would hide the pinkness of her cheeks.

"Up on the bridge, with his men. They'll lie low with us at Glenrowan for a bit, so rouse yoursel', ye slugabed. I shall sup at my own table this evening, or know the reason why. Aye, and sleep in my own bed! A muddy ditch may be good enough for you heathenish MacLeods, but 'tis not my idea o' comfort!" he teased her.

Glenrowan, she discovered less than two hours later, was not half as imposing as Dunvegan. It was, however, far more beautiful.

While her ancestral home squatted defiantly

upon its mount of craggy black rocks like a brooding hawk upon an ugly aerie, surrounded on three of its sides by the gray crashing sea, Glenrowan was a crannog, a glowing golden jewel of a keep that soared from a manmade island in the center of a natural lake.

The lake itself was cupped by a broad and lovely glen, forested with rowan trees and alive with red deer and other game. Swans sailed like miniature ships across its lake, which gleamed like a looking glass in the afternoon light.

The gatehouse, flanked by round guard towers, was reached by crossing a narrow causeway of land, shored up by slabs of stone. Riders and wagons could pass easily to and from the keep, yet it could still be readily defended.

Furthermore, the lake itself ensured a ready supply of drinking water that could not be easily drained, in the event of a siege.

Small wonder the English had ambushed Gray's father while he was hunting and far from his donjon, Skyla thought, casting a shrewd eye over Glenrowan's fortifications. No MacKenzie laird could be pried from his keep, as long as the causeway was manned.

As their horses clattered into the bailey, the Clan MacKenzie ceased its labors and surged forward to meet their horses, eager to welcome their laird and his brothers home. They were also eager to get their first look at the MacLeod lass who was to be the MacKenzie's bride—or so they believed.

As she looked down at their unfamiliar faces, it struck her for the first time that she knew no one but Gray here.

She would be quite alone at Glenrowan, surrounded by a clan that, for the last century, had feuded with her own.

And without allies, she would find no escape from this place—not without careful planning.

"My lady?" a red-faced young woman began determinedly, elbowing her way through the throng to reach her horse. Fresh-cheeked, plump, yet surprisingly determined, she thrust a posy of wildflowers under Skyla's nose. "For you, my lady! Welcome t'Glenrowan! The MacKenzie said I was to be your serving woman, if it please ye? I am called Mary Jean, my lady."

Skyla took the flowers from the breathless girl, and buried her nose in their fragrant pastel faces. The sweet innocence of their scent, their cool velvety petals, made her heart ache for innocence lost.

"It would please me, aye. I'm sure we shall do verra well together. Thank you, Mary Jean," she murmured warmly, reaching down and squeezing the girl's hand. It would be nice to have at least one friend in this place, and the girl's sweet, plump face was open and friendly, indeed. " 'Twas verra kind of ye t'gather these for me."

Mary beamed, shooting her giggling friends a triumphant smile over her shoulder. Her expression was adoring as she gazed up at her mistress. "Och, not at all. 'Twas my pleasure, milady! If there's anything ye need—anything at all—ye have only t'ask your Mary, my lady."

And so her captivity began.

"Whist! She looks a mite long in the tooth t'me, laddie," Graham's Uncle Archibald declared dourly that evening in the great hall as he hobbled around her.

Freshly bathed and wearing a kirtle of simple gray-blue wool that Mary had borrowed for her from somewhere, Skyla was forced to stand there and fume as Graham and his uncles carried on as if she were elsewhere, or deaf, at the very least. "Ye'll only get ten years of childbearing oot of her, I'm thinking. Can ye no' find a younger woman t'wed ye?"

The old goat peered down his beaky nose at her, intent as a hawk. "How many winters have ye seen, woman?"

"Twenty, sir," she retorted through clamped jaws and gritted teeth. She tossed her auburn head in defiance, and shot the old fool a frosty glare. Two spots of crimson burned in her cheeks.

"Twenty! There, ye see? I told ye, laddie.

Open your mouth, woman. Show me your teeth."

"I shall not," she declared, clamping her jaws shut. Woe betide the man who tried to pry them apart! "I am the lord of the Isle's daughter—not some spavined nag at a horse fair. I willna be treated in this fashion!"

His uncles had gone too far this time, Gray thought with a gusty sigh, hiding a grin. Skyla was furious at being prodded and gawped at. Anger showed in every line of her slender body. He hid a smile. Unless they watched themselves, his paternal uncles, Archibald and Kenneth, were in for a spirited exchange he sorely doubted they'd win. Or, if they pushed her to the edge, God help them, a bloody nose apiece!

"Hrrrrrmmph. As I said, boy, she's long in the tooth and has a waspish temper, besides," Archibald declared with every evidence of glee. "Mark my words, laddie. She'll prove a shrew as a wife. Aye, and a scold, too. Wed her at your peril! Whist, were I you, I'd send her home to her father!" Archie MacKenzie said emphatically.

"If you were my bridegroom, sir," Skyla shot back, bobbing him a mocking curtsy, "I would go—and gladly! In truth, I can think of nothing that would make me happier!"

"What's that? Why, ye impudent wee besom! I've a mind t'—"

"Now, now, Archie," Kenneth cut in. "Give the lassie a chance. True, she's older than most brides, but . . . och, she's verra bonny, is she no'? And that red hair promises a carnal nature—"

"—and a bad temper, too!" Archibald cut in, smacking his lips with satisfaction.

"Och, never mind her temper. Spirit's a fine thing in a woman—and in a man's bed. Besides, will ye look at that bosom? And the fine firm arse she has on her? Whist, 'tis like a ripe peach, waiting t'be squeezed! In truth, the lassie's built for warming a mon's bed and bearing him lusty bairns. Is she not, Morag, my pigeon?"

The old fellow pinched the midwife's scrawny buttocks. Morag, several decades beyond being a lass herself, responded by coyly tittering and primping as she slapped his hands away, showing the gaps between her long teeth in the process.

"Och, that she is, Kenny, lad. That she is!"

"There. D'ye see, Archie?" Kenneth Mac-Kenzie declared, jabbing an elbow in his twin brother's ribs. "What more could our laddie ask for? Now, leave our two turtledoves be, do! They'll be wanting to plan their nuptials, I shouldn't wonder—unless they were marrit on Skye?"

The thrifty old devil cocked a bushy white

brow in Skyla's direction, plainly hoping the expense of the wedding feast had been borne by the bride's father, and the Mackenzie coffers spared.

"We were not," Skyla ground out through clenched jaws, not bothering to conceal her relief.

Archibald's face dropped. "A pity! A verra great pity . . ."

"What's wrong wi' her, nephew?" Kenneth—the more astute of the pair—asked. He nodded his whiskery chin at Skyla over the rim of his mug of mead. "Ye said the MacLeod lassie was hot t'wed ye, before ye went t'fetch her home, did ye not? She doesna look t'be burnin' for ye now, m'boy—! Far from it! 'Tis the face my Sheilagh was wearing, the day she learned I'd taken Morag as my leman. The miserable auld shrew never shared my bed nor smiled from that day, until the day we laid her in her grave!"

"Are ye sure she was dead when ye did it?" Skyla wondered aloud, shooting the old man a venomous glare.

"What do ye mean by that, woman?" Kenneth demanded hotly, his jaw jutting in a quarrelsome fashion.

"Shoo, shoo, the three of ye!" Gray declared before either of them could resort to blows to solve their differences. "Skyla's no shrew—are ye, ma doo?"

The Gaelic endearment meant "my dove," but a woman less like a dove at that moment would have been hard to find.

"She smiles often enough, Uncle. But right now, she's a wee bit tired—and verra fashed at me. Someone murdered her uncle, ye ken, and blamed me for it. Ye canna fault the lass for not wanting to wed her uncle's murderer! Or at least, the mon she believes is one."

Kenneth MacKenzie's eyes narrowed. He stared at Skyla as if he hadn't really noticed her before and sucked thoughtfully on his gums.

"Does she now? How so? Seems t'me a bride should trust the mon she's t'wed," he suggested mildly, after giving the matter a few moments' thought. "And accept his word, when 'tis given her, as she'll soon accept his vows."

"You're right, Uncle," Graham murmured, shooting Skyla a long and level look. "As always, ye give sound counsel."

"Ohhh, pish!" Skyla muttered under her breath, damning the furious color that rose up her cheeks. "Any more o' this, and I'm going t'hurl!"

Her expression of relief was almost comical as the ancient twins—Graham's father's much older half brothers—bade them a good evening and hobbled off to their chairs by the hearth and an unfinished game of chess.

"Congratulations, ma sonsy. Ye've passed the final test. My uncles approve of ye."

"Ha! Then I'd hate to hear what they say when they dinna approve! Still, their likes or dislikes change nothing. I'm not marrying ye, MacKenzie."

Graham laughed as he handed her a brimming goblet of wine. "Here, sweeting. Drink this. 'Twill soften that 'shrewish' temper of yours."

Skyla accepted the goblet with an impatient snort. She was about to set it aside, untasted, when she thought better of it and drained the cup in a single swallow.

The fine feast of roasted mutton and all the trimmings had left her growling belly pleasantly filled. The sweet wine would bring a good night's rest—her first in a proper bed since leaving Dunvegan so unexpectedly.

"Ye have a rare appetite for a lassie," Graham observed, chewing a mouthful of coarse dark bread as he regarded her. "But I agree with my Uncle Kenneth. MacKenzie men like their women with meat on their bones, we do. A fine fat wench keeps a mon warm at night, aye?" He winked.

"I am not fat," she said softly. *Too* softly by far. "Perhaps you should find yourself another woman?"

129

Gray chuckled. "I think not. We'll do well together, you and I, once ye come to your senses. Both at table, *and* in our marriage bed," he added in a lower, sensual voice. He reached out to take her hand between his, but she snatched it away.

"Devil take ye, MacKenzie! That I'm here means nothing! There will be no marriage, no table, and of a certainty, *no marriage bed*! My father will send his men t'bring me home within a day or two, you'll see," she declared with a toss of her auburn head. Her cool, smoky eyes blazed, hotter than ever before. "Ye may think you can keep me here, MacKenzie, but ye can't. Not without great cost to ye—'fine fat woman' or nay!"

"A pity," Graham murmured, leaning back with a sigh in the carved chair he'd placed alongside hers. "I'd hoped this could be done wi'out bloodshed."

"Bloodshed?" Her brows arched in dismay.

"Aye. That is what you meant by great cost, was it not?" he asked innocently. "That your kinsmen will be after my blood for stealing you away? If they come, I'll have t'defend mysel', will I no'? Blood will be spilled, lives lost, on both sides. A pity, as I said, when there's a less . . . bloody solution, one that's easily come by, aye?"

"What solution is that?" she asked warily.

The MacKenzie was as crafty as a fox. She must never forget that.

"Send a messenger to Skye wi' a letter for your father, lassie," he urged. "One that says ye chose me for your husband long ago, and mean t'wed me. Ye're able to write, are you no'? If not, my priest will pen the missive; then you may make your mark at the bottom," he offered generously.

"Make my mark? How dare you! I have a fine hand, I'll have ye know!" she flared. "What did ye expect? That I was an ignorant unschooled lummox, as well as a—a 'long-toothed, waspish shrew'?"

Her hackles were up. Indignation hummed in every taut line of her body.

Several of the gathering turned to stare in the direction of her raised voice.

"On the contrary, my laird," she went on. "My brother and I shared a tutor when we were small, and I was quicker to learn then Alec ever was.

"But I digress. May I remind you that I am not your guest here, but your prisoner, sir? A pampered one, I admit, but a prisoner nonetheless! I refuse to pretend otherwise!"

"My prisoner?" Gray shook his head. "Not so, lassie." His brilliant blue eyes danced with wicked glee. Her cheeks were flushed, her gray eyes full of sparks.

Exhausted or no, she had never looked more spirited nor more vividly lovely than she did at that moment. His stones ached with wanting her. His heart hurt with the need to hold her. To lose himself in the fiery softness of her body. Yet the sun-furrows at the outer corners of his eyes deepened as he smiled.

"There are no locks upon your chamber door. No bars at your latchets. Neither chains nor manacles bind your bonny limbs," he pointed out. He cocked his ebony head and eyed what little he could see of those bonny limbs with a wolfish grin, then took her hand between his own and drew it to his lips. "In truth, madam, you seem in perfect health, for a prisoner. A rose in fullest, lovely bloom."

He ducked his head. His lips tickled her skin as he kissed her inner wrist.

She sucked in a breath, for it felt as if his fairy kisses scorched her flesh. When she looked down, she expected to see a brand there. A scorch mark in the shape of his lips upon the delicate blue tracings that led straight to her heart.

But there was nothing, she realized, her tawny brows arching in surprise, although she could still feel his kiss upon her skin . . . and in the farthest reaches of her heart, if truth were told.

"My lady," Gray added in a lower, huskier

voice. His eyes were dark now, a turbulent blue under ink-black brows. "You are as free as the wind t'nest or fly, as ye see fit. It is my hope that Glenrowan will become your home. Not your cage."

"You lie, MacKenzie!" She wrenched her hand free of his fingers with a great show of distaste. "One of your women has attended my every step since first I came here. When I took my rest, she slept nearby, ready to spring to her post the second I awoke. She dressed my hair, brought me fresh garments . . . in truth, at all times, she was closer than my summer shadow. What is that, pray, if not a—a gaoler or a spy?"

He chuckled. "A truly devoted servant, my lady—and my second cousin, Mary Jean Mac-Kenzie. True, the lassie's a mite . . . overeager. But since she begged t'serve ye, what was I to say?" He threw up his hands in defeat. "Never mind. If Mary displeases ye, I'll find another t'serve ye."

His tone made her feel unkind, blast him. She tossed her head.

"Och, never mind! Mary Jean will do well enough." In all honesty, she liked the girl. "But what of the guard who watches the causeway at all hours? Is he yet another 'cousin' of yours, my laird?"

"Indeed, no." He grinned. "Lachlann is my Uncle Archie's son-in-law."

"With so many sentries, how may I leave this place, should I wish to sally forth? Sail across the wretched lake, like one of your swans? Or sprout wings, to soar over Glenrowan's walls?

He chuckled. "I dinna doubt ye could sprout wings and fly, heavenly angel that ye are, ma sonsy. And Lord knows, ye're lovely as any swan." He stared at her pale, swanlike throat, which begged his kisses, yet staunchly resisted the urge.

"However, it would be easier for ye to ride wherever you wish t'go. Flying might set idle tongues to clacking that ye dabble in witch-craft, aye? And Lord knows, I've trouble enough, wi'out that. Though I allow," he added, almost as an afterthought, "that ye've bewitched me, madam. . . ."

He trailed his fingertips down her forearm, barely touching her sleeves. The blue wool seemed to sizzle. Indeed, even such a light caress made her shiver. Gooseflesh sprang out upon her arms.

She swallowed. Why could she not ignore the wretched man? Why could she not remain unmoved by his efforts at seduction?

Because you're not unmoved, ye silly besom! came her answer. Because the mon's touch makes ye melt like butter in the sun. Because a word, a glance, turns ye soft and wanting, deep in your belly. But most of all, because, in your secret heart, you know that you lo—

No!

She would not say it. Would not even think it!

"Dinna count your chickens too soon, Mac-Kenzie!" she hissed, pulling her arm away. Her gray eyes flashed. "I'm not your bride now—and nor shall I ever be! How many times must I remind ye?"

Standing, she walked away from him with a haughty toss of her dark red hair. Yet . . . her fingers strayed to touch where his lips had caressed her as she walked away. And when they did, she felt weak at the knees all over again.

"Or, failing wings, ma sonsy witch," he called after her in an almost bantering tone, "ye could bind me ever deeper with a lovespell. Charm me with honeyed words and kisses t'set ye free."

He sounded so hopeful, looked so droll, she almost laughed.

"Kisses, ye say? Sweet words?" she asked, halting. She shook her head. "I think not, sir! Such ploys would serve only to bring me to your bed, yet do nothing to secure my freedom!"

"Aye," he admitted with disarming honesty, a wicked smile wreathing his striking face and playing about his sensual mouth. "They would."

Against her wishes, she caught herself staring at his lips. Oh, God. How did he do that? What made her fingers itch to trace the dimples at their corners? To smooth the ball of her thumb over his fuller lower lip, then replace it with her mouth and with her kisses . . .

She flicked her head in annoyance. Why could she not stop thinking about the rogue, no matter how she tried? Was he a warlock in his own right? Had he the power to weave glamours about her? To command her every thought?

"Would warming my bed—*our* marriage bed—be so awful for ye, my sweet?" he asked in a low, taunting voice. "Once upon a time, you enjoyed my kisses, aye? And you were eager to become my bride." His voice was low. Husky. "Have ye forgotten that, my sweet?" he asked in a silky, sensual tone that played havoc with her breathing. "Don't ye remember how it is between us? The fire we kindle together?"

She flushed, remembering only too well how eagerly she had kissed him on the shores of Lochalsh. How loath she had been to leave his arms. Dear God! The blaze they made had threatened to incinerate them both that day. . . .

But that moment seemed a lifetime ago now. As distant as the moon.

"I have forgotten nothing," she whispered. "That was before your kinsmen killed my own."

His complexion darkened. His shoulders stiffened. "Tell me, my lady. How shall I prove to you that I am innocent? That neither I nor any member of my clan took part in Douglas MacLeod's murder?"

"You may do so easily, my laird. Bring the guilty party before me! Let me hear from his own lips that you are innocent."

"Is my sworn word no' enough for ye, then, lassie?" he growled, angry that she would question his word, once he had given it. Had she been a man, he would have challenged her for the insult. "I had honor t'spare two weeks past!"

Unable to meet his accusing look, she turned her head aside and whispered, "Not in this."

Anger darkened his throat. His hands clenched into huge powerful fists at his sides. "Ye dinna mean that, ye stubborn wee baggage. Look at yer cheeks. Pink wi' guilt, they are! Nor can ye look me full in the eye and accuse me t'ma face! But if 'tis Dougie McLeod's murtherer you're wanting for your dowry, then by God, 'tis he ye'll have. But first, I will have your sworn word, my lady."

"Mine?" She frowned. "Upon what matter, sir?"

137

"That ye'll wed me when I deliver your uncle's murderer to ye. Do it now. Swear it again!"

"Wed ye?" she sputtered. "I made no such promise!"

"Och, but ye did. On the shores of Lochalsh, when I asked ye t'be my bride, remember? Ye took an oath t'me that day, and sealed it with a kiss. Just as ye did that day in the great glen, ten years ago! 'Now joined by blood are we, so joined forevermore will be.' Remember?

"Ye were most eager to give me whatever I asked for that day, in return for the stag's life, aye? Do it again now. Swear ye'll wed me, if I give ye what ye want. Swear here, before our good company," he urged.

He gestured at the MacKenzie clansmen, seated at the trestles below his own table, and at the servants scattered about the great hall.

All of them had stopped what they were doing and were eyeing their lord and herself expectantly, Mary Jean, Jamie, Ian, and Gray's uncles among them.

They had been eavesdropping, she realized.

She drew a deep breath. "Very well. I will marry you, on one condition, my lord Glenrowan. That you bring me proof the guilty party isna you, nor one of your kin." Her expression said she doubted that day would ever come.

"Done, by God!" Gray vowed, bringing his fist down onto the trestle before him with such a thump, the goblets, candlesticks, and Skyla all jumped.

He and his obstinate bride were as good as wed, he thought, congratulating himself!

"You, Hamish. Fetch whiskey! Your lady and I would share a dram t'seal our bargain."

"Straightway, sir," the grinning servant promised.

Hope! he thought, eyeing Skyla as a hungry cat eyes a plump mouse. 'Twas a heady aphrodisiac!

Now all he had to do was find Dougie's murderer, and she was his. . . .

Ten

Sleep would not come to her that night, despite her exhaustion and the wine. She tossed and turned on the feather pallet, her restlessness underscored by the soft snores from Mary's pallet across the tower chamber.

Silly girl, Skyla thought fondly. Mary had staunchly denied being weary, yet had fallen asleep the instant her head touched the bolster, just as Skyla's little sister, Catriona, often did.

Skyla sighed. If only she could fall asleep so readily. Her fitful doze beneath the bridge had refreshed her somewhat, but had not been the deep sleep her body badly needed. And now, she was too restless to sleep at all.

Tossing aside the wool coverlet, she stepped into her soft kid slippers, wound a woolen arisaid about her shoulders, and climbed the steep spiral staircase that led up and out onto the battlements.

The sounds of wild revelry and the skirl of the pipes reached her from the great hall below, despite the late hour, signifying that the feast the servants had prepared to welcome the laird and his promised bride continued. But tonight, the "promised bride" preferred to be alone with her thoughts.

A sharp wind buffeted her as she stepped out onto the battlements. It tossed her hair, lifting it in a great dark cloud about her shoulders. The fringed hems of the tartan flapped this way and that, molding her borrowed night rail to her body.

Hugging herself about the arms, she made her way to the crenellated walk. The stone felt icy beneath her slippers. The wind carried the promise of autumn on its breath, as crisp and cold as cider brought up from the cellars. Yet tonight, she welcomed the chill. Cold helped to sweep the cobwebs from her thoughts and sharpen her resolve.

Above Glenrowan yawned a sable sky, strewn with tiny stars, sequins sewn to a costly mantle of midnight-blue velvet. Below, the lake that moated the keep was smooth as black glass, except for where it was broken by wind-blown ripples, rimmed in gilt by the light of a full moon.

Beyond the lake lay the glen itself, and the dark rowan woods for which Gray's keep had been named. By daylight, she had noticed the trees were heavily hung with the scarlet rowan berries used by some in the making of jellies and tisanes—and by others in the brewing of potions and the casting of spells. The supple rowan also yielded the finest wood for bows.

But tonight, the dark masses of the rowan woods were somehow mysterious and threatening. Who knew what dangers lurked within their shadows? Wild creatures like the badger, the fox, the rabbit, and the stoat—or other wild creatures that were far more dangerous: Sassenach soldiers, bristling with daggers and swords, as they had been that afternoon. . . .

"Lady."

Startled by that low, single word, and the scrape of a boot on stone, she gasped and twisted around. Her hand flew to her heart.

A tall figure formed a darker shape in the shadows, just an arm's length away.

"Who goes there?" she called. Her voice sounded thin and frightened to her ears. Small wonder that it did. Her heart was pounding.

" 'Tis William Wallace, my lady," the man murmured as he stepped forward into a shaft of gray moonlight. "Forgive me if I startled ye."

"Nor did you, sir," she lied. "A good even' to ye. We missed your company at supper. Have you eaten?"

"I was not hungry, madam. Please, you must forgive my absence at your table. I am poor company of late."

"Come, sir. I find that hard to believe," she said, forcing her voice to sound light and teasing.

"Nevertheless, it is so. Nay, nay, you do not have to cheer me," he protested when she would have insisted. He smiled. "Though it is most kind of you to try."

"What—what are you doing here, sir?"

"I came up here to pray, madam. And to be alone with my thoughts. As, I suspect, did you?" He cocked a questioning brow at her.

"I did, yes," she admitted. "But since you came here first, I shall leave you to your devotions." She gave him a shy, uncertain smile. "A very good evening to you, my lord Wallace."

"My lady? You are afraid of me!" he said softly when she would have hurried off.

"A little, perhaps," she admitted, turning back toward him.

"For what reason? If some deed or word of

mine has frightened you, then I ask you to forgive me, for it was never my intent."

When she refused to answer, he wondered aloud, "Was it what Hartford said in the woods? Did you understand what he said?"

"In truth, very little, milord." She had understood more of what had been said to Graham, especially the part about him and the loathsome constable sharing the same . . . well, the same woman. Not surprisingly, that part, in particular, remained sharp and clear in her mind.

What woman had they shared? she had wondered immediately. *Who? And when?* She was not naive. She knew men, many men, were of a baser nature than women. That, like stags, they were in constant rut. Nonetheless, she could not bear the thought of Gray bedding someone else—in truth, she was even jealous of those he had bedded before they'd met again. . . .

Wallace spoke again. "Perhaps my inclination to solitude and melancholy would make better sense if I explained?"

"Really, my lord Wallace. You have no need to explain yourself to me, sir."

"I know that. But . . . I would like to."

"Very well, then. By all means, continue, sir."

"I was but newly married, ye ken?" he began, smiling a wistful, sad smile. "My bride, Marron, and I had been sweethearts since we were children. She was a beautiful woman and I loved her dearly, but we could not live together as man and wife. The English had declared me an outlaw, you see, and placed a price upon my head."

"How so?" she whispered.

"A few years before, my father had refused to swear fealty to King Edward. The English killed him for it, and I had made it my . . . business . . . to see that they paid for his murder tenfold! The sheriff of Lanark was particularly . . . displeased with my outlawry. His efforts to arrest me forced me beyond the pale. The forest became home to me and my merry band—my brother, little John, and the others.

"We made frequent forays from our forest stronghold to ambush passing travelers and 'lighten' the fat purses of the English."

Here, he allowed himself a faint smile.

"The coin we took, we gave t'feed the Scottish poor! Such deeds won us the bitter enmity of the local sheriff, who swore he would see me hanged for my crimes."

"So, I visited Marron only after dark, then slipped away when the coast was clear. Somehow, Lanark got word that I meant to visit my bride that last night. We were abed when I heard his men battering down the door and roaring my name. I slipped out the back and

146

fled for the forest, thinking 'twas a fine jest to play upon the sheriff. But Lanark had the last laugh, God rot him. He ordered his men to fire the cottage. It burned t'the ground with Marron in it."

"Sweet Jesu!" Markedly paler now, she crossed herself.

"Aye. 'Twas so. I had my revenge of Lanark and his men not long after. The bastards paid in blood for what they did that night. But their deaths meant nothing, for the woman I loved was gone. And vengeance couldna bring her back to me. Life is precious and verra short, my lady Skyla," he added, looking her squarely in the eye now. "I pray that you remember it.

"We canna tell when our days—or the days of those we love—shall come to an end. I beg you to remember that. You love Glenrowan. I see it in your eyes, though your lips tell another tale. Soon, he will fight at my right hand," he went on, "in battle against the English. Love him now, lady. Love him for as long and as well as you can, for who knows how that battle may end?"

His words made her skin prickle, as if someone had walked over her grave.

Her grandmother had prophesied that her betrothed would someday "stand at the Hammer's right hand," had she not? And the Wallace was called the "Hammer of the English," just as King Edward was known as the "Hammer of the Scots."

"Only our Good Lord knows who will prevail that day," he went on. "For that reason, if no other, I beg ye. Set aside what your head tells ye. Forget your pride, forget revenge. Listen t'your heart, instead. Love him, lady. Wed him. Make him happy. Hold him fast to ye for all the days God gives ye together."

With that, he turned abruptly on his heel and marched away, toward the stairs—though not before she had seen the moisture that glistened on his cheeks.

"Sir!" she called after him. "Wait!"

He froze in mid-stride. Without turning his head, he murmured, "Aye, lady?"

"I—I canna take away your sorrow, sir, nor return your love to ye. But in my prayers, I shall ask God t'help ye accept His will."

He nodded. "You are kind, my lady," he murmured. "I thank you for it." With that, he nodded and left.

Eleven

Skyla sighed as windblown ripples stirred the glassy lake below her latchet.

Just a few short weeks ago, she had watched elegant Glenrowan swans gliding by like Viking longships. But now, the Swans had heeded some inner call and flown south for the winter.

She had watched them lift into the sky one evening, just as the setting sun splashed the sky with pink and gold.

Forming a perfect arrowhead formation, they had wheeled away, headed south. She had not seen them since.

The swans' departure left her saddened and

feeling more alone than before, although in all honesty, she was never truly alone, thanks to Mary.

The girl waited hand and foot upon her, hung upon her every word, served her every need. In truth, she was in all ways devoted to her.

As the days passed, Skyla began to return Mary's affection, little by little. Closer to her own age than her Dunvegan nurse, Moira, had ever been, the girl had quickly became both friend and confidante—as well as Gray's loyal advocate.

"Can ye not take the MacKenzie's word about your uncle, then, madam?" Mary would implore her as they worked at some piece or other of sewing.

That morning, their work was a pair of breeks they were patching for his lairdship.

Since Gray's mother had died, several years before, there had been no gentlewoman to tend to the household's sewing or to see to ordering the servants as a chatelaine should.

As a result, Glenrowan had sprouted holes in every conceiveable piece of cloth or garment, from the laird's hose to the linen tablecloths.

Skyla had made it her mission—or penance was a better term—to remedy both matters and bring her knowledge of sewing, fine embroidery, and the proper running of a household to Glenrowan while she was in residence.

She considered it a penance because in all honesty, she was not accomplished at either plain sewing or fancy embroidery. In truth, her stitches were more often large and ugly and very apparent, than invisible, as she would have wished them to be.

However, it was something to do, and it needed doing, and since everyone seemed to wholeheartedly appreciate even her smallest efforts, however inferior, she continued them.

"Why should I take Laird Graham's word?" Skyla demanded impishly, answering Mary's question as she glanced over at the plump girl.

Mary's brown eyes were huge with worry in her fresh-complexioned face. Furthermore, she was blushing—proof, Skyla suspected, that the girl was more than half in love with the master of Glenrowan herself.

"Weell, he's verra honorable, the MacKenzie, aye? And his word is his bond. I know he wouldna lie, not to you, my lady. A fool could see he loves ye dearly!"

"Hrrmph. So ye keep telling me. But ye dinna make prisoners of those ye profess t'love, Mary Jean," Skyla sternly reminded the girl. "Ouch!"

She sucked at the finger she'd poked with the needle as a tiny droplet of blood appeared.

"You, a prisoner, my lady?" Mary giggled, seeming to find the idea vastly amusing. " 'Tis nonsense, madam! There are no bars at your casements. No shackles aboot your wrists! Why, madam, you're no more of a prisoner here than—than I am, say!" Mary declared with merry peals of laughter.

"Did his lordship tell ye to say that?" Skyla demanded, for Mary's words had a distinctly familiar ring to them.

"No, dear madam. 'Tis just—common sense. Why, look at you!"

Appearances notwithstanding, however, Skyla still thought of herself as a prisoner, although—as Mary was ever quick to point out—she was fed, watered, and entertained like some pampered songbird within the tapestried cage of Glenrowan's walls.

Furthermore, if she was completely honest with herself, for the past six weeks, her every wish had been fulfilled. Every wish, that is, except for the one wish all prisoners wanted granted above any others. To go free! To return to her beloved Isle of Skye and her mother, the Lady Shona. To her papa. To her brother, Alec. To Rowena and their little sister, Catriona. To be far, far from Graham and his Highland stronghold, his wild clansmen, and his eccentric uncles, forever!

Or, so she told herself . . .

She would, of course, miss Mary terribly, if she were to leave Glenrowan now. And she would never learn all the recipes for healing simples and woolen dyes that wicked Auld Morag had promised to teach her. The midwife's knowledge of herb lore far outstripped Skyla's grandmother's.

Then there was the master of Glenrowan himself, for—despite the Wallace's urgings that night on the battlements—she had yet to approach Graham, or to take back her rash, proud vow that she would never wed him.

Och, aye, if she were to leave here now, she would miss Glenrowan, too, though in a different way. As one missed a tooth that suddenly ceased to ache, or missed the throbbing when a sharp thorn was finally drawn from a badly poisoned foot.

He was both aching tooth and thorn, and more. . . .

She sighed. Her feelings were so confused. Her fickle heart wanted one thing one moment, and something else entirely another.

On the one hand, she told herself she hated Graham now, and so went to great lengths to avoid him. She ignored any affectionate overtures on his part. Refused invitations to go riding with him, or to share games of chess, and covered her ears rather than listen to his undoubtedly dreadful lute-playing in the solar.

When she sat by his side at the laird's high table each evening, in the seat of honor reserved for the clan chieftain's lady, dressed in a borrowed kirtle with an arisaid of the Mac-Kenzie plaid pinned at the shoulder, she also refused the tender morsels of game, poultry, or salmon he offered her on the point of his eating knife.

Nor did she so much as glance his way when the steward poured her a goblet of sweet wine from the vineyards of France. Or when a servant brought her bowls of warm scented water and clean linens with which to wash her greasy fingertips after eating.

Nay. She would not openly acknowledge his existence.

Privately, secretly, a very different state of affairs existed. For, deep in her heart of hearts, she was acutely aware of Graham as a man.

In truth, the depth of her female response to his maleness shocked her, for she had never thought of herself as either wicked or wanton. But her thoughts, as far as Gray was concerned, were often both.

His lilting burr reminded her of the fragrant peat fires they had burned at Dunvegan, and of the smooth dark burn of her father's aged malt whiskey.

Aaah, that voice! Its sensual timbre possessed a magic that fanned the sparks of her innocent desire into roaring flame.

Even the most innocuous word he uttered

left her breathless and wobbly-kneed. His endearments, the way he said her name, reached deep inside her, like a caressing hand. One that teased heat and pleasure throughout her belly and between her thighs, just as a lover's caresses might do.

"Skyyyla, ma doo," his whiskey voice murmured in her darkest, wildest fantasies. "I want ye, ma sonsy. Yield t'me, ma bonny lassie. Yield all!"

In truth, a handful of Gaelic endearments from Gray were more potent than a hundred kisses from other men, she was certain.

His looks pleased her, too. Och, aye! Very much.

She loved the thick sooty locks that fell boyishly across his brow in hooks and swirls, or snaked over a faded plaid thrown over his powerful shoulders.

She enjoyed watching the play of cord and sinew beneath his bare chest, too. Watching those same muscles ripple and dance beneath close-fitted linen whenever he drilled with his clansmen in the bailey made her mouth dry up.

And never had she seen such strength as when he swung his weighty claymore between both powerful fists, or wrestled with his fellow warriors there, all of them roaring and bellowing like young bulls.

Her attention would stray to the powerful

Penelope Neri

muscle of leg and thigh revealed when his kilt
hiked up . . . and linger. If she caught a chance
glimpse of lean, hairy flank or hard muscular
buttock, her nostrils flared and her breathing
quickened.

She could not help wondering, as she lay
awake in her lonely bed each night, unable to
sleep, how it would feel to be pinned beneath
that powerful male body. To be taken by him,
whatever "taken" really meant. How would it
feel if those strong, callused hands caressed
her bosom with the same exquisite gentleness
with which he fondled his hounds?

But her imagination refused to go beyond that
moment, to her fantasy's logical conclusion.

Sometimes, she caught him watching her
speculatively in return, over the rim of his
tankard. Or else eyeing her from across the
smoky hall.

At such times, his MacKenzie blue eyes were
always bright with laughter—aye, and with
love—in the flare of the torches. Wicked merriment glinted out at her from beneath a fringing
of thick charcoal lashes, and the corners of his
mouth would curve up in a wistful smile.

*"This has gone on long enough! Have done
with your wee games, lassie!"* his expression
seemed to say. *"Remember what we had together
and love me! Let me love you!"*

And if—for a fraction of a moment—their

eyes chanced to meet, it felt as if she'd been struck by a lightning bolt—seared to the very bones.

Her poor heart faltered in her breast. Ba-boom, ba-boom, ba-ba-ba-boom, it went, before thundering on. She forgot to breathe—forgot to think! She had to look away.

The world tilted on its axis.

The torches flared and guttered, filling her vision with streamers of gold.

But somehow, she managed to carry on without going back on her promises, or yielding, although her knees were weak with longing and she had the oddest feeling in her belly, as if a swarm of butterflies had been trapped inside it, and they were now trying frantically to escape.

As the days passed, she began to learn more about Gray—little things she had not known before. What pleased him, and what did not. What brought him joy or made him frown.

In truth, she memorized every detail of his looks, his gestures, his moods, his temper, and his character, what he chose to eat and what disgusted him, every detail much as a starving man gobbles up morsels of bread.

She wondered sometimes if she was looking for some huge flaw in him. An enormous fault in the man that would justify believing the worst about him.

But to her chagrin, she saw little she did not like—and far too much that endeared the rogue to her!

The sweet way he cupped his chin whenever he grew thoughtful, for example. Or the way the sun-furrows creased the outer corners of his eyes whenever he squinted, so that her fingers itched to trace each one, and plant a kiss upon his eyelids.

His fairness in all matters, large or small, was admirable, as was the way he asked no more of his clansmen than he was willing to give himself.

She noticed, too, his deep love for his family, especially his younger brothers, and how he protected all those who had the right to the laird's protection, from the smallest pot boy to the old midwife, Morag.

In truth, he treated every living creature with respect and gentleness, be it man or woman, graybeard or youth, hound or horse, kit or hawk. Not at all what she would have expected from a cold-blooded murderer, the tiny voice of reason whispered, but she turned a deaf ear to it.

When Gray fondled his pointers' sleek brown heads or stroked their velvet ears and spotted coats, she longed to feel his hands on her. Oh, how her treacherous body ached to be caressed just so! She burned for his kisses. Hungered for embraces like those they had shared when he'd asked to wed her. Or for the savage kisses he'd stolen on the moors, when he'd carried her off. Kisses he did not beg her for, but took, as if they were his right.

At the time, they had seemed such small delights. Trifles to be enjoyed, then forgotten moments later. But, now that they were denied her, everything had changed. How precious such sweet nothings seemed!

But perversely, she gave the object of her affection no outward hint that her feelings for him were unchanged, and as powerful as ever. Quite the contrary.

She turned away when he wanted her to look in his direction. Frowned when he made her want to smile. And, when he bade her come nearer, she went elsewhere.

If his disappointed expression was anything to judge by, Gray believed she scarcely knew of his existence. But she did. Och, aye, she did!

And, although she still plotted ways to escape Glenrowan, doing so had long since become an intellectual challenge, rather than a true goal on her part.

Like it or not, she was here to stay. . . .

Graham peered gloomily into the dregs of ale that remained in the bottom of his pewter mug, as if the answers to all his problems lurked there. He sighed heavily.

With every passing day, he looked for some sign that Skyla's icy indifference was melting. A smile or a glance that would give him reason to hope. But thus far, he had seen no indication of a thaw.

The lady was as lovely as ever, yet she remained aloof, detached, cool, and haughty, speaking only when spoken to, looking in his direction only if she had no other choice, as if the very sight of him disgusted her.

And yet, to everyone else, she was gracious and free with her gentle words, from the second cousin he had appointed to serve her, to his brothers, Ian and Jamie, who had come to believe the sun shone from the lady's eyes. The latter were, or so he jealously fancied, both half in love with her themselves, if for no other reason than because she had mended the holes in their moth-eaten garments.

But instead of her coolness driving him away, perversely it drew him like a lodestone, so that he followed her as closely as day followed night.

When she spoke, he hung upon her words as if they were crystal. He took advantage of any excuse to serve or touch her in some way, whether it was to offer her his arm as they went into the great hall to dine, or to seat her beside him at the chieftain's high table.

If he offered her a tempting morsel from the

Thrill to the most sensual, adventure-filled Historical Romances on the market today…

FROM 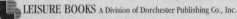 LEISURE BOOKS

As a home subscriber to the Leisure Historical Romance Book Club, you'll enjoy the best in today's BRAND-NEW Historical Romance fiction. For over twenty-five years, Leisure Books has brought you the award-winning, high-quality authors you know and love to read. Each Leisure Historical Romance will sweep you away to a world of high adventure…and intimate romance. Discover for yourself all the passion and excitement millions of readers thrill to each and every month.

SAVE AT LEAST *$5.00* EACH TIME YOU BUY!

Each month, the Leisure Historical Romance Book Club brings you four brand-new titles from Leisure Books, America's foremost publisher of Historical Romances. EACH PACKAGE WILL SAVE YOU AT LEAST $5.00 FROM THE BOOKSTORE PRICE! And you'll never miss a new title with our convenient home delivery service.

Here's how we do it. Each package will carry a 10-DAY EXAMINATION privilege. At the end of that time, if you decide to keep your books, simply pay the low invoice price of $16.96 ($17.75 US in Canada), no shipping or handling charges added*. HOME DELIVERY IS ALWAYS FREE*. With today's top Historical Romance novels selling for $5.99 and higher, our price SAVES YOU AT LEAST $5.00 with each shipment.

AND YOUR FIRST FOUR-BOOK SHIPMENT IS TOTALLY FREE!*

IT'S A BARGAIN YOU CAN'T BEAT! A Super $21.96 Value!

LEISURE BOOKS A Division of Dorchester Publishing Co., Inc.

GET YOUR 4 FREE* BOOKS NOW— A $21.96 VALUE!

Mail the Free* Book
Certificate
Today!

---

4 FREE* BOOKS 🌸 A $21.96 VALUE

*Free * Books Certificate*

YES! I want to subscribe to the Leisure Historical Romance Book Club. Please send me my 4 FREE* BOOKS. Then each month I'll receive the four newest Leisure Historical Romance selections to Preview for 10 days. If I decide to keep them, I will pay the Special Member's Only discounted price of just $4.24 each, a total of $16.96 ($17.75 US in Canada). This is a SAVINGS OF AT LEAST $5.00 off the bookstore price. There are no shipping, handling, or other charges*. There is no minimum number of books I must buy and I may cancel the program at any time. In any case, the 4 FREE* BOOKS are mine to keep—A BIG $21.96 Value!

*In Canada, add $5.00 shipping and handling per order for first shipment. For all subsequent shipments to Canada, the cost of membership is $17.75 US, which includes $7.75 shipping and handling per month.[All payments must be made in US dollars]

Name _____

Address _____

City _____

State _____ *Country* _____ *Zip* _____

Telephone _____

Signature _____

If under 18, Parent or Guardian must sign. Terms, prices and conditions subject to change. Subscription subject to acceptance. Leisure Books reserves the right to reject any order or cancel any subscription.

Get Four Books Totally
F R E E* —
A $21.96 Value!

(Tear Here and Mail Your FREE* Book Card Today!)

PLEASE RUSH
MY FOUR FREE*
BOOKS TO ME
RIGHT AWAY!

Leisure Historical Romance Book Club
P.O. Box 6613
Edison, NJ 08818-6613

point of his own eating knife, he would let his fingertips linger upon the inside of her delicate wrist, where a tracing of pale blue veins ran beneath creamy skin.

Or else he caressed her boldly, brazenly, stripping the garments from her with hot eyes, until she froze him with a frigid glance or—worse!—looked away and yawned, as if he bored her.

To his shame, like the basest lecher, on several occasions he had purposely crowded against her in some narrow spot, so that her hips brushed his side, or a breast was crushed momentarily against his upper arm.

But, except for a quick intake of breath, or a slight pinkening of her cheeks, she reacted not at all, while he had been plagued with guilt for his actions, rather than deriving pleasure from them.

There were times, however, when he wondered if she was playing some elaborate game of her own invention. Moments when he would have sworn upon a heap of holy relics that she enjoyed his illicit caresses and heated glances.

At such moments, a certain light in her gray eyes hinted that she would not spurn bolder advances on his part, should he dare to offer them.

But, since the lady gave him no overt encouragement, blast her, he could never be sure she would not box his ears or bloody his nose again, if he were to touch her.

In truth, the lassie blew hot and cold, like some fickle wind! And what man could read the wind, let alone a maiden's mind?

And so, he held his tongue, resisted the urge, and clung steadfastly to his vow to preserve her honor as his own.

He would not bed her until they were man and wife, not even if his celibacy killed him!

Draining his mug, he grimaced as the bitter dregs shriveled his palate.

Just thinking about her made his staff uncomfortably hard.

"I hear your betrothed has denied ye her chamber, brother. They say she willna meet with ye alone, but has her ladies there at all times to vouchsafe her honor," Jamie began from across the trestle as they broke their fast that morning. "Any truth t'the rumors?"

"Aye," Graham confirmed in a clipped tone. "There is."

He impaled his brother with a jaundiced eye over the expanse of white linen cloth between them.

"However, the chaperones were *my* idea, not the lady's."

"Were they, by God?" Jamie exclaimed.

His dark brows lifted in surprise as a servant

set bread, porridge, cheese, cold capon, and beer before him.

"Then you are to be commended on your restraint, brother," Jamie murmured, raising his pewter tankard in salute. "The Graham I remember would have tossed up her skirts in a twinkling, and fretted about wedding vows after!"

"Ye mock me, despite your flattery," Graham growled irritably. "My lady is gently bred—not some easy slattern t'be tupped for a riband or two. So, watch your tongue, brother. Honorable or nay, I can still loosen those bonny white teeth for ye, do ye insult her," he warned.

He stood, his large hands knotted into fists, his handsome features twisted into a scowl. The two black eyes and broken nose that had been Skyla's dowry had long since faded, yet the skin where they had been was still a yellowish-green hue. And, although the slightly crooked angle at which his nose had set had not spoiled his looks, the ferocious scowl did.

Jamie rolled his eyes. He had seen bonnier gargoyles on the cathedral in Edinburgh.

"Sit down, mon, do! Take hold o' your hot temper. There's no cause for ye t'pick a fight with me! I was but pulling yer leg, aye? And— since the lassies like my smile as it is, I'll thank ye to leave my teeth exactly where they are!"

Graham grunted, but offered no further comment as he sat again and resumed his moody contemplation of the inside of his mug.

"So. You love her, but the lady will have none of you unless ye find her uncle's murderer," Jamie continued in a thoughtful way, correctly guessing the cause of his brother's foul temper. "I wonder. What are ye to do?"

Gray shrugged broad shoulders. "Prove mysel' innocent, if I can, and woo my way back into her favor and into her heart. If not . . . well, I can be verra patient, if it pleases me. I'll wait, for however long it takes."

"For what?"

"For her defenses to crumble! She loves me, Jamie, as I love her. I know it here," Gray insisted, jabbing a thumb in the direction of his heart. "And in here." He jabbed his forehead.

He did not point any lower, to that other burgeoning proof of his affection beneath his kilt. A cockstand, after all, was proof of lust, not love!

"And because she does," he went on, "sooner or later, she'll come to her senses. Then we shall wed."

"Please God, we'll survive ye both, in the meantime," Ian added, grinning as he joined them at table. "And that the lady is yet young enough to give ye bairns."

Spearing a wedge of Jamie's cheese on the

point of his eating knife, he took a generous bite from it. "Hmmm. Good morrow to ye, brothers," he mumbled through a mouthful. "This . . . here . . . fine cheese."

"Dinna talk wi' your mouth full, ye blasted savage," Gray said, glowering at him. "If ye've no manners, go break your fast with the bluidy English, aye?"

"Dine wi' the enemy? Well, now, that's a fine way for a man to treat his own brother." Ian's eyes sparkled in his cherubic face. "Especially when that brother brings news that is bound to interest the laird."

Gray's dark brows lifted. His blue eyes, so like Ian's own, narrowed suspiciously. "He does, does he? And what is your news? Has the Wallace sent word? Is he raising an army?"

" 'Tis not of the Wallace I bring ye word, but of the murder of Douglas MacLeod!"

Graham perked up. "Do ye, now. Well, then. Let's hear it. What have ye heard?"

"I spoke with the shepherds up on the croftings. They shared their fire with a traveling tinker some three days past. Word in the Highlands is that ye killed Douglas over a woman. One ye were both bedding. Ye'll not be happy t'hear her name, I'm thinking. 'Twas Fionna MacRae."

Gray's brows lifted. "Was it, now? Then Will Wallace was right," he added thoughtfully.

"Aye, so it would seem," Ian agreed.

Fionna, the bane of his childhood. Gray had not given the sly wee baggage so much as a thought since the day his father, Adam MacKenzie, exiled her from Glenrowan at her own father's bidding, several years ago.

At that time, rumors had flown that she was with child, without benefit of wedlock. Her wanton dalliance with the English soldiers at Fort Edward had cost her her good name, her home, her family, and her clan's protection. Had it been worth it? he wondered.

The last he'd heard of her, she'd been earning her coin on her back, servicing the soldiers at the garrison under Sir Roger Hartford, the English constable. He had later heard she was Hartford's leman.

Had she lied to her Sassenach lover? Had she told him she was once Gray's mistress, too? Given Hartford's crude remarks in the forest—about the two of them sharing the same quim—he thought so.

"I'm thinking 'tis high time I paid the woman a visit, aye? Where do we start looking for her?"

"She keeps a tumbledown croft in the hills above Lochalsh. 'Twas there, in her bed, that Douglas was found murdered. 'Tis a wonder we saw naught of his murderers, we were that close that day!"

"What day? What are ye talking about? That close to what?" Graham questioned, puzzled.

"To Fionna. Her cottage." Ian shook his head, exasperated. "Don't ye remember? It was her—the woman bathing in the burn the Sabbath we went to press your suit on Skye. That woman was Fionna! We passed right by her cottage that day."

"We did?" Startled, Gray frowned. He vaguely remembered his brothers and the others making ribald comments about some barebreasted wench they had surprised washing herself in the stream.

Had the woman really been Fionna? Apparently so. He would have to rely on Ian's judgment, for his thoughts that day had been all for Skyla—and for the two corbies that had been a portent of the misfortune soon to come. . . .

"According t'gossip, Sir Roger, MacLeod, and yourself were all regular visitors to her bed," Ian continued with a disparaging shake of his head. "Or so Fionna was wont to tell anyone who would listen. She claimed ye were terrible jealous of the other two and wanted her all t'yourself. She says ye murdered Douglas MacLeod in a jealous rage, when ye caught him in her bed. Ye would have killed her, too, had she not fled. Or so she's saying."

"Is she, by God?" Graham's voice was frightening by virtue of its very softness, its utter lack of emotion. His eyes had turned a hard, cold blue. Pitiless. Glacial.

"Strikes me 'tis high time I had a word with Mistress MacRae and put an end t'her lies," he went on.

"Paagghh. Ignore them, mon! Let them die their own deaths," Jamie suggested. "Trying t'silence them will only lend them substance. 'Tis but your word against hers, after all. The word of a laird, a chieftain, against that of a soldiers' whore. A traitoress who sells herself to Scotland's enemies."

"So she does, Jamie. But 'twas my dirk they found in a murdered mon's belly!" Graham reminded him hotly. "And that murdered mon just happens t'be my lady's uncle."

"I ken. But, think it through, laddie," Jamie said soothingly, his eyes intense. "The woman had ready access to whatever took her fancy whilst she was one of us here at Glenrowan.

"That it was your dirk in MacLeod's belly strikes me as no accident, but it doesna prove you're the murderer. If the lassie is a thief, as well as a whore, she is more than likely a murderer, too."

Ian grunted, for once in agreement with Jamie. "Well said, brother. I agree. But what interests me is why the MacRae woman is spreading lies about the two of ye being lovers?

What has Fionna t'gain by linking your name to hers and thus to MacLeod's murder?"

"Revenge, mayhap?" Graham suggested. "She was sweet on me once, I know, but I spurned her in favor of Skyla."

Ian grinned and punched his shoulder. "Ha! You are bonny, brother, but no' bonny enough t'drive lassies to murder! Besides, why now? Why not years ago, when ye first sent her away? And why Dougie, rather than you—or her rival for your affections?"

Gray shot him an evil scowl. "I dinna ken, brother. Nevertheless, I've a mind t'ask Fionna MacRae a wee question or two."

"Ask away, if ye must. But take your lady with you to hear her answers. Prove to her you have nothing to hide," Jamie suggested.

"Better yet, pretend you have," Ian suggested with a wicked grin that gave his angelic features an evil cast. "And bid her stay home! Women are contrary creatures, especially when they are vexed with a man, are they not? Bid them come, they go. Bid them smile, they frown. The lady Skyla, lovely though she is, will prove no different, I warrant. Ask her to accompany you, she will refuse."

"You're right," Graham agreed reluctantly. "She will."

"So, ye bid her stay here at Glenrowan with her maid, while ye go grouse hunting with us.

169

Forbid her to accompany you, and she will want to come, as surely as the sun rises each morn, God bless her! A silver sixpence on it!" The small silver coin he drew from his sporran winked in the gloomy hall.

"Done!" Graham agreed. The sixpence was as good as his. Skyla would not come. He knew it.

Skyla slipped the hood of soft leather from her hawk's dainty head. The perfectly manned bird stiffened with excitement. The pupils of its cruel golden eyes contracted as it sensed the hunt—and the kill—close at hand.

Ahead of them, chest deep in hazy purple heather, a dappled hunting hound froze in its tracks. Its black nose was aimed at the bushes directly ahead of it, where a grouse crouched in hiding. One of the dog's front paws was lifted. Its docked tail had gone rigid.

Casting her hawk skyward, Skyla moved quickly around the frozen dog as her father had taught her, while the hawk hovered in place high above, waiting for the hound to flush the bird.

Skyla gave the call. The hound moved forward. Seconds later, the grouse broke from cover with a frantic flurry of feathers.

The hawk wheeled and swooped through the air. So swiftly did it drop onto its prey, Skyla could hear the wind whistling through its wings.

She knew a moment's exhilaration in the instant before the hawk plucked the grouse from the ground, killing it instantly.

Perched atop her quarry, the hawk began tearing feathers from the grouse as she awaited Skyla's arrival.

"Verra good, my lady." One of the kennel lads nodded his approval. " 'Twas a swift, clean kill."

"Aye, Hamish, it was," she agreed, her cheeks flushed with exertion and pleasure. "I've never seen a better hunting hound, nor a hawk that was better manned!"

"Och, 'twas not my doing, my lady," the youth said. " 'Tis himself. The MacKenzie, aye? There's no beastie at Glenrowan that hasna been tamed to our laird's hand, but for—for—!"

Hamish, the groom and falconer's lad, fell abruptly silent. He hung his head. But the sheepish look he shot her made the high color in her cheeks deepen, for some reason. Nor would he meet her eyes.

Why? she wondered. What had the lad been about to say? That every creature at Glenrowan had been tamed to his master's bidding, *with the exception of herself?*

"Aye, Hamish," she shot back, tossing her dark red hair. "There's one beastie that yet remains untamed by your fine laird's hand. *Mysel'*—thanks be t'God!"

Now it was the youth's turn to blush.

"Your pardon, my lady! Truly, I didna mean to offend ye, or imply anything o'the sort—!"

"No offense taken, Hamish. Here. Add this to the game bag," she urged, handing the dead grouse to him by the neck.

The hawk, now hooded again, was perched upon the lad's gauntleted wrist, tearing at the scraps of raw meat that were its reward.

"Aaah. Will ye just look at her! There's no prettier sight than a comely woman flying a hawk!" Ian murmured with a gusty sigh. "By the bye, ye still owe me that sixpenny piece, remember?" Ian prodded Graham as they watched Skyla man the hawk. "Unless ye mean t'welsh on our wager? It wouldna be the first time."

"Hmmm?" Gray murmured, ignoring the insult. His thoughts were leagues away. Or more properly, a few lengths hence.

As Ian had observed, Skyla made a bonny sight with the breeze lifting her fiery hair. The sunlight glinted off the dark red strands as if they were flames.

Dressed for the hunt, she wore a MacKenzie hunting plaid of muted greens and blues, pinned at her right shoulder with a silver brooch.

A deep-green kirtle of soft wool clung to her supple curves. With her cheeks glowing, her gray eyes bright, her hair billowing on the wind, she cut a handsome figure.

Imagining that fiery hair spread across his pallet, instead of furling on the wind, or wrapped about his throat as they made love made his innards clench with lust.

He tossed Ian the small silver coin.

"Here, blast ye. Take your coin and have done, will ye no'? I'll hear none of your I-told-ye-sos."

"Ah-ha! Pricks your pride t'be wrong, does it not, brother?" Ian crowed jauntily. Catching the coin on the fly, he tested its silver on his teeth as Gray, ignoring him, rode off toward Skyla.

He flung a foul curse over his shoulder that only deepened Ian's grin.

"Tsk. Tsk. Father Andrew will gi'e ye a hefty penance for such blasphemy at your next confession!" he muttered. "Ye'll be muttering Hail Marys till the moon turns blue!"

What had Gray and his youngest brother been talking about? Skyla wondered idly as she watched Graham approach. Her? More likely than not. They had both been eyeing her from time to time as they talked, although they had only done so when they thought her attention was elsewhere.

In fact, Milord Glenrowan had been acting oddly all morning, for some reason.

An imp of mischief possessed her as his gray horse plodded towards hers over the moor. Perhaps she should give him something to worry about?

Truth was, she had grown heartily sick of being mewed up within Glenrowan's walls for weeks on end, plying her needle or concocting herbal remedies with Auld Morag. She was bursting to do something outrageous, something fun and exciting and completely unexpected.

Something that would draw Graham's undivided attention! Why, the wretched man had practically ordered her to stay in her bower and tend to her womanly duties this morning, while he went hawking. After weeks of urging her to accompany him hither and yon, why had he suddenly insisted she stay behind at Glenrowan? she wondered.

"Women," he'd informed her with a scowl, "lack the patience needed for hunting wi' hawks. Better ye keep to your bower, with your women, lassie. Tend to your sewing."

To his credit, he had made no unkind comment about the linen shirt she had darned for him just the day before. Nor had he teased her about sewing up the armholes, claiming she had thought they were especially huge holes in need of darning, when in truth, she had thought nothing of the kind.

"On the contrary, milord," she protested. "I dinna wish to seem boastful, but I am verra skilled at hawking. Much more so than at . . . oh, darning holes in tunics, say? My lord father often used to take me hawking with him when I was a little girl." She had sounded wistful.

"Even so, I think not." His scowl was like a thundercloud wreathing his handsome face, with the promise of more foul weather to come.

"Oh, come, now, brother," cajoled Ian, the youngest and most handsome of the three MacKenzie brothers. He even shot her an encouraging wink. "I am persuaded the Lady Skyla could be the very soul of patience, do you but allow her to accompany our hunting party."

"Thank you, sir!" she said gratefully, shooting Graham a triumphant look. "You are right. I can be the very essence of patience, when it suits me, although I would not wish to seem boastful of my prowess."

"Och, God forbid," Gray added with no little sarcasm.

"I really am skilled at hawking," she added quickly.

"Ye own some small skill, I have no doubt. Even so . . . the sky has the look of rain about it," Graham insisted, casting Ian an unfathomable glare. "Ye'd be soaked. Ye'd probably catch an ague in yer chest."

"Nonsense. 'Twill be a mere . . . sprinkling," Ian said airily, dismissing the prospect of dire weather and favoring Skyla with an indulgent smile.

She beamed back at him.

"Besides, I'll not melt, even in a heavy downpour, sir, nor yet fall victim to your wretched ague!" she promised gaily, grinning back at Ian as if they were co-conspirators in some grand plot.

Outnumbered and outmatched, poor Graham was at a loss for a reply.

"Good. Then it is settled, my laird. I shall join you shortly in the bailey," she declared, the matter done with. "Please have Hamish saddle my horse."

"If you insist, my lady," Graham agreed, tight-lipped.

"Oh, but I do, aye," she replied, her chin jutting pugnaciously, her gray eyes unblinking as they met his.

And so, join them she had.

She suspected the reason Gray had not wanted her to accompany them was because he had feared she might try to escape him.

But in all honesty, the thought of escaping had not occurred to her for ages . . . until just now. Until she'd realized: This was what he had been expecting all along. An attempt to escape!

A wicked smile deepened the dimples in her cheeks. Perhaps she should give him exactly what he was expecting?

And so, with a peal of naughty laughter, she quickly sped back to her horse, hoisted up her skirts, and flung herself across its broad back.

"Get up there!" she cried, tearing the reins from the groom's hands.

She urged the dainty white palfrey into a trot, then a rapid canter that quickly carried her far from the small hunting party.

Her sudden break for freedom drew Gray in pursuit immediately, just as she'd known it would.

The race was on!

By the time Gray decided she really was trying to escape, she had put considerable distance between the two of them.

Her cream-colored mare had its head down and the bit between its teeth. In a matter of moments, it was galloping full tilt across the rolling moors, its mane and tail streaming behind it like banners of ivory silk.

Had the mare bolted? Gray wondered. Perhaps a rabbit had hopped up from a rabbit hole, right beneath its nose, and startled it. That must be it. No sane rider would press such speed from his mount, up here on the high moors, where a rabbit hole could break a horse's leg or a fall snap its rider's neck in two.

"Get up, there! Yeeeeaaah!" Digging in his heels, Gray leaned low over his stallion's neck and gave it its head.

He had to stop her, before she broke her daft wee neck!

Such heady speed exhilarated Skyla. Never before had she ridden a mount as fast or as hard as this.

She liked it fine, she decided as the mare thundered beneath her, gobbling up great strides of turf each time its hooves drummed the ground.

The unbelievable speed stole her breath away, and loosened her hair from its plaits so that it streamed behind her on the wind.

The moors, the hazy blue mountains in the distance, the pine and fir woods became a blurred frieze, a never-ending tapestry of color and indistinct form.

Truly, she felt free as a bird! A peregrine hawk, swooping and screaming as it cut through the air, swift as any arrow!

Moving fluidly, horse and rider as one, she soared over grassy hollows and low prickly gorse bushes with hardly a pause, then splashed on through a wide burn where icy brown water sang over smooth black pebbles. The horse's hooves struck the turf with a dull drumming beat that matched the steady thunder of her heart.

A ring of crumbling standing stones rose from the hillside up ahead of them, she saw as the mare strained up the steep incline toward them.

The huge stone monoliths appeared to have been placed there in a stone ring by some sorcerer's art. But, before she and her mount could reach them, something slammed into her from behind.

The breath driven from her, she toppled from her horse's back, landing heavily across something as bulky and solid as a side of beef.

For a moment, she sprawled there, locked in her assailant's arms, shocked into stillness for a second or two, before the steep incline sent them both tumbling over and over, like a rolling log, back down to the very bottom of the hill.

There, they finally came to a halt.

Before she could gather her thoughts, catch her wind, or scramble to her feet, she found herself quickly flipped over, onto her belly, and pinned there.

"Not sae fast, my slippery wee salmon!" Gray rasped. He was furious.

"Let me go! Get off me, ye great dolt!" she ground out, panting and red-faced. "I dinna— *oooof!*"

179

Held forcibly in place by what felt like a weighty knee planted in the small of her back, Skyla sprawled facedown in the scratchy turf and heather, unable to move a finger, let alone a limb, in her own defense.

From such a vantage point, everything seemed larger than life. Small stones were as big as boulders, blades of grass were enormous green swords. Worse, she could see an earwig—as monstrous as any dragon from this perspective—trundling relentlessly toward her.

It was headed, she was suddenly convinced, directly up her nose!

"Get off me!" she ground out, an edge of panic in her voice now.

"Did ye think you'd escape me so easily, ma wee bannock?" Graham murmured thickly.

His breath, hot in her ear, sent shivers down her spine.

"Or that I wouldna come after ye, eh? Skyla? Skyla! Lassie, speak t'me! What have ye t'say for yoursel'?"

More frightened by the prospect of the insect crawling up her nose than she was of the man pinning her to the grass, Skyla opened her mouth and screamed:

"Earrrrr-wiiiiig!"

Twelve

"Whist! Name-calling doesna fash me, lassie," he scoffed.

She could hear the laughter in his voice, and it infuriated her.

"Call me dolt, call me earwig—call me whatever ye will—I'm no' letting ye go!"

She writhed beneath him like an eel, tossing her head, flailing her arms and legs, trying desperately to unseat him.

"Aye. Go ahead. Call me all the names ye've a mind to, lassie," Graham panted, still applying weight to the small of her back, "for sticks and stones may break ma bones, but insults willna hurt me!"

"Devil take your wretched sticks and stones, you thick-skinned oaf—! Just—just get it away! For the love of God, get it away—else let me uuuuup!"

He set his jaw, wounded—despite his claims—that she would call him an oaf. "I will free ye, and gladly, once ye swear ye willna fly again, my dove."

"I swear, ye great dolt!" she shrieked. "Now. Please. Do it—! Do it *now*! *Let me up!*"

She could see the earwig out of her right eye now. It was only two hands' span from her face, trundling toward her with sinister purpose between the giant blades of coarse grass.

Its tiny plates of black armor were glossy in the light. The pincers at its rear end looked like a master torturer's tongs and were waving about, searching for something to pinch. Something like her poor little nose. Or a tender lip . . .

"Just—just let me up. For pity's sake, sir, let me *up!*" she squealed.

Her toes drummed the turf. Her head shook from side to side, so that her dark red ringlets tossed wildly about.

"Swear to me, then!"

"Aye, aye, I swear! I swear!"

"On what do ye swear?" he persisted in a

taunting, teasing tone, wanting to laugh at what seemed to him her childish display of temper. Now that he had her exactly where he had wanted her for so very long—beneath him—he was determined to savor the moment. Loath to end it. Eager to draw it out for as long as he could.

His mouth was very close to her ear now. If he chose, he could nibble her delectable pink lobe as if it were a sweetmeat. A tiny pink grape, mayhap? Or a sugared plum? Or else he could press his lips to the warm downy skin of her nape, and fill his nose, his lungs, with her elusive female fragrance and—

"*Ugh!*"

He grunted, doubled over in pain as a lucky backward punch landed solidly in his middle.

"Graham MacKenzie, if ye dinna let me up this instant," she ground out, "I willna marry ye, not if ye live t'be a hundred—no matter what bluidy evidence ye bring me of your innocence. I swear it on my granddam's life, so help me God!"

So vehement did she sound, so fierce did she look, he rocked back on his heels.

The very instant his weight left her body, she sprang up and began slapping at her face and hair, grimacing horribly as she danced about like a madwoman, first on one foot, then the other, as if taken by a horrible fit.

"What is it, lassie? Have ye lost yer wits?" he asked, black brows lifting in surprise.

"Nay, ye haggis-headed half-wit!" she shouted. "An earwig crawled up my nose!"

It had—she just knew it!

"A—what?" he echoed in disbelief. "Where?"

"An earwig! An earwig!"

"Up your nose?"

"Aye! And don't ye dare laugh at me, Graham MacKenzie. If ye laugh—if ye so much as smile—I'll punch your nose for ye, see if I don't!"

"Och, lassie, I'm no' so bad as all that," he said soothingly, trying to keep the laughter from his voice. "Come here t'me, woman. I'll slay yer wee beastie for ye."

He drew her gently to him and tilted her lovely head back.

A pert little nose. A narrow pair of nostrils. Nothing more—certainly no earwig.

He stared at her soft mouth, transfixed. At two rose pink lips, perfectly formed, the lower a bit fuller, lusher, poutier than the top. Earwig be damned! God help him, he wanted to bite that lip himself.

" 'Tis gone," he murmured huskily, fully aware of the warm slender curves pressed to his. Filling his arms.

"Are ye . . . certain?" she murmured shakily, lifting worried gray eyes to his. Her fingers closed over handfuls of his linen shirt, as if she needed to hang on to him to keep herself from falling.

"Aye," he murmured, lowering his dark head, "I am."

What he was about to do went against every vow he'd made. But in that moment, he could not help himself. He must have the taste of her, or go mad.

Her eyes closed as he covered her mouth with his. Her long, curling lashes hovered above glowing cheeks like tawny moths. The moths trembled, ever so gently, against his cheek as he deepened the kiss and touched his tongue to hers.

The very earth moved beneath him. Choirs of angels sang. Pipes skirled and drums rolled.

Skyla made a small, contented purring sound. Sliding her arms around him, she leaned against him, letting his chest bear her weight.

"Gray," she whispered, pressing herself against him. "Oh, Gray, Gray, what's happening to me?"

"Aye, lassie, aye. I ken how ye feel. I feel it, too."

The breathless way she whispered his name pushed him over the edge into an abyss of lust, of desire.

Lost in the taste, the feel of her, he lowered

her gently to the hollow beneath them, where shadows spread like spilled wine over the dimpled turf.

Following her down, he caressed her, his hands shaking as he feverishly stroked the soft curves that were, oh, so blessedly different from his body.

Her hair smelled like wildflowers, he thought, dazed, as he buried his face in the dark red floss. A man could drown in the scent of hair and skin that smelled like heather, wet with dew.

As he held her, his heart brimmed over with love. So much love, he feared it would burst. His loins ached from wanting her.

"Have done wi' teasing me, lassie," he urged roughly, thickly, holding her by the upper arms. "Wed me tonight! Gi'e yourself to me of your own free will, before I take ye, will ye, nill ye, and my honor and yer own be damned."

"Dinna ask it! What I want doesna matter anymore. I—I canna," she whispered, placing her finger across his lips and turning her head away.

She pressed her palms against his chest, pushing him from her.

Inches that felt like leagues opened up between them.

"How I feel for ye has nothing to do with this, don't you see? It never has! Marrying ye means

186

betraying my family. My own flesh and blood. It doesn't matter if I believe in you, or even whether I love you. *I canna do it, Graham*. Not until I can prove to them that you're not—"

"Your uncle's murderer?" he finished for her. He sounded bitter and angry, but he no longer cared. "So ye've said. Many times! But—what about you and me, Skyla? Will ye deny the love ye once swore for me? Do our lives, our happiness mean nothing now? What if—what if I canna bring you the proof you ask for? What then? Will ye cast me aside like a—like a stub of burned-down tallow? Will ye find another mon ye dinna love, and marry him instead? Well? Will ye?"

"Graham, please, I—"

"No. Enough of your excuses, woman," he said, cutting her off. "Whatever excuse ye make, it all comes down t'the same thing, aye? Ye dinna love me enough t'wed me on faith alone. Like doubting Thomas, ye must have your proof or have none of me. Then, so be it. I shall pray to God that the time will come when I want no more o' ye!"

He towered over her for a moment or two longer, before he turned on his heel and strode away, his black hair furling on the wind, the MacKenzie plaid flapping about him.

His expression was closed, unfathomable by

the time he reached Ian and Jamie, who had ridden after the runaway horses and were now leading their mounts back to them.

"What is it" James asked, eyes narrowing. "Ye look like Old Nick himsel'."

"Keep your opinions to yourself, blast ye," Gray growled. "And while ye're at it, mind your own bluidy business."

Wresting his horse's reins from Jamie's hand, he mounted up and rode ahead, leaving Ian to cup his hands and help Skyla to mount her own palfrey.

"He is not vexed at you, sir," Skyla murmured as she settled herself on the saddle, "but at me. I have hurt him, I fear. And yet . . . my conscience is divided, and gives me no choice!"

"He loves ye, my lady. He will recover," Ian assured her, his cherubic face creased with concern for her.

"You are kind, sir. But I dinna think so. Not this time."

And, knuckling a tear from her cheek, she rode after them.

They reached Fionna McRae's croft soon after the nooning, and tethered their horses close to the burn where Ian and Jamie had seen the woman at her bath.

The hut was the humblest, crudest of dwellings, little more than a cave someone had carved from the brow of a hill above Lochalsh. But no one lived there now. Gray sensed it. The place already wore the desolate air that a dwelling acquires when no one has lived there for some time.

The plank door was gone, too, Gray noticed, stepping over the flagstone threshold. He ran his fingers down the coarse lintel. The leather hinges were not ragged, as if worn by weather and time and usage, but cut cleanly, as if by a blade.

The MacLeods had probably pressed the cottage door into service to carry MacLeod's body home to Skye.

Inside the small dwelling, Gray was forced to duck his head to keep from bumping it on the cobwebby bits and bats that hung from the rafters.

Mice scattered in all directions to evade his feet. A string of neeps, long gone moldy, brushed his cheek. Another string of what looked like watercress or dried herbs scattered about his shoulders in powdery flakes.

The hearthstone was heaped with ashes. Over it hung an iron flesh-hook for the roasting of meat or game. A kettle could also be hung from it for porridge or soup.

The bed in the corner was poorly hewn and held a pallet from which most of the straw had escaped. Its soiled linen bore a huge rusty stain.

Douglas MacLeod's blood? Probably. He fancied he could still smell the metallic tang of it on the musty gloom.

"She's bolted," Jamie decided, looking about him. "And why run, if ye've nothing to hide?"

"Jamie's right. 'Tis proof of her guilt, wouldn't ye say, Gray?" Ian suggested eagerly, shooting Skyla a pointed look as she followed them in.

"I might, aye." He bent to retrieve a ragged shawl from the cottage's dirt floor. "*If* she'd left of her own free will."

"What makes ye think she didna?" Ian asked, looking around the cottage. There were no signs of a struggle. He was obviously wondering what Gray had seen that he had not.

"He means these." Crouching down, Skyla picked up the pair of worn leather shoes Gray had spotted, carelessly tossed in a gloomy corner.

In the Highlands, where most women went barefoot all their lives, except to their weddings, shoes like these were a rare possession, despite the holes worn in the bottoms.

No lassie in her right mind would have left such riches behind—not if, as Gray said, she had left of her own free will! Nor would any woman willingly leave her shawl. Yet this one had apparently left not one, but both treasured possessions.

"Aye," Graham agreed, flashing Skyla an irritable look. "That's right."

"She knew ye'd come looking for her, aye?" Jamie said. "Your honor as a man left ye no choice, once she's pointed the finger at you as Dougie's murderer. Soooo. Mayhap the lassie fled in fear of ye, and didna pause to take her possessions with her."

"Hmmm." Jamie's explanation was plausible, but for some reason, Gray doubted that was what had happened.

Fionna had always been a planner, a schemer. Leaving behind something of value, however small, was not in character with the sly, greedy wench he'd known. Besides, how long did it take to gather up shoes and shawl? A heartbeat, no more.

"I've a feeling we'll never know. She's—"

"Dinna move, sirs! Lady!" hissed a reedy warning voice from the open doorway.

The four of them spun around as one, to see a thin figure silhouetted against the rectangle of bright light that filled the doorway.

"Move a hair," the voice cautioned, "and I'll slice ye from gullet to bowel!"

Thirteen

"We have no fight with you, laddie. Put up your dirk."

"You're him, are ye no'?" the lad—for a lad it was—exclaimed in surprise. "The MacKenzie of Glenrowan! She said ye'd come!"

"She?"

"My . . . mother. She doesna like for me t'call her mother, ye ken, but she is, anyway. This was our croft, aye?"

"What happened to her? Where is she?"

"We lived here all the time, except for when . . . except for when mam was away at the fort, or when she sent me off t'hunt game," he finished, without answering Gray's question.

His eyes slid away and would not meet Gray's own. Gray knew then that the lad meant those times when his mother had men with her, and had seen fit to be rid of him for a while.

"How old are ye, laddie? Twelve? Thirteen?"

"I'm ten winters," the boy said proudly. "But I'm tall for my years, am I no'? Like you—! Stay back!" The dirk in his hand wavered, but he gamely brought it up, jabbing it threateningly in Graham's direction. "Just because I'm talkin' to ye, it doesna mean ye can best me!"

Graham threw up his hands in mock surrender. "I wouldna dare t'try," he vowed softly. "Laddie. How is it ye know my name?"

"Easy," the lad scoffed, showing strong white teeth despite his scrawny build. "My mother told me how ye looked. She said yer eyes were bluer than a robin's egg. She was right. They are."

"But why? Why did she describe me?" Gray asked, those striking eyes narrowed now.

The boy rolled his eyes as if Gray was a simpleton. "Why else? Because you're my father, o' course!"

"Your *father*?" Dark brows shot up in surprise.

"Aye! Och, she told me all about ye. How ye used her, then cast her aside when she told ye she carried your bairn in her belly. About how ye made her father send her away, so that ye could bed another lassie and not be reminded of your bastard bairn. That was when I decided," he finished with a determined air.

"Decided what?"

"That if ye came here, I would kill ye, *Father*."

It was chilling to hear a child speak so calmly of killing anyone, but especially the man he clearly believed had sired him.

"Did ye now," Gray said softly. "And what if I told ye I'm not yer father. That I canna be your father, because I did not do with your mother what must be done t'make a bairn. Ye ken what I'm talking about?"

"I'm no' a wean!" He flushed and squirmed. "Of course I know!"

"And? Would ye believe me?"

"No. She said you did." His jaw came up. "My mother wouldna lie t'me."

"Did ye ever see me come to her here?"

"Noo," he admitted shakily and with obvious reluctance.

"But ye did see other men?"

"Some, aye."

"And where is your mother now?"

"Gone! Long gone! The Sassenachs came, and took her away wi' them. She didna want t'go, ye ken. She wanted t'wait for ye—but they made her.

"I hid and watched until they rode away. Mother was crying and she was fighting them, so they tied her wrists and—and they—they—! There—there was nothing I could do!" he finished, his expression defiant. "I wanted to help her, but—there was nothing."

He did not add that he'd been afraid that they would hurt him if they found him. They could see it in his frightened eyes and gaunt face.

"No one's blaming ye, laddie. Come. Put up your dirk. If you're really my son, we should talk, you and me, aye?"

Indecision flickered in the boy's brown eyes. He ran a hand through straggly foxy-red hair.

"All reet then. Do ye have aught to eat? I'm awfu' hungry! Hungry enough t'—*stay where you are!*" he quavered shrilly as Graham took a step toward him.

Graham froze, throwing up his hands and pretending to comply as one of the grooms stepped up behind the lad.

Before the boy could duck past him, young Hamish hooked a powerful arm around the boy's neck, catching him in a headhold. He grabbed his bony wrist and squeezed until the rusty dirk dropped from his fingers, then caught him by the ear and pinched.

"Owwwch!" the boy cried, trying to twist free. "My lug!"

But the groom would not release him.

"What shall I do wi' him, my laird? Snap his scrawny chicken neck?" Hamish taunted as the lad shrieked in terror.

"Enough, Ham. Let him go now. But, boy—?"

"Aye?" the lad asked sullenly, chafing his sore wrist with his one hand, his ear with the other, and glowering at Hamish.

"That's 'Aye, my laird' to ye, laddie," the groom prompted, cuffing the boy's ear with his own free hand.

"Aye, my laird!" the lad sang out smartly, shooting the groom another murderous glare.

"Mark well my words. Try to run from me, and I'll catch ye and give ye to him," Graham added, nodding his jaw at the groom.

"Oof! Aye—my laird!" the boy added belatedly after Hamish nudged him in the ribs.

Graham nodded. "We're away home to Glenrowan, then! But first, what is your name, lad?"

" 'Tis Dougie, my laird."

"After his real father," Skyla added softly, meeting Gray's eyes above the lad's head. "My uncle. Douglas MacLeod."

"MacLeod! How do you know?"

"He's the image of him! His mother must have known who fathered him. Why else would she name him Douglas?"

"And yet she told the boy it was me, when we were never once lovers. Why would she lie about it? Why so many lies?"

197

Skyla shrugged elegant shoulders. "When love curdles like spoiled milk and becomes hatred instead, anything is possible. Did ye cross her? Scorn her?"

Graham shook his head. "Nay. She was a plaguesome wee besom when we were children, forever tattling on me to my father and following me about. Most of the time, he took her word that I'd been up to mischief, and walloped my arse for my transgressions." He grinned. "But I hardly knew she existed, once we were grown."

"No? I'll wager she knew of *your* existence, my laird!" Skyla said with feeling, remembering how handsome Gray had seemed to her, even as a little girl. She thought silently, And what could be worse than to lose your heart to someone who never even knew you were alive?

Small wonder Fionna's love had turned to hate—and, or so Skyla was beginning to believe, a need to hurt the man who had hurt her.

He had done so quite unintentionally, not by using her, nor by casting her aside, but by being completely unaware of her existence.

Could Fionna have known of her and Gray's courtship? she wondered suddenly. And knowing, could she have engineered Douglas's death to look like murder at Graham's hands, in order to deepen the hatred between the MacLeods and the MacKenzies, and to keep her and Gray apart forever? By strengthening the feud between their two clans, was she trying to ensure that Skyla and Graham would never be wed?

It was a question that only Fionna could answer, and she was nowhere to be found.

Fourteen

As they sat at supper a few evenings after their
visit to Fionna's cottage, one of the causeway
guards came to speak with Graham.

The guard brought news that a stranger
named Angus MacLean had arrived at Glenrowan's gates, seeking the MacKenzies' hospitality. He claimed he carried a message for the
master of Glenrowan from the Wallace himself, and offered the golden ring he wore as
proof that he came from Wallace and no other.

Pro Libertate, the Wallace motto, was
inscribed inside the ring in curling letters, Gray
saw. It was the password he and Will had

agreed upon before Will left Glenrowan, to prove any messenger the Wallace might send was really who he claimed. Better safe than sorry, these days. Not all Scots were loyal to Scotland, after all. Some had turned their coats and become spies for the bluidy Sassenachs, in return for English estates and Longshanks's thirty pieces of silver.

"Bring him here," Graham ordered, thoughtfully turning Will's ring on his own finger.

Moments later, an enormous Scot was ushered into the hall.

"We bid ye welcome to Glenrowan, Angus MacLean!" Skyla heard Graham say to the man, but as they exchanged greetings, her attention was caught by the little children who had scampered inside after the huge newcomer.

They congregated about the door like a litter of pups, Fionna's son the oldest and tallest among them, standing a little apart from the rest.

Dougie MacRae was watching, wide-eyed and fascinated, as the huge newcomer—a feathered bonnet atop his head, a claymore strapped to his side, a dirk tucked into his scuffed boots—crossed the hall like a mighty ship in full sail.

When MacLean reached the dais on which the laird's high table had been placed, he swept off his bonnet, pressed it to his heart, and made an extravagant bow.

At first, Skyla could discern no reason for the wee lad's fascination with the newcomer, but then it suddenly struck her. Could Dougie MacRae have mistaken him for her Uncle Dougie? she wondered. Did that explain the boy's wide eyes, his slack jaw? Why he'd paled as though he'd seen a ghost?

It would not have been difficult to confuse the two men momentarily, she decided, for they bore more than a passing likeness to each other. They were similar in height, both heavily bearded, and of almost identical coloring. Her uncle had not been a slender man, either, although he could not lay claim to the stranger's huge girth.

No doubt the boy had often seen Douglas MacLeod, she thought grimly. Her uncle had surely been a frequent visitor to Fiona's croft house—and her bed—while he yet lived, and not without reason, she supposed, for her lady mother had once told her, years ago, that he could no longer share his wife's bed. The midwives of Dunvegan had warned Aunt Alison that carrying another babe could well mean her own death.

Uncle Douglas had loved his delicate wife very dearly, although she had borne him no children, and so he had left her bed and slaked his male needs with women like Fionna MacRae. And with Fionna, he had apparently fathered his one and only child, a boy he did not even know was his.

Skyla sighed. The nagging questions that still surrounded her uncle's death continued to haunt her, robbing her of any future with Gray, as well as destroying her peace of mind. Where would it end?

Graham had insisted Fionna's bastard child should accompany them back to Glenrowan, despite the lad's fierce protests to the contrary. Once there, he had been given over into the care of Glenrowan's cook, Sorcha.

She, though not the most motherly of women, was kindhearted, and would at least see that the lad was given food and clothes. Barren herself, Sorcha had a soft spot for bairns and weans. After only three days of regular victuals in his belly, the lad's scrawny face was already much fuller.

"Will ye look at the wee lad!" Gray had murmured outside Fionna's cottage that day. "Half-starved, he is! See the hollows under his eyes? Those scrawny arms and legs? Take off that ragged shirt, and ye could count his bones through his skin! He's not eaten since his mother left, I'm thinking."

And so, to Skyla's surprise—and despite both brothers' protests—Gray had brought home the son of the woman who had not only hated

Gray, but had lied about his being the boy's father.

Amazed by his kindness, Skyla had asked him why he had done so.

"The lad is your enemy, sir," she had pointed out. "He wanted to kill us all. Why bring this small assassin into your household, when you already have five hundred mouths to feed?"

"That wee scrap, kill us?" Graham had scoffed, grinning for the first time since their confrontation earlier that day.

He'd ruffled Dougie's foxy red hair, and his Mackenzie blue eyes had sparkled like twin stars in his wicked, handsome face. "I think not. He's nae bigger than a flea, after all—and scared witless beneath this fierce face he's wearing.

"Besides, he knows only what he's been taught by his mam, do ye no', laddie? And since Fionna taught him to hate us all, God bless 'er, he knows only hatred."

Gray had rolled his eyes. "Sooner or later, he'll discover we're his friends, not his enemies. When he does, I'll try t'settle him wi' his mother's kin, if we canna find Fionna."

"With the MacRaes? Surely ye jest, sir." It was a rare family that acknowledged its byblows in this day and age. Surely the MacRaes were not so different from other men?

"Aye. *If* they'll take him in. They may surprise ye, lassie. He's of their blood, after all, and auld Eric MacRae has no grandbairns. Happen he'll welcome an heir t'carry on his line, bastard or nay. If not, then the wean can stay wi' us at Glenrowan till he's grown. No child should starve, when a laird has it in his power to feed the brat, as do I. And dinna look at me like that, lassie. I havena lost my wits!"

"I—I didna say you had," she protested, thinking exactly that, yet admiring him even more for his kindness, nonetheless.

Kindness. It was a rare quality in a chieftain. One that was too often dismissed as unimportant or viewed as a weakness rather than a worthy or admirable trait.

"You—you are verra kind, sir," she'd said aloud.

"Aye," he teased. "I am. 'Tis a pity ye didna notice it sooner, lass."

"But . . ."

He cast her a sharp look. Something in the tone of her voice had struck a chord. "What now?"

"Tell me truly. Is Dougie your . . . ?" She could not finish the question.

"My get, you mean?" He shook his head. "Nay, lassie. I canna be his sire. For one thing, ye said yerself he bore a striking likeness t'your uncle. And for another, as I told the boy, I never lay wi' his mam. Although, unlike yersel', she was verra willing t'bed wi' me."

He had grinned and winked, as if he thought she might be, well, *jealous*. And he was right. She had been jealous—and more than a little, too! Not only because Gray might be the lad's father, but also because she simply could not bear to think of him bedding the MacRae wench. Or kissing her. Or holding her in his arms. Or looking at another woman the way he sometimes looked at her.

And so, angry again, she'd tossed her head and looked away, wondering why, if she did not care for him, as she claimed, it hurt so blessed much to think of him with another woman. Any woman . . .

"Steward! Another trencher for our guest. Meats! Victuals!"

Graham's bellows jolted Skyla back to the present, returning her attention to the newcomer.

"You, Ranald! Wine!"

"Straightway, my laird."

"And you, Ross! Another platter of meats!"

"Hrrrmph. By your leave, my laird," the stranger murmured in his host's ear, inclining his head. "I'd prefer a wee drop of the . . . er . . . the water of life, if ye'd indulge me? I've a—

er—delicate palate, aye? And wine—excellent vintage though it may be—is apt t'sour my stomach."

Skyla turned away to hide a smile. A man less likely to have a delicate palate than the newcomer would have been hard to find.

Angus MacLean stood a strapping two tailor's lengths, perhaps more, in his dusty boots. His enormous girth was kilted with yards of faded MacLean plaid, so that he resembled a small pavilion, swaying from place to place, as he moved about.

His red hair was long and wild as a barbarian's. His orange beard was full and frizzy, its bushiness hiding, she suspected, a number of chins. His cheeks were ruddy, the eyes above them a light clear blue that sparkled with roguish merriment amidst a webbing of creases.

He looked the sort of fellow who would relish pinching the serving lasses' bottoms, or playing the Lord of Misrule for the Yueltide revels.

"Whatever pleases ye, MacLean," Graham told him as he waved him into a seat. "Ye'll not be disappointed with our *uisque beatha*, I vow. Come! Be seated. Ye've ridden some distance, aye? My brother tells me ye bring word from my friend, William of Elerslie."

"That I do, sir. That I do. And from Sir

Andrew de Moray. I've covered many a league since I left the Wallace's camp two days hence," Angus confirmed, hitching up his plaid as he took his seat at the table. The bench bowed under his great weight as he sat.

"And how is the Wallace?" Graham asked, throwing himself down into the chieftain's carved chair. "In good health, I trust?"

"Verra good, though spoiling for a fight wi' the English, as always." Angus chuckled, slapping his beefy thighs.

Graham exchanged glances with Jamie. His brows lifted in inquiry. "And? Is there a battle in the offing?"

"Och, aye. And a bluidy great big one it promises to be, too, by all accounts! Even as we speak, the Moray is amassing an army t'the north, to fight alongside the Wallace and his Lowland men."

"Tell us," Graham ordered. His handsome face was stern and grave now. "But first, the dram I promised ye, t'wash the dust from your throat. Traveling is thirsty work, aye?"

"Och, aye, that it is, very thirsty. God bless ye, sir."

Neither man spoke while the steward splashed water-of-life into goblets. Angus drained his in a single greedy quaff.

"Aaaah. 'Tis well aged, my laird," he wheezed

209

hoarsely, then beat on his chest with his fist a time or two. His eyes watered. "Verra well aged," he spluttered.

"You were saying? The battle Wallace is expecting?" Graham reminded him, gesturing for their goblets to be refilled.

"I was, aye. Now. Where shall I begin? "Did ye ken that King Edward—auld Longshanks—has taken ship for France?"

When Graham nodded that he did, Angus continued. "Well, before he sailed, Edward sent his armies north to Scotland under John de Warenne and Hugh de Cressingham."

"Cressingham! That fat auld sow!" Archie snorted disaparagingly. Cressingham was well known and hated north of the Borders for his enormous bulk and his enormous cruelty.

"Aye, sir. The very same, sir! Well, Longshanks told Warenne and Cressingham that while he was in France, they were t'squelch the plaguesome Scots' rebels who'd been refusing t'pay his bluidy taxes! In a word, sir, oursel's!"

As everyone within hearing distance tittered, MacLean spat onto the rushes, drawing a look of disapproval from Skyla, who did not like the disgusting habit of spitting.

"There! That's what I think of Longshanks' taxes. Aye, and of the man himself, God rot him! I spit on them both! Bleed our people dry, he would, if we let him. And—while he was

ordering Warenne and Cressingham about—
Longshanks also bade Robert the Bruce take
up arms against his fellow Scots! Naturally, the
Bruce refused, God bless him!"

"Whist. Never mind all that. Ye talk too
much, ye great hairy bag o'wind! How big an
army d' they have?" old Kenneth MacKenzie
pressed. "How many of the bastards are coming to the Highlands? Ten, eleven hundred foot
soldiers?"

"Och, 'tis a wee bit more than that, Grandfather," Angus told the old fellow with a wink,
rearranging his sporran and tossing a picked
mutton bone over his shoulder to the hungry
hounds that waited nearby. "The English claim
an army of fifty-thousand strong, but I—"

Kenneth's jaw dropped. "Great God
Almighty! Fif-fifty *thousand*?"

When Angus nodded, the old man crossed
himself, visibly shaken. "Holy Mother of God!
That many?"

"Aye—or so the English would have us
believe. T'be truthful, however, my laird—good
sirs," he added for the uncles' benefit, "Wallace's spies put their numbers at half as many."

"Twenty-five thousand, then. Not all infantrymen, surely?" Graham asked.

"Mostly infantrymen. But they have Welsh
archers, and heavy horse, too," Angus confirmed.

211

"Even with five-and-twenty thousand, the English will still outnumber our force, three to one," Graham pointed out, sending a lad for his charts.

They were maps he'd drawn himself over the years as he went from place to place, and he had taken great pride in making them as accurate as he possibly could. In fact, he had copied many similar charts for Will Wallace's own personal use. For a battle commander, such charts were invaluable.

Fifteen thousand, fifty thousand, it made little difference, he thought as they waited for the boy to return with them. The English army would far outnumber the ten thousand or so Scots the Wallace and the de Moray could muster. Sweet Jesu! The clans would be mowed down like stalks of barley before the scythe. What the devil was Will thinking of, to jeopardize the lives of so many Scots?

Gray knew himself for a chieftain with courage aplenty. He did not fear dying for a cause in which he believed or to protect his loved ones. But he would not blindly offer up his clansmen to their enemies, like lambs offered up in sacrifice. Other lairds might lead their clans into a battle they could never hope to win; one that could result only in the slaughter of every last Scot. He would not. Impulsive he might be, but he was no fool!

To Graham's way of thinking, freedom was too dearly won when it cost the lives of so many good Scottish men, and left widows and little children behind to fend for themselves in the miserable aftermath of war. He knew from past experience that fending for themselves too often meant starving to death.

"Aye," Angus answered his question. "But . . . the Wallace has a plan." His blue eyes gleamed. He smiled, wetting fleshy red lips with his tongue. "And a worthy one it is, too, for it takes full advantage of English arrogance!"

"It does, does it?" Graham murmured, all ears now.

Will was a resourceful fellow. Over the years, Gray had come to respect him, and found Will's "plans" well worth listening to, whether they involved scrumping apples from English orchards just over the Scottish Borders when they were lads, or planning strategies of war as grown men.

With a gesture of his arm, Gray swept the goblets and platters from the tabletop and spread the first chart the boy handed him across its surface. "Here, MacLean. Show us where the English are camped this night."

Angus stepped forward. Thoughtfully stroking his bushy red beard and chewing on a fleshy lower lip, he scanned the parchment for a moment or two, then stabbed a grubby finger at a point on the map.

Skyla strained to see, but could not make out the name of the place.

"See these meadows here . . . by the river?"

"Aye." Graham grunted.

"That's where they are."

"Ah. And the Wallace's plan?"

Angus grinned. "Och, aye, the plan. Weell, we all ken that if the Sassenachs want t'conquer the farthest reaches of our bonny Scotland, they must pass through . . . here t'get to us in the Highlands," he began, stabbing his finger at a spot on the map again.

"Through the Forth valley, he means," Archie explained for the benefit of those standing behind who could not see.

Kenneth shot him a quelling glare. "Hold yer tongue, ye old dolt! Ye dinna ken what you're talking aboot."

"I do, too! There's a bridge across the river thereabouts. Right about here, aye, here it is. A wooden bridge," Archie added. "Verra narrow. Am I right, laddie?"

Birdlike, he looked over at Angus, his rheumy brown eyes very bright, his long hair a wild, snowy bush about his head.

"Right you are, Grandfather. Right as rain! A very narrow wooden bridge. But even so, Will says he can make the Sassenachs cross it!"

Angus declared. "Fifty *or* twenty-five thousand o' the bastards!"

"And once they cross it, the Wallace and his army will cut them down to the last man!" Archie was almost crowing with glee, jittering about on rheumatic knees. " 'Tis a fine strategy! I like it well!"

"But, how? How will he make them cross by the bridge? Has he taken leave of his senses?" Graham demanded, stern-faced and unimpressed. "I know the place myself. There's a fine ford upstream, at Kildean, here, some distance above the bridge. The water isna deep. Fifty men could cross at once, wearing heavy armor.

"No man—not even the daftest Sassenach—would try crossing a narrow bridge with the enemy waiting on the other side. Not when there's a broader, easier ford close by."

"Mayhap not. But cross it they will, for the Wallace has challenged their manhood to cross if they dare!" Angus declared with a triumphant flourish. "The English answered that they would, for God was on their side, and that the Scots would perish, t'the last man." Angus added, "They dinna believe we Scots can prevail against so many o' them."

"And Will's answer?" Gray sorely doubted it had been polite.

Angus grinned and winked boldly at Mary,

seated next to Skyla. The lassie blushed bright pink and was suddenly all atwitter, fidgeting about and fussing with her hair.

"There are ladies here, my laird," he continued, reluctantly looking away from Skyla's maid and back at Gray. "I canna repeat what he said, word for word, but I can tell ye what he meant.

"The Wallace bade them come. He bragged that he would meet the bluidy English face t'face—and that they would pay for the wrongs they've done the Scots, tenfold!

"Unless, that is, they were afraid of him, and had neither the balls nor the spleen for a wee brawl with his laddies . . . ?" Angus threw back his fiery head and roared with laughter, hugging himself about his ample belly, which jiggled alarmingly.

"Fighting words, indeed," Graham agreed with a small, quick grin.

The English were an arrogant lot who considered themselves above other men. And they had hated the boastful Wallace—an even prouder Scot—and the sneak attacks he'd waged on them over the years. Not only had Will Wallace and his family rebelled and refused to swear fealty to their King Edward, he had made the English look like fools in the process.

His scathing challenge to their manhood

must have been like a red rag, waved before some five-and-twenty thousand furious bulls. God, what he would have given to be there—to have heard them.

And, risky as it was, Will's plan was not entirely without merit. If they were to send some of their Scots to defend the ford, and deployed the rest of their number at the bridge, they could pick off the English as they crossed it, two by two.

"Where is the Wallace camped now?" he asked.

"He and his army marched out of Dundee yesterday, my laird. When I left them, they were planning to cross the Tay, then camp in the hills of Cambuskennet, closer to Stirling. The Wallace said ye'd find him there, and t'tell ye he had other plans for the Sassenachs," Angus added with a frown.

Clearly, he was not privy to those parts of the Wallace's great plan himself.

"He says he'll explain when ye join him," he added.

Will's message had not said "if" he joined him, but "when," Gray noticed. How like his friend, he thought, shaking his head. An embittered, lonely man, made more so by the death of his bonny bride at English hands, the Wallace lived for only two things—freeing Scotland and the complete and utter destruction of the English.

"Good people of Glenrowan, I am of the mind to march to Stirling, and join the Wallace there in the fight to free our beloved Scotland!" he said when his people grew quiet under his raised hand. "But I will order no man to follow me into what may prove a bloody death for us all," he added.

"The English number in the thousands, as McLean has told ye," he continued softly.

They watched him, spellbound by his words, their eyes filled with a mixture of dread and excitement.

"And by contrast, our numbers are few. In truth, the odds weigh heavily against us." He paused to allow the full measure of his words to sink in.

"Although your chieftain, I will command no man to follow me into this battle. Instead, I ask each of ye to look into your own hearts and make the choice. Will ye follow me? Or will ye stay and tend the loved ones we leave behind?" He paused. "Should ye decide to stay, I will think no less of ye for it. Nor shall any man malign you or call you coward."

He looked around the gathering, at the circle of pale faces. At eyes that glittered too brightly in the flare of the torches. At mouths that worked soundlessly.

Some of the women were already weeping, as were some of the men. Others stared ahead, unseeing, their eyes unnaturally dry, their jaws set hard, their bodies stiff with fear.

"By God, I'll follow ye, Gray! T'hell and back, if ye ask it!" his brother Jamie declared with relish. "The Clan MacKenzie will shine again, by God!"

"We shine, not burn" was their clan motto.

Gray's own eyes felt suddenly moist. A knot caught his throat. "Aye, laddies. Shine again, we shall!" he murmured.

"We're all behind ye, Gray," Ian promised. "We'll follow ye to the gates of hell and beyond, if need be—will we not, Jamie? And what say you, lads? Are ye for it, or against it?"

"For it!" their close companions shouted.

"Who else among ye will fight with us?" Gray bellowed, springing up onto the trestle table to address them all. His thunderous voice reached the farthest corners of the hollow hall, rose to the smoky rafters and the racks of antlers and iron sconces that branched from the walls as he strode the length of the trestle. "Who else will join the war for Scotland's freedom?" he demanded.

"Here!" cried one man. "I'll go!"

"Guid man!" Gray approved with a broad grin.

"And me! Ye can count on me, my laird!" yelled another.

"Here!" shouted a third.

More and more shouts circled the hall until

they became a single roar that clamored to follow the laird of Glenrowan into battle against the enemy English.

When the last man fell silent, all the male members of the Clan MacKenzie who were old enough, still young enough, or healthy enough to do battle had thrown their lots in with him and the Wallace.

As he looked around the hall at his clansmen, at the smiling faces all around him, his heart swelled with love and pride for these loyal, courageous men who would follow wherever he led, unquestioning. It was, he imagined, like the love a father felt for his children.

"From the depths of my heart, I thank ye, good men and true of Glenrowan, as our bonny Scotland will someday thank ye. Now. Find your beds, kiss your women, or return to your feasting, my friends! Eat! Drink! Dance! All of ye, make merry, for at first light, we march south t'Stirling! Piper, gi'e us a tune, laddie! One to stir the heart and light a fire in the blood!"

As the thrilling skirl of Robbie's bagpipes swelled and filled the hall, a pibroch that called the clan to arms, Graham felt the call in his own blood, and in his loins.

He glanced over at where Skyla had been seated earlier, eager to see her response, but her chair was empty.

She and her maidservant were gone.

Crushed with disappointment, he turned to see if she was elsewhere in the hall, and caught a glimpse of her skirts as she passed from his view, taking the stone staircase that led up to her bower above the hall.

His cousin Mary was hurrying after her.

Her face had been white as whey when last he saw her. As pale as the other lassies as she watched him rally his followers. Her gray eyes had glittered with unshed tears.

Seeing the telltale sheen, he had hoped—for one fleeting, joy-filled moment—that she might beg him not to go. That her fear for his safety might move her to admit that she loved him. But alas, she had done neither.

Where he was concerned, the lassie was a locked door. One he now believed would never be opened, not to him.

Heavy-hearted, he bade a servant set more whiskey and victuals before his uncles, his advisors, and Angus MacLean, then made his excuses and slipped out by a side door, taking the outer stone staircase to the battlements.

Each man needed to prepare for the coming battle in his own way. So would he prepare his head and his heart. In quiet and solitude.

"My lady! Wait for me!" Mary was puffing, her plump face red-cheeked as she hurried up the steep stairs in her mistress's wake. "Will ye no' let me comfort ye, madam?"

"Nay. Go away," Skyla sobbed. "Ye canna help me. No one can, not with this. Please, Mary. Just leave me alone! Just—just leave me—!"

Lifting her skirts, Skyla sped past her chamber door and ran on alone, up the steep stone staircase, to the keep's battlements, leaving Mary staring after her.

Once there, Skyla sank to her knees on the cold stone and opened her mouth, letting the anguished wail she had held in check for so very long escape her.

Hugging herself, she rocked back and forth as she wept. Great rivers flowed down her cheeks; scalding tears that quickly chilled in the wind.

She loved him! She loved him with all her heart! But on the morrow, he would march away, leading his clansmen into battle against a bloody foe who far outnumbered the Wallace army. A battle that would surely take his life.

He would die, never knowing how she felt.

Stubborn, obstinate creature that she was, she had chosen her course. Had sworn to be loyal to her family rather than believe and trust the man she loved. Unlike the supple rowan or willow, she had told herself she would not bend, that bending—yielding—was a weakness, even though losing Gray would break her in two like a brittle twig.

She had loved him ever since he was a gangly lad, and she a little girl. Had never, ever stopped loving him. She had known it the spring day they'd met again in the woods above Lochalsh. Had known it the day they carried her uncle home upon a crude door. Had never stopped loving him, even when they had named a MacKenzie—*her* beloved Mac-Kenzie—her uncle's murderer.

She loved him. She loved him with all her heart, she thought, swallowing over the huge lump that clogged her throat. She would always love him. Why could she not simply tell him so? All she had to do was say . . .

"I love ye, Gray!" she blurted out to the starry September sky, studded with a billion pulsing points of cold white light. "God help me, I love ye!" she told the inky shadows. "I always have. I always will," she told the pale moon as it swam in the gleaming black lake below the keep's walls. "I beg ye, please. Dinna go t'Stirling. Dinna leave me. I couldna bear it if ye should die! I'll do anything—anything at all! Just say you'll stay here, wi' me, where 'tis safe. . . ."

Her broken words tumbled from her lips like water tumbling from a millrace. They spilled,

crystal clear, into the wine-sweet autumn air—
and straight into Graham's heart.

"Sweet Mary be praised," he exclaimed,
unable to believe his ears. His heart leaped in
his chest. His voice was rough and choked with
emotion as he stepped from the deep shadow
of a wall, into silvery moonlight, to stand
before her.

"I never thought to hear ye say those words,
my love. My heart!"

"Wh—what are ye doing here?" she
exclaimed, startled. "Who gave ye leave t'spy
upon me!"

"Shoo, shoo, lassie. Enough. Have done wi'
yer act. I didna come up up here t'spy on ye,
but to be alone and t'think. The prospect of my
lads dying is not one I take lightly, ye ken. Nor
should any laird."

"Nay. It takes a brave man t'admit it, sir," she
told him shyly, sniffing back her tears. "F-few
lairds would."

"Lassie," he began hesitantly. "What ye said
about—about loving me. 'Tis true, I didna come
up here t'spy on ye, but—Well, I couldna help
but hear ye! Lassie, did ye—did ye mean it?"

His MacKenzie blue eyes were troubled.

"I said . . . I said only what is in my heart,
sir," she whispered. "That I—that I love you!"

As she said the words, it was as if a great
stone had been lifted from her heart.

Taking her hands in his, he raised her to her feet, and drew her into his arms.

"Aaah, Skyla. Lassie. My love . . . my dearest love. I feared never t'hear ye say those words t'me again."

She pressed her face to his chest, soaking his breachan with her tears.

"I canna help mysel'. I love you!" she whispered again through tears that clogged her throat and brimmed in her eyes.

The sweet words trembled in the air between them, like a ballad sung by a minstrel, or the dulcet notes of a plucked harp as it played a melody of love.

"I didna want to. I didna mean to, but I—I do! I canna help mysel'!" she whispered.

"Aye, lassie. Aye. I know how ye feel. I love you, too, wi' all my heart and soul! I've never stopped loving ye, even when ye didna trust me."

"Truly?

"Truly. Shoo, shoo, ma bonny wee dove, have done wi' yer tears. Dinna redden your wee eyes wi' weeping. Come here to me, ma doo," he murmured, using lilting Gaelic like a lovesong.

Hooking a finger under her chin, he tilted her face to his.

She was pale as a lily by moonlight, and twice as fair, he thought as he looked down at her. The tears on her cheeks glistened like dew, lovely enough to make stones weep.

He cradled that face between both hands and dipped his head to gently kiss her, full on the lips.

"There's still time, lassie," he murmured in her ear when he ended the kiss, smoothing the soft down of her neck with the ball of his thumb. "We may yet exchange our wedding vows and share a marriage bed, if it please ye. 'Tis not too late for us."

The way she curled her arms about his neck, the way she clung to him, fiercely as ivy to a wall, was the only answer he needed.

Tonight, he thought, his heart leaping with joy in his chest, after weeks of fearing it would never come to pass, he would claim his bride!

And so, taking her hand in his, he led her back down to the hall.

They were dancing reels in the great hall when Gray and Skyla returned, hand in hand, like sweethearts, oblivious to the knowing glances and the nudges exchanged as they came in together, aware only of each other.

Smiling down at her, Gray led her into one of the intricate circles of men and women that, like cogs in a machine, moved in opposite directions over the rushes.

"I've a mind t'dance with my betrothed, just this once," he answered her questioning look, "before we're wed. Come, lassie. Show me! Are ye as graceful as ye're bonny? If ye dinna step on my toes, I'll wed ye."

Laughing, she followed his lead. Catching up the hems of her kirtle in her left hand, she tucked her right inside his large one and skipped after the other dancers, whose plaids and tartan arisaids were flying.

"Well, lassie. Will ye miss me while I'm gone?" he asked as, heads cocked to one side, they linked arms and promenaded in a stately circle about the hall. "Will ye think of me? Will ye fash yourself that I've been spitted on a Sassenach spear? Or pricked by an English bodkin?"

"Dinna jest about such things!" she scolded with a shudder, giving his broad chest a little thump of reproach as she passed by him.

"Nay? Then say it, lass. I want t'hear ye say it. Will ye?"

"Aye. I'll miss ye, MacKenzie," she admitted softly. She looked away, unable to look him in the eye, terrified he'd see how deeply her fears for him ran. How deathly afraid she was that he'd be killed in the coming battle. "B-but I shall pray and fast and beseech God to bring ye safe home to me. To all of us here!"

"And? What ye said on the battlements? Will ye wed me tonight, before our clan? Ye've had a wee while to regret your words while we danced. What say ye now?"

227

There was no hesitation this time. As her gray eyes lifted to his, he saw the love that shone like burning brands in their depths, and his heart swelled with joy.

"I will, sir," she said firmly. "I'll wed ye here and now, before this guid company, if it please ye."

"Prove it!" he challenged with a teasing grin, his eyes twinkling.

"As you will, then. Good sirs! Gentle ladies! Hear me!" she cried, clapping her hands to silence the pipers, the drummers, and the jinglers with their bells, and to halt the dancers skipping to and fro all around them.

The bagpipes squealed into silence like a strangled cat.

"Your laird has offered me marriage this night," she told them in a clear, ringing voice, "and I have accepted his suit. What say you all?

"Will ye welcome me as your chieftain's bride?" she asked on the sudden hush. "Will ye accept me as your lady and the chatelaine of Glenrowan?"

"Aye! That we will! Wed him, lassie!" cried one fellow after what seemed to Skyla an endless silence. "And may the Guid Lord bless ye both!"

"Send him awa' with a night t'remember, lassie!" cried another, bawdier soul.

Her cheeks turned bright pink and the people laughed, delighted by her maidenly modesty.

"Aye. Rouse the priest! Summon him here!" cried still another.

All of them roared in agreement, "Aye! Fetch the priest!"

"Do you believe me now, my laird?" she teased Gray, smiling as she looked up at him. "The good people of Glenrowan insist upon our marriage, so how shall I refuse them? We shall be wed this very night!"

"Dinna jest wi' me, lassie. Not about this," he warned. Dark-lashed, vivid blue eyes searched her face. His grip on her upper arms tightened. "I couldna bear it. If ye dinna mean it, say so now."

" 'Tis no jest, my fine dear laddie," she murmured huskily, touching his cheek. "I shall become your bride tonight, or ken the reason why."

Her love for him shone like stars in her eyes.

"Make haste!" she urged. "Summon Father Andrew straightway, sir." Her voice was throaty with emotion—or was it desire? "We have waited long enough, aye? No more, I say! Not another hour. Nor yet another minute!"

"Steward!" Gray bellowed. He threw back his head and whooped with laughter, his grin stretching from ear to ear. "By God, man, to me—and quick about it! I'm to be wed this night!"

"Here, sir!" Hamish sang out, red-faced and puffing as he came at a run.

"Rouse Father Andrew from his cot. Bid him don his vestments and hasten here straight-way. Tonight, he shall celebrate a marriage between mysel' and the Lady Skyla. Right here, before our people. The chapel is too small to hold us all."

Hamish beamed. "My felicitations to ye, my laird. And to you, my lady," he added, making a bow to Skyla. "Our keep has been too long without a lady's gentling touch," he added as he hurried off.

"God willing, ye'll bear our nephew a lusty bairn wi'in the twelvemonth," Uncle Archibald prophesied loudly, hobbling forward to buss Skyla on both cheeks with his whiskery lips. "And another the year following. Both toms and bettys, aye?"

"Amen!" roared the onlookers in bawdy approval. "Both lads and lassies!"

Skyla's cheeks deepened to a fiery crimson. Yet she was smiling, nonetheless. In truth, she could not help herself. Their delight was contagious.

"Come! Fill your cups and lift them high, good people of Glenrowan!" urged Uncle Ken-neth, who had overheard his nephew's instruc-tions to the groom. "Our laird and his lassie are t'be wedded this night. May the Good Lord bless them both! Slainte!"

"Slainte!" They roared the Gaelic toast. "Good health!"

Glenrowan's blackened rafters rang with their cheers.

"Ye've been queen of my heart since ye were a wee lass."

Gray began their vows less than an hour later, before the Clan Mckenzie and its septs, all of whom had assembled in the great hall below. Noisy just moments ago, they were hushed now, straining to catch every word.

Graham's heart was in his eyes as he looked down at Skyla. Truly, she was the goddess of the harvest, a Samhain bride. A wreath of hastily gathered russet and yellow wildflowers, braided with ears of barley and oats, crowned her loose auburn hair. A topaz-colored kirtle clung to her slender figure. Over it, she wore a surcoat of russet, embroidered with gold thread.

Auld Morag and Mary witnessed the nuptials, clinging together and sniffing back happy tears and blowing their noses on their kerchiefs.

"I've loved ye since that day in the great glen. I love ye now. For as long as I draw breath, I'll love ye, lassie. 'Tis why I take thee for my bride, Skyla MacLeod of the Isle of Skye," he murmured as he slipped his mother's golden wedding ring, etched with rowan buds and leaping stags, onto the third finger of her left hand, where the vein led straight to her heart.

" 'Tis you I want to bear my bairns and sit wi' me by the hearth when we are old and toothless."

Eyes twinkling, he stretched his lips over strong white teeth and grinned at her like a gummy old man, looking very like his ancient uncles in the process.

Skyla laughed through happy tears as Father Andrew clucked his disapproval of her bridegroom's antics.

"Ye're mad, MacKenzie," she mouthed. "A lunatic, in truth!"

Gray grinned, but his smile was quickly replaced by a serious expression.

"Aye," he agreed, searching the lovely face she lifted to his. "Perhaps I am. But will ye take this lunatic as your husband, to have and hold from this day forth, Skyla MacLeod?"

"I will, and gladly, sir," she promised, grown suddenly shy. "For I've loved you just as long, though I couldna admit it, not even to mysel'. Till the last breath leaves my body, I will love ye." She smiled up at him.

"I'll be your loving bride. Your loving *wife*. I'll share your bed." Then she blushed and her

232

hand trembled within his. "I'll bear your bairns."

"My *many* bairns," Gray said, grinning. "All of them lads!"

"—Our many bairns, be they lads or lassies," she agreed.

Her gray eyes shone. Her lovely face glowed, radiant as any candle.

"I'll live with ye and laugh with ye and love ye for as long as we both may live," she said. "And, when the world seems dark and threatening, I will know that there's a haven in your arms. The only fortress I shall need from this night forth."

"Amen," he said softly.

Their eyes met. Their hands, crossed and clasped in the ancient symbol of infinity, tightened their grip.

Love everlasting, their eyes said.

Love forevermore, their linked hands promised.

Love eternal, their hearts sang in a Highland lovesong that was older than the hills—yet new and tender as the buds on the rowan.

Father Andrew removed the embroidered stole from about his neck. Loosely, he knotted it around the couple's clasped hands as a symbol of their joining.

"God has joined this man and this woman in

holy matrimony tonight. Let no man sunder their most blessed union," he said firmly, adding, "Amen."

The onlookers crossed themselves and echoed the word. "Amen."

"And now, my laird Glenrowan, ye may kiss your bride t'seal your pledges!"

The onlookers howled bawdy approval as Graham clasped Skyla's glowing face between his hands and bussed her so soundly, her feet left the rushes.

Seconds later, feasters hoisted Graham up onto their shoulders, lifted his protesting bride onto other shoulders, and bore the newlyweds once around the great hall, then to the laird's bedchamber.

Someone—probably Mary or Morag or both, Skyla thought, dazed—had slipped away ahead of them to prepare the chieftain's bower for the night to come.

Apple boughs crackled on the hearthstone, filling the chamber with a spicy, fragrant aroma. Dried lavender, rosemary, and other scented herbs had been scattered amongst the rushes strewn over the flagstones. Tapestries sewn with gilt thread and vivid silk warmed the cold stone walls. Fur pelts were heaped before the crackling fire.

On a small scrivener's table beneath the

latchet was a silver flagon of sweet wine and a platter of honeyed oatcakes.

"Our thanks for your good wishes, my friends. Ye may leave us now," Graham urged the noisy, laughing company, anxious to be alone with his bride.

"I said," he declared in a louder, ringing voice just moments later, "that your lady and I have no further need of you this night!"

Ian grinned and elbowed Graham in the ribs so that the wind was driven from him.

"Oof!"

"Are ye certain about that, brother?" he asked with an unusually bawdy wink. "I'd be happy t'—" His voice trailed away as Graham glared, freezing him in a single icy glance.

"Get out, little brother, before I plant my boot on your arse! All of ye, *go!*" he thundered.

"Weeelll, since ye ask so sweetly . . ." Jamie teased, still laughing at Ian's pained expression. He bowed. "A very good night to ye, dearest sister," he murmured, kissing the air above Skyla's hand. "In truth, my brother doesna deserve such a gentle angel as—"

"*Go!*" Graham thundered, shooting him a murderous glare. "Out, I say!"

"I know, Jamie," Skyla responded, her gray eyes sparkling with laughter and excitement. Such bawdy exchanges were common at weddings, no matter the social standing of the happy couple. "But I love the rogue!" She sighed. "What's a puir lassie to do?"

"What, indeed?" Ian said, laughing. " 'Tis fortunate ye didna choose me t'wed, instead of my ugly brother here, my lady. There's many a maid will go smiling to her bed tonight because of it."

"Aye—smiling because she sleeps alone, and not wi' you, ye young braggart!" Gray growled, cuffing him. "Be off with ye!"

Ian laughed, evaded his fist, then bear-hugged Graham's head. "Every happiness to you, brother—and a very good night to you and your lady wife."

Both brothers hurriedly left the bedchamber, herding the stragglers through the door, before closing the door behind them.

Their departure left the newlyweds alone with the old priest.

Raising his hand, Father Andrew drew the sign of the cross with his thumb in the air above Graham and Skyla's bowed heads, then did the same to bless their marriage bed.

"May your union be fruitful, my children," the priest murmured as, yawning, he toddled to the door. "A very guid night to you. God bless ye both."

Carefully, Father Andrew closed the heavy door behind him.

Silence reigned in his wake.

"Praise be, we are alone at last. I feared we should never be rid of our company," Gray said softly in the ensuing hush. "Will ye come t'bed now, wife?"

They stood there, hands joined, gazing at each other and grinning like two who have found buried gold, and cannot believe their good fortune.

"The MacKenzie of Glenrowan has a powerful hunger t'bed his bride," he murmured, gently inscribing circles on her palm with his index finger.

"And so he shall, husband. Very soon," she promised breathlessly.

"Nay," he countered, his voice thick, his tone urgent.

In the fire's flickering glow, he no longer looked kind. He looked dangerous, powerful. The Dark Knight of legend, come to wicked life!

A delicious sensation tugged and twisted deep in her belly. Anticipation? Desire? A delicious mingling of the two?

"Not soon. Not later. Not some other time. *Now!*"

Wrapping a hand through her tumbling hair, he tugged her toward him.

Fifteen

His hand still tangled in her auburn hair, he backed her up against the door Father Andrew had just gone through, and kissed her soundly. Thoroughly.

"I'm no dainty mon," he said between kisses, his voice husky with lust and desire—and with love. "But I swear, lassie, I willna harm ye, except what I must, t'make ye mine. Do ye ken what I'm trying t'say?"

"I do," she said, her voice unsteady, laughing softly as she went up on tiptoe to press her lips to his throat. "Ye mean when we consummate our marriage, aye?"

239

Penelope Neri

"Aye." A shudder ran through him. She understood. "Well, then. Good enough. Now. Off wi' your clothes, lassie!"

"What?" she shot back indignantly. But giggling, she started to oblige him, nonetheless.

The moment the words had left his mouth, he cursed himself for an overeager fool. What had he been thinking?

Night after night, he had planned how sweetly he would seduce her, given half a chance. And yet, when the moment was finally upon him, he had treated her as callowly as any green lad with his first wench! He had not intended to begin it so soon, nor so directly. First, he had told himself, they would share a loving cup of wine, and perhaps a honeyed morsel of oatcake, and then he would remove her garments with infinite slowless, until she was breathless with anticipation.

But instead, the words—and his heart's desire, along with them!—had spilled from him, of their own accord.

He groaned, wanting to kick himself for his stupidity. The last thing he wanted was for Skyla to fear him, or to fear this part of their marriage. To think of him forever after as some rutting male animal that wanted only to mate her. If he frightened her now, she might never come to enjoy their bedsport. And marriage to her without it did not bear contemplating.

240

"Well, my laird? Dinna just stand there, wi' yer eyes sae big! Help me off wi' my sark! My hands are trembling so, I canna undress myself," she whispered, shivering as she pressing her burning forehead to his chest.

"Do ye really want me to?"

"Aye! Didn't I say so?"

"Really?"

"Really! Are ye deaf, mon? Make haste, ye great lummox!"

He grinned. "Verra well, then! If 'tis what ye want!"

One by one, Gray drew the garments from her body, baring her slender limbs and creamy skin a little at a time, so as not to scare her, while cursing the aching ridge of hot flesh beneath his breachan that nudged her hip and urged him to make haste.

He was, a part of Skyla's mind registered, no stranger to the intricacies of female dress. Her husband's hands were deft and knowing as he loosened ribbons, unfastened laces, removed sleeves, or eased her kirtle and sark down over elbows and hips, and she could not help wondering where he had come by his expertise.

He did not stop until she stood shyly before him, as bare as on the day she'd been born, save for the harvest wreath of flowers and grain that crowned her lovely head, and the curtain of dark auburn hair that spilled almost to her waist.

"My bonny bride, in truth," he breathed, holding her at arm's length to admire her nude loveliness. To touch his fingertips to the tiny coraline buds that steepled each ripe, round breast, and played hide-and-seek with strands of her dark-fire hair. "My beautiful, *beautiful* wife!"

She shivered as he ran his finger down the valley between her breasts. Closed her eyes and let her head tip back as he skimmed her abdomen, her flat, almost concave belly, until he reached the tiny thimble of her navel.

There, he halted, his breathing shallow.

Easy, laddie, easy. Soon enough, Gray told himself. Dinna scare her.

"Gray?" She frowned. "What's wrong wi' ye? Why have ye—why have ye stopped? Do I—do I not please ye? Is that it?"

"Not please me?" he said. "Look at yerself!" he urged, turning her by the shoulders to face the looking glass of polished silver.

He could not swallow. Could not draw a deep breath. Could not utter whole sentences, for the loveliness of the woman who stood before him. How, in God's Name, could she think she did not please him?

Her breasts were ripe as pears, tipped with coral pink berries like sugar plums. Her long supple torso nipped in at the waist, before flaring into lush, womanly hips that were made for bearing bairns—*his* bairns—or for cradling her man when they made love. A triangle of soft auburn curls hid the folds of her virgin quim.

He groaned as his shaft stirred, nudging her sleek thigh through his plaid with a vigor all its own. His stones ached with the denial he had been forced to practice for so many long weeks.

"How can ye think ye dinna please me, woman?" he whispered hoarsely. "If ye pleased me any more, whist, I'd be dead!"

Skyla tossed back her glorious mane of hair and laughed. Bubbly, earthy laughter that made his gut tighten anew.

"Ye're a bluidy liar, MacKenzie! There's a part of ye that is nowhere near dead—though I wager 'tis stiff as a corpse!"

He threw back his head and roared with laughter himself. "Hark at ye, woman! Is that any way for an innocent lassie t'speak to her mon on their wedding night? *Is it?*"

He caught her eye.

She giggled.

He grinned.

"I'll show ye who's a corpse and who isna, ma bawdy wee lass," he vowed.

Unwinding his breachan, he let it fall, then pulled his shirt up and over his head.

Magnificently naked himself now, he tossed it aside and reached for her, his body all cords and sinew and lean hard brawn. "Come here to your laird, my lassie."

Catching her about the waist, he swung her up and carried her to their bed like an outlaw.

When they lay facing each other, side by side, he tilted her chin. Her dewy lips parted under the hungry pressure of his mouth as she clung to him. She yielded her lips. Opened her mouth beneath his in mute yet loving surrender—as she would soon surrender her virgin body to him.

Their eyes met as he kissed her, smoke drowning in MacKenzie blue. His eyes were the bonny gentian of harebells and stormy Scottish skies. Hers were the soft, smoky gray of the mist that hung over the loch, and of the gloaming that drifted and roiled over banks and braes like a woolly gray fleece.

To gaze into those dark-lashed eyes was to gaze into his soul, she thought suddenly. One unmarred by either murder or deceit, but clear as any pool. Why had she not noticed before?

"Ah, Skyla. My love. My bride," he murmured. His hand drifted down her throat. His long fingers grazed her collarbone, curved over and around the fullness of a breast.

"Mmm. Ye taste like berries and fresh cream," he murmured moments later, gently flicking both damp nipples with his tongue.

Her nipples became rosy pebbles at the first brush of his lips.

"D'ye ken how I've longed to be inside ye?" he murmured, adding thickly, "T'touch ye, taste ye . . . here." With that, he slipped his hand between her thighs, groaning as he found her wet and ready.

Dipping his dark head, he swallowed her gasping breath in his mouth and took her lips in a long and tender kiss as he explored her silky secrets.

She uttered a low moan and let her head fall back as she closed her eyes.

The flower garland tumbled from the bed to the rushes as she did so, shedding bright petals and ripe kernels of grain across the pallet as it fell.

"Ye're sae beautiful, my love. Sae wet. Sae tight. I dinna deserve such a bonny bride."

"Nor I such a husband," she whispered, pressing both palms against his chest.

With a languorous motion, she smoothed her hands over the powerful bare chest that swelled beneath her fingertips, delighted when his small flat nipples puckered. Emboldened, she slid her arms all the way around him, thrilled by the raw strength and power of the well muscled body in her arms.

Sweet Jesu. She could scarcely speak, could not think straight, for the magic his hand was

245

weaving! She tossed her head on the coverlet and gasped as his fingers probed deeper. She was light-headed with pleasure, whimpering as the tension built unbearably.

His touch sent fire shimmering through her, over her, into her. Waves and ripples of heat that robbed her of breath and thought.

Plunging her fingers into his thick black hair, she pulled his head down to hers and pressed her hips against him. Against the sweet invasion of that maddening hand that teased and taunted but would not bring her ease.

"More!" she murmured on an urgent, greedy breath, her lips tingling. "Kiss me till I canna speak! Till I canna breathe. Kiss me till I'm— I'm tipsy on your kisses!"

"Is that all ye're after?" he asked, amused. Laughter danced in his vivid eyes as he looked down at her. Shadow and light chased each other across his handsome face, lending him an air of danger and of mystery. "More kisses?"

"Aye, my laird," she lied.

Her breasts rose and fell rapidly with the shallowness of her breathing. What was wrong with her? She seemed to be melting from the inside out, like butter left too long in the sun. Her arms and legs were heavy and languid. A throbbing pulse had started, deep in her belly.

"Och, there's more than kisses to it, lassie. Far more than kisses."

A powerful man, a rugged warrior, he nevertheless caressed her gently, fingers splaying over her snow-white throat to cradle her head as he captured her lips, like a hummingbird sipping honey from the throat of a lovely flower.

Sliding his body lower, he cupped each breast between his hands and suckled them in turn, like a bee drawing nectar from a blossom it fears to bruise.

"Are ye tipsy yet, my bonny?" he asked at length, his own breathing unsteady, his voice thick as he gently nudged her legs apart to nuzzle her belly.

"Aye," she replied shakily, her fingers knotting in his hair. "But if ye've a mind to kiss me again, I willna stay ye."

He laughed. "Aah, but it's not kisses I'm after, ma doo. Not anymore." So saying, he pushed her thighs apart and ducked his head between them.

She screamed as he made love to her there with his mouth, his tongue doing a lazy dance that made her writhe in pleasure, spiraling her higher and still higher until she soared free, over the edge, on wings of pleasure.

He waited until she had recovered a little, until her eyes were open and she had returned from that lofty place. And then, taking her hand, he placed it over his jutting member.

" 'Tis time for the two of us t'become one, wife."

"Aye. Oh, aye!" she agreed shakily, curling her fingers about him.

Her small nipples ruched like gathered velvet beneath the rough ball of his thumb as she stroked him, tentatively at first, then with growing confidence.

His manhood felt like steel under velvet to her touch. *Hot steel. Hot velvet.*

A thick, tortured groan escaped him.

"Now, lassie. I must have ye now."

He scorched a necklace of feverish kisses about her throat. Tucked others in the shadowed hollow at its base. Hid still others behind her ears, upon her downy nape, on the sweet innermost curves of her white thighs.

Kisses—kisses everywhere!

Blood churned and frothed like a waterfall in her veins. Like honey, drizzled from the back of a ladle, unraveling in endless ribbons of pleasure.

"My love!" she whispered as his hand sleeked over her thighs, again seeking the treasure between them.

He found it, and with a thick groan, he teased the tiny jewel of her womanhood with his thumb as he drew her tongue into his mouth. He again pleasured her with his hand, building her desire, preparing her body for their first coupling.

"Aaah." Her cry was throaty. Her eyes were closed, her head tipped back. The pulse in her throat beat erratically beneath flawless skin as he eased his fingers into her untried flesh.

Her fingers clamped over his arms as she clung to him, like ivy to a wall. In truth, had she not been pinned to the bed by his weight, she would have floated bonelessly up to the smoke-blackened rafters like a wisp of thistle-down, swirled on a lazy zephyr.

"I love ye," he whispered, sliding his hands beneath her buttocks. Lifting her astride his flanks, he wound her legs about him.

Clamping both hands over her bottom, he carried her across the chamber, leaving the massive bed with its hangings of ruby-red velvet for the heap of pelts before the hearth.

Candles guttered with their passing. A log dropped on the hearth, scattering ashes and sparks about the hearthstone.

Neither of them noticed.

Skyla moaned against his lips. Her fingertips fluttered delicately against his chest, like a butterfly wanting desperately to land but afraid to do so.

"Aye, my lovely, 'Tis safe for ye t'settle there, so close to ma heart," he murmured, kissing her fingertips. " 'Tis where ye belong. Just as I belong here, inside ye."

A shudder moved through him as he tipped her backwards, onto the furs. Pressing her legs apart, he knelt between them. Ducking his dark head, he tasted her again.

She stiffened beneath his mouth. Her slim fingers knotted in his hair. She cried out as fireflies of pleasure flickered through her a second time. "Oh! Oh!"

His shaft bucked, demanding, impatient as he knelt between her legs. He slid his hands under her hips.

"I love ye, lassie. Never doubt it!"

And with that promise, he thrust strongly forward.

A cry escaped her as he broached her maidenhead in one swift thrust.

"Yer mine now," he murmured. "My bride. My wife. My woman—and my only love."

He began to ride her, deepening his possession with every lunge.

Her world narrowed to his broad shoulders, and to the gray stone walls of the chamber that framed them. To the flickering play of light from the fire's dying embers and the luxurious caress of ermine and coney, wolf and fox beneath her.

Covering a breast with his hand, Gray fondled the taut mound until the rosy peak rode high and hard upon the creamy crest.

" 'Tis done, lassie. 'Tis done," he whispered. "No more hurting for ye, dearling. Henceforth, ye will have only the pleasure of it all."

"Only the pleasure," she whispered, arching up against him. "Only the pleasure. . ."

And pleasure there was, indeed.

She awoke with a start in the gray hour just before dawn, fearing he had already left for the south, and war.

But no, he was still deeply asleep beside her, his face pressed into the angle of her throat and shoulder, his warm breath fanning her cheek, his heavy arm curled around her.

Jet-black hair spilled across the linens, framing his striking wind-browned face, which was now swarthy with the night's beard shadow.

Leaning back, she studied him in the shaft of moonlight that spilled through the arrow-slit. The perfectly formed lips. The long, slim nose, the broad brow. The vivid blue eyes, closed now, with their fringing of sooty lashes, the straight black brows that gave his face its character. The hard jaw and squared cheekbones that would ensure he kept his striking looks into old age, long after his ebony hair had turned silver.

251

There was no longer a splinter of doubt in her mind, she thought as she stroked his rough cheek, his thick black hair, a muscular shoulder. She belonged to him. Wanted to stay with her handsome laird forever. To hold and be held by him for the remainder of their lives. For eternity.

If only she could bind him to her with cords of love so strong, he would never leave her. Let Will Wallace fight the Sassenachs without her husband, she thought, filled with resentment.

"Dinna leave me," she whispered to the shadows. "Graham, my braw laddie, dinna go. Dinna fight. Stay here!"

MacLean's arrival and all their talk of the coming battle had caused a terrible fear to bloom inside her like some malevolent weed, fed and watered by her love for him.

It was the price every woman who loved a warrior must pay for loving her man. The bitter knowledge that she could lose him forever to Mistress War.

And yet, in her heart of hearts, as the daughter of a warrior chieftain herself, Skyla knew she had no choice and neither did he.

Graham would leave in the morning because he must. He would not be the honorable man she loved, nor a worthy laird to his clan, if he stayed safe at home while others fought for Scotland's freedom. Others could choose their destiny, but not him. Not the chieftain. He had been born to lead in his father's stead, and lead he must.

A tear rolled down her cheek and dripped off her nose.

"Shoo, shoo. Dinna greet so, my lassie. I'm nearly drownin', aye?"

He was awake, she saw. Eyes wide open. Watching her. He reached out and caught her to him. Twining his hand in her hair, he kissed her softly, soundly, full on the lips.

"I'm no' greeting," she insisted, sniffing.

"Wee liar. Ye are, too. And I ken why. Ye'll not be the only wife at Glenrowan wi' swollen eyes on the morrow, I'm thinking. Just remember. I'll come back to ye. I swear it."

"Ye canna swear! Ye canna! Not about this."

He grinned, leaning on one elbow now. "I can—and do. I'm the MacKenzie, aye? Anything's possible for a bluidy MacKenzie!" He grinned and winked at her. "Besides, I've you to come back to. For a wife like yoursel', a mon would defy anything—even death! Now, up wi' ye, ma wee slug a bed."

To her amazement, he stood and, still naked, held out his hand to her.

"Up? Why? Where are we going?"

"Up t'the battlements, to watch the sun rise. 'Tis a bonny sight t'see. Here. Tuck this around ye, my lady of Glenrowan."

He wrapped his heavy woolen breachan around her. Its sheer weight and bulky folds made her giggle.

He patted her bottom through its bulk. "Dinna make fun of your husband's plaid, wife, else I'll be forced to wallop your pretty wee arse for ye!" he threatened.

"Ye would, would ye? Then ye'd have t'catch me first, would ye not?" she challenged, scampering from the chamber and up the stone staircase ahead of him.

The night air was as crisp and chill as a draught of cider from the cellar, the sky paling from ebony to charcoal as they tumbled over the last step.

"I win!" Skyla crowed, tossing her hair back, eyes sparkling in the otherworldly gray light.

"How can ye be the winner, when you're the prize?" Gray asked softly, dropping the armload of furs he'd brought with him to the cold stone and following them down.

Tugging her down after him, he pulled the breachan up, over them both.

Side by side, they snuggled together, gazing up at the glorious night sky, spangled with stars.

"Look how many of them there are! Thousands of tiny silver rowels," she exclaimed, awed.

"Aye. And would ye look at that moon? Such a slender crescent of light. Like a curved blade . . . aye, a Saracen blade! And do ye see that star, next to our lady Moon? 'Tis the evening star. First to peep out each night, last to fade each morning."

"Hmm. They're as beautiful as any jewels. But . . . why did ye bring me up here, Graham?"

"I wanted ye to see the stars and the Highland dawn. I used to come up here with my tutor, Brother Benjamin, when I was a lad. On clear nights like this, he taught me the names of all the constellations.

"I want ye to come up here when I'm gone. Gaze up at the evening star and remember tonight, and know that wherever I am, no matter how far away that might be, somewhere, I'll be gazing up at that very same star and that very same moon, and thinking of ye. Missing ye. Loving ye. Aye, and counting the moments till we're together again."

In his own way, he was already telling her farewell, she realized sadly. Each word he uttered was like a thorn that pierced her heart.

Her lovely features crumpled. Her lips quivered. Tears brimmed in her eyes, threatening to spill over.

"I dinnna want ye to go. I canna bear it. . . ."

"Aye. I ken. And I dinna want to leave ye. . . ."

"But you must."

"Aye," he agreed heavily. "I must."

"Och, I was such a fool! I wasted so many

weeks we could have spent together! Oh, Gray, hold me!" she whispered. "Hold me tight. I'm sae frightened for ye."

Shivering, she threw herself into his arms and clung fiercely to him. He kissed her cheeks, tasting her tears on his lips.

"Dinna greet, lassie. Dinna greet. I'll be back, ye'll see," he crooned, stroking her back, smoothing her hair. "We are marrit now, my sweet, both in word and in deed. When I leave Glenrowan in the morning, I'll carry ye with me, in my heart, until we can be together again."

The plaid slipped from her shoulders. It slithered down her back and soon lay forgotten beneath them. Their kisses intensified. Their breathing quickened.

And, somewhere between that first kiss and the last, the night became dawn. The evening star faded into the saffrons and pinks of dawn . . .

. . . and consolation became true passion, once again.

No matter how desperately the newlyweds tried to hold back the dawn, the sun rose on the new day as it rose every morning. The only difference was that this, their first together as man and wife, might well prove their last, a nagging little voice insisted fearfully.

All too soon, the men of Glenrowan were up and ready to go. The MacKenzies and their septs, close to five hundred men in all, would join Sir Andrew de Moray's army of Scots from the far north on the banks of Loch Lomond and from there march southeast to Stirling together.

Many of the clansmen were yawning and bleary-eyed and feeling the worse for the liquor they had swilled. Some had sat up all night over mugs filled with the water-of-life, or beer, or mead, and exchanged tales of past battles and feats of heroism.

Their women had also sat up and gone sleepless that night to darn their men's torn or worn breachans or to patch their tunics by the poor light of a tallow candle stub. Their eyes were red-rimmed, both from the strain and from their tears.

None of it seemed real, and yet preparations were being made nevertheless.

Their few horses had been groomed and brought out, and were now whisking their tails and stamping, eager to be off. Blankets and sacks of provisions were being piled onto carts, along with bread loaves, all of them baked overnight in Glenrowan's ovens.

Yet to Skyla, it seemed like part of a bad dream. It was not until the men of Glenrowan assembled in the bailey, some of them little more than fresh-cheeked lads whose voices had hardly begun to change, that the reality of what was happening truly struck home.

She became quiet and withdrawn, watching Gray as he moved about, issuing a command here, a word of advice there.

It was left to Skyla to reassure the women-folk who were to be left behind that their husbands, sons, and brothers would soon be coming back, victorious and unharmed. She checked countless times to make sure the men had everything they needed, or could ever possibly need. It was expected of her, as the mistress of Glenrowan, and she did not shirk her duties as their lady.

Yet there was also a part of her that watched the way her lord husband grinned, and responded to the tiny voice inside her head that said to remember that smile, to remember that look, that certain way he had of angling his handsome head and laughing at her, for she might never see that smile, that look again.

When it was time for good-byes, she clung to him until the very last moment, her belly queasy with dread that she would never see him again. She wanted to cry, but how could she, when she must set a good example for the others?

Gray wrapped his arms around her and kissed her so hard, her head spun. "I'll be back before ye know it, my lass," he murmured, tucking his foot into the stirrup to mount his horse.

"Fare thee well and may God speed ye safe home to us, my lord husband," she whispered brokenly, looking up at him through a blur of tears.

When he was settled in the saddle, he kissed his fingertips, then reached down and touched them to her lips. She grabbed his hand and pressed it to her cheek like a kitten. Kissed it.

"Remember. We'll be gazing at the same stars," he murmured.

"Aye," she returned, forcing herself to smile. "The very same."

Then he turned his horse's head to the gates of Glenrowan and rode his mount around the men, to their head.

Drawing his claymore from its scabbard, he brandished the polished weapon.

"To Stirling!" he roared. "We shine, not burn!"

"To Stirling!" His men took up the cry, jostling forward to follow their laird as he rode through the gates and on, across the causeway.

The women streamed after them.

Mary started to follow the others, waving her kerchief and blowing kisses to burly Angus MacLean, but she turned away when she realized her mistress had turned and was running back inside the keep.

"My lady!"

"Go with the others! I forgot something! I'll be there in a moment."

True to her word, she made her way to the front of the throng as it reached the far bank of the lake. She thrust her way through the men and women to Gray's horse.

"Here, my lord!" she cried. "A talisman to bring you good fortune and ensure your safe return!"

With that, she handed him the narwhal's horn that they had found amongst the flotsam and jetsam so long ago.

Obviously moved, he said nothing as he took it from her, instead mutely linking his fingers through hers.

"I love thee." He mouthed the words, his heart in his eyes as he looked down at her.

"As I love thee," she whispered back.

And then he was gone, and the men on foot were tramping after him. One fellow took up a rousing song and the others joined in.

In what seemed like only moments, they had reached the brow of the nearest hill, then vanished as they passed over it.

The men of Glenrowan had marched away to fight a battle for Scotland's freedom. To the women was left the waiting and weeping. With a heavy sigh, Skyla asked herself which was easier, but she already knew the answer in her heart.

Sixteen

" 'Tis a bonny place, but not much t'be dying for, I'm thinking," Ian observed with a shudder a sennight later.

He was looking down at the river plain where the two great rivers, the Forth and the Clyde, came together to form the gateway to the north of Scotland, and at the gently rolling green hills that surrounded the strategic point.

Though he was trying desperately not to show it, Graham suspected Ian was nervous about the upcoming battle—his first of any great size. And, Gray prayed fervently, the last, for all of them. For all of Scotland!

"There's nothing wrong wi' being afraid, laddie," he assured him, gripping Ian's shoulder. "Only a fool goes into battle unafraid.'Tis fear that keeps us alive."

"Aye? Then what about courage?" Ian asked with a faint smile now. "There would be no heroes, wi'out courage."

"Courage is what we draw upon. 'Tis what makes us go on, despite our fear."

"He's right," Jamie agreed, joining them. "Dinna fash yersel', laddie. Ye'll not dishonor our name. Once the fighting starts, it all happens so fast, ye dinna have time t'be scared. Gray? A word wi' ye."

"What is it?"

"Ye're t'ride at the Wallace's right hand. He says make ready t'mount up. His spies report the English are forming ranks. Cressingham means t'cross the brig!"

"Does he, now?" Graham grinned.

His brothers grinned back.

He knew what they were thinking. That Cressingham's great weight, combined with the weight of his huge horse, might well bring down the bridge without a single arrow needing to be loosed, or a claymore lifted on their part!

"Are our lads tucked snug in their bolt-holes?"

"Aye—and raring t'go!" Jamie grinned.

"And go we shall, my friends, once we've been given our blessing. Aye, Andrew?" Wallace promised as he and Sir Andrew de Moray joined them. "Brother Marcus?"

With his great height and his proud bearing, the Wallace was a worthy champion for Scotland's freedom. His manner was calm and collected, yet his eyes blazed with the true patriot's fire and his voice rang with the authority of the born leader.

Not for the first time, Graham wondered fleetingly what manner of priest his friend would have become, had fate not torn him from the Church and the priesthood he had entered, and forced him to become a rebel warrior instead.

One to inspire the fiercest pagan to convert, he had no doubt.

Kneeling, the Scots bowed their heads as the Wallace's tonsured friar moved among them in his brown habit, a silver crucifix held aloft, giving them the blessing of men about to go into battle, with no certainty that they would survive it.

It was quickly done.

In but moments, they crossed themselves and muttered "Amen." Then Graham strode over to where his horse waited, circling nervously and tossing its head, so that the groom was hard put to hold it.

The big gray stallion could smell the excitement—and the fear—that rode the wind this morning, Gray thought, stroking its velvety nose to calm it.

Aye, and neither of them wanted to be there, he thought ruefully.

Leaving his bride the morning after their wedding was the most difficult thing he had ever done.

He wanted the battle soon fought and won, so that he could go home to his beloved Skyla, and begin their future together as man and wife. He drew the veil she had given him as her favor from inside his shirt, where he carried it, close to his heart.

The gauzy sea-green folds had captured her scent. Elusive. Provocative. Female. *Skyla*. He buried his nose in its softness, and was immediately back at Glenrowan, his face in her perfumed hair, his lips brushing her throat as they lay together, limbs entwined, fingers linked, hearts beating as one. . . .

"Are ye thinking of me, ma sonsy lass?" he mused aloud, squinting as a sunburst of dazzling light reflected off a shield or perhaps off the polished armor of the English knights encamped across the valley. Is that why I feel ye with me sae strongly? he asked himself as he took the reins from the groom and vaulted up into the saddle. His fingers brushed the narwhal horn he'd tied to it for good fortune.

The sensation of her presence was so real, he fancied he could smell the delicate herbal-and-flower fragrance that always surrounded her. Yet when he turned, fully expecting to see her standing there, smiling up at him, her arms outstretched in loving welcome, there was no one there but other grim-faced, determined Scots like himself.

The Wallace and his army, drawn from the south of Scotland, and Sir Andrew de Moray and his force, made up of Highland Scots, from the far north, had met and made their camp here on Abbey Craig. The great mount of earth formed a perfect lookout point from which to survey the flat flood plain below that would become, in a matter of hours, the battlefield.

From the mount's foot, the ground dropped sharply away. Through it wound the river, which snaked back upon itself in a vast loop.

As Ian had observed, it was a bonny spot, with the gray stone of Stirling Castle looming high atop the hill, and the pretty abbey and small croft-houses scattered about.

Seeing it this morning, with the sun shining and the bright silk banners of the English fluttering in the warm breeze, the emerald grass along the riverbanks dotted with grazing sheep like balls of thistledown, others must surely have questioned the wisdom of doing battle to hold such a tranquil spot, much as Ian had done earlier. As he had said, it did not appear worth dying for.

Appearances notwithstanding, however, the area was of vital importance, for it was truly the gateway to the north of Scotland. Whoever controlled this point had the ability to conquer and dominate the farthest reaches of the Highlands.

For that reason, the bridge must be held, the enemy turned back, at all costs.

As for the brig itself—or bridge, as the English called it—it was just as Angus MacLean had described it that night at Glenrowan.

Built of wood, it was so very narrow, only two horseman could ride across it, side by side. Any man could see that attempts to cross with the enemy waiting at the far end would prove suicidal.

Moreover, the going was soft, the ground muddy on the other side, where Scots awaited the English. Maneuvering the weight of man, horse, heavy weapons, and armor was almost impossible. Any horse would be up to its fetlocks in the mire in moments. Surely the Sassenachs, however arrogant, would not be foolish enough to try it, would they—?

"Dinna fash yersel', mon. I know the enemy as well as I know my own hand. The Earl of Surrey will come."

Sir John de Warrene, Earl of Surrey, led the English army.

"Or he will send his 'wee' Cressingham ahead of him, t'do his dirty work," Will added as he rode up alongside him. "Tell your lads t'be ready for the signal, aye? T'stand firm, until they hear my horn, then charge!"

"Let them come! I dinna give a tinker's damn who's the first to die! Whoever crosses that bridge, we'll be waiting for them, by God!" Angus MacLean vowed.

"That we will. Our fine Surrey and his fat henchman will catch more than taxes from this wee burn!" Sir Andrew de Moray declared with a wink. "And I'm no' talking about the salmon!"

Others hearing Moray's jest laughed heartily, caught up in the battle-fever of the moment, and in the almost feverish excitement that pervaded the Wallace's camp as the men of the clans dug in.

As part of the ambuscade, some hid themselves amongst the reeds and marsh grasses that lined the banks of the rushing, roaring Forth—de Moray's "wee burn." Others went upriver, to lie in wait at the wide ford where most of the enemy were expected to cross.

On every side, Scots were making last-minute preparations for the coming battle. Many wore faded breachans and coarse shirts, some were barefooted, others' feet were crudely bound in strips of leather.

Some still honed their dirks or the blades that topped their long and deadly shiltrons to a razor's edge on a handy whetstone. Others painted their faces for war in the old way of the warriors of yore.

It was common knowledge that the English feared the Scots' wildness and their barbaric ways. So be it, Gray mused. If painted faces and howling Gaelic war cries could chill the enemy's blood, then so much the better!

The Scots possessed no armor, no chain mail, few horses, and precious little food. Most were on foot and carried only clubs of wood, staffs, slings, and other crude weapons they had fashioned for themselves. Still, they had Highland hearts and Highland pride and the fierce desire to be free of their English oppressors. That, coupled with a fearsome appearance and a reputation for unparalleled savagery—deserved or otherwise—could well prove the most valuable weapons in the Scottish arsenal.

"Cressingham's crossing! Make ready!" The warning rippled through the Scottish ranks like wind rippling through reeds.

Graham glanced over at Jamie and at Ian. "Well? What say ye? Are ye ready, laddies?"

"Ready!" came their resounding shout.

"We shine, not burn! A Mackenzie! A Mackenzie!"

A second later, William Wallace blew a long winding blast on his horn. The melancholy note floated far and wide over the grassy flood plain.

And so, the battle began.

Skyla, Mary, and her two older sisters, the mischievous Wilda and the ever-talkative Sonia MacKenzie, were weaving at their looms the first time she sensed him. His presence was so real, she actually twisted in her seat and rose halfway to greet him.

"Thank God! You're safe!" she exclaimed as she stood up. The shuttle fell from fingers grown suddenly slack. Her hand flew to her throat. "My—my lord? Where are you—?"

There was no one there, she saw, feeling foolish and perplexed.

"What is it, my lady?" Mary stared at her, startled by her cry. She looked over her own shoulder. "Who—who are ye talking to?"

Skyla frowned, confused as she looked about her. There was no one there. And yet . . . how could that be? she wondered, the fine hairs on her nape standing up and prickling. She had heard Gray call her name, as clearly as a bell.

She looked up, realizing Mary, Wilda, and Sonia were staring at her, their expressions puzzled.

271

She drew her hand across her brow to dispel the sense of unreality that had come over her.

"Forgive me, my ladies. For just a moment, I thought . . . well, I thought my lord husband had come home . . ."

Her voice trailed away as she realized the foolishness of what she was saying. There were only the four of them in the solar. They would think her mad.

" 'Twas but wishful thinking, my lady," the Lady Wilda murmured gently, squeezing her hand. "Nothing more. Dinna fash yersel' "

Her lovely green eyes were full of sympathy.

"Laird Graham will come home t'ye soon enough, bringing our braw laddies with him. You'll see."

"Of course," Skyla agreed, shaken despite her words.

Gray's voice, his presence had been so—so real. The sensation of his lips brushing her throat, his voice in her ear. The dear familiar scent of him in her nostrils . . .

Could she have imagined it?

"Are ye thinking of me, ma doo . . ." she had heard him say.

She sighed. Her shoulders sagged.

It must have been her imagination. What other explanation was there?

Graham had been gone only a sennight, but already she felt as if the heart had been torn from her breast. Did missing him so terribly explain why she was imagining things?

She pressed her fingertips to her belly, hoping her lord's babe grew beneath her heart even now, living proof of the passion that had flared between them on their wedding night. A passion born of love.

Or was her condition, like imagining her lord's return, more of what Wilda termed "wishful thinking"? The Good Lord knew that she wanted so dearly to give him a son and heir!

Still, wishful thinking or nay, it was very possible she was with child, for her blood link with the moon had been broken. Her monthly courses, due a week ago, had yet to flow, and there were none of the usual signs that they were imminent. No cramping pains in her belly, no aching breasts, none of the throbbing headaches she sometimes had.

Auld Morag, Glenrowan's midwife, said the signs were promising. She was already cheerfully predicting a bairn for the MacKenzie and his bride in the month of June, the Year of Our Lord 1298, despite the other women's whispered protests that it was far too early to be making predictions of any sort.

"I know what I know," Morag told them all with a dark and mysterious look. "Our laird Glenrowan is virile as any stallion, just like his father and his uncles before him. How could ye

273

not be with child, my lady, wi' such a mon fer yer husband?"

Making the excuse that she needed some fresh air, Skyla left the other women to their weaving and climbed the stairs up to the battlements.

A fresh wind was blowing off the lake, sending glinting ripples scudding across its surface. The distant mountains wore streamers of lavender and gray mist like old women dressed in gauzy veils. The rowan woods were scarlet with the changing seasons, so that everywhere she looked, the beauty of the Highlands gladdened the eye and lifted the spirit, but not her eye, nor her spirit.

She would not feel truly glad nor uplifted about anything until her husband returned.

Every night since Graham left, she had come up here, to the battlements, as he'd asked, to gaze up at the moon and stars and think about him. Closing her eyes, she had wished with all her heart and soul that her love would find him and, like some powerful spell woven for his protection, keep him safe from all harm, wherever he might be.

She had come back to this same place at dawn, too, and been awestruck by the flamboyant beauty of the dawn sky; by the vivid saffron yellows and rosy pinks that beat back the charcoal clouds of night, and heralded the glorious dawn. The evening star was always the last star to fade from that breathtaking sky.

Just then, the wind changed direction, blowing hard against her back, tossing her hair in all directions. She stepped forward, intending to stand in the lee of a stone embrasure, out of the wind, when she gasped and sidestepped to avoid treading on the person huddled at her feet!

Dougie MacRae had come here before her.

"What do you here, laddie?" she asked gently, crouching down to speak to him. "Ye belong below, in the kitchens, where 'tis warm for ye."

Dougie slowly rose, pressing his back against the stone column and shooting her a wary look, as if he feared she might cuff him. He would have ducked past her with only a frightened glance in her direction had she not grabbed his shoulder.

"What is it, laddie? Are ye afeared of me?"

He hesitated, as if he had to consider her question before answering, then lunged forward, meaning to dive past her, to wrench his arm free.

"Laddie! Wait!" she cried, hanging onto his arm. "Tell me. What is it ye fear? Who is it ye fear? I willna hurt ye! No one here will hurt ye!"

"*He* will! I know he will! That's why he came back! T'get me!"

"Who, child? Who?"

"The big man," he babbled. His eyes were round as brooches in his narrow face, his foxy red hair disheveled, as if he'd just awoken from a nightmare.

"The big man wi' the beard! The man she killed! I saw him! I saw *them*. I was watching, ye ken? I sometimes watched what they did together, me mam and the men who came. She stuck ma father's dirk in his belly—the one wi' the stag hilt, ye Ken? She said the dirk was for me, when I was grown, t'remember my father by. But she used it! The big man's eyes rolled back, an' there was blood everywhere."

He shuddered violently, reliving the memory, his eyes wide with remembered horror. He shook his head from side to side.

" 'Twas on her skirts. On her face. Some of it were spattered across ma hand. *My* hand, mistress! Och, sae much blood! 'Twas like the winter cull, when they slaughter the pigs for the salting, aye? And I knew her sin would blight my soul, as it would blight hers. . . .

"After the McLeods came to take his body awa', she went and washed hersel' in the burn," he went on. "She kept humming the same wee scrap of a tune, over and over, as if she'd gone mad . . .

"The big man was dead when his clansmen carried him out the door, mistress. But now, he's come alive again! How can that be, my lady? Why will he not stay dead? *Why?*" he sobbed.

"He *is* dead, Dougie. Ye dinna have t'fear him. Tell me. Where was it ye saw him again? Here?"

"Aye. In the great hall, my lady. He came t'speak wi' my fath—wi' the MacKenzie himself!" he hastily corrected himself, his eyes sliding uncomfortably away from hers.

"'Twas him what brought word from the Wallace, aye? And every night since that night, he's filled ma dreams. I can find no rest for fearing that he's come for me!"

Angus MacLean. The child had mistaken MacLean for her uncle. That was how Dougie's "dead man" had come alive again.

And, if what the boy had said was true—and she had no reason to think it was otherwise—this innocent child had witnessed her uncle's murder at his mother's hands! Had actually seen Fionna MacRae plunge Gray's missing dirk into her uncle's belly!

Dougie's account of her uncle's death was proof that Gray was innocent!

"I close my eyes, an' I see him, over and over again! Please. Dinna send me away, mistress. I beg ye. I'll starve if ye send me awa'!"

"'Tis naught but a bad dream, laddie," she told him, cupping his grubby tear-streaked face between her hands. "Douglas MacLeod is truly dead. The man ye saw, his name is not Douglas at all. 'Tis Angus MacLean, and he is another man entirely. True, they look alike, but they are not the same man."

"Nay?" he piped.

"Nay."

"How do ye know that, my lady?"

"I know because the man who died was my Uncle Douglas."

"Douglas! That's my name, too!"

"Aye, I ken. When I was your age, he used to dandle me on his knee. He would let me do all manner of wonderful things that my lord father forbade me to do." Remembering, she smiled. "Things my father thought better suited to my brother, like hawking and swordplay."

"Aye. He were good to me, too, he were! He gave me a whistle once. Said he'd carved it himsel', just for me." He grinned. "He wasna like me mam's other men, always ready wi' a clout or a kick. Mam used to laugh all the time when he came t'our cottage."

And laughing, she had stabbed him, Skyla thought, wondering why—if her uncle had made Fionna smile—she had still seen fit to kill him.

She doubted she would ever know.

Dougie MacRae's head jerked up. "My lady? Do ye think—do ye think I'll ever see her again?" His voice broke.

She stroked his foxy red hair, wishing she could tell him that he would, for all that she had no love for the missing woman herself. But she sorely doubted it.

"I dinna ken if ye will or nay, Dougie," she said instead. "But whatever comes, the Mac-Kenzie says there'll be a place for ye at Glenrowan. He'll no' let ye starve. Perhaps ye can live with yer mam's kin? Wouldn't ye like t'meet your grandsire and your aunts and uncles?"

He scowled and looked doubtful. "I would not! They willna want the likes of me. They'll spit on me and call me a bluidy bastard. You'll see. That's what they all do." He was trying to be brave, she could tell, but his lower lip quivered uncontrollably.

"Time, laddie. Give it time," she murmured softly, squeezing his shoulder. "It heals most hurts."

What else could she tell him? She could not alter the fact that he was illegitimate, or that the world was not a kind place for children to grow up without a father's name to protect them.

"Now. Run along with ye! Go down to the kitchens and break your fast. I'm sure Sorcha has something good for ye to eat? Scones, mayhap, or a bannock or two wi' jam?"

"Aye, mum. She feeds me till my belly's fair t'bursting, Mistress Sorcha does!" His grin was broad and merry. Never had he looked more like her uncle than he did at that moment, she realized with a pang of sadness as she followed him down the stairs, returning to her ladies in the solar.

Seventeen

Almost forty leagues to the south, the battle for Stirling Bridge was all but over. And, although brief, it had been bloody.

In but an hour or two, and armed only with makeshift weapons, the Scottish army had triumphed over the enemy English! The gateway to the north had been defended. The Sassenachs under Surrey had either died, or turned and fled back whence they came.

Hated Cressingham was among the first to fall. His heavy destrier had quickly become bogged in the mire, as they had known it would.

As Cressingham struggled to ride his horse out of the muck, the Scots had erupted from their hiding places in wood and bush, reeds and water, and attacked him and his men-at-arms.

In but moments, Cressingham had been torn from his charger's back and slain.

Once they had ridden across the brig to the other side, the English knights and men-at-arms who followed after Cressingham found themselves hopelessly trapped between ambushing Scots and the loop of the river, unable to either attack or put up a solid defense.

One after another, the Sassenachs were dragged from their horses and forced to fight for their very lives.

Almost all of them lost that fight.

In the aftermath of the battle, Graham rode his weary stallion across the river plain, the emerald grass strewn now with bodies, twisted in the obscene postures of war, and dead or dying horses.

His heart was in his mouth as he searched the dead for his brothers. As he rode, he looked at the faces of the fallen and prayed that, unlike Sir Andrew de Moray, who had been badly wounded in the battle, his brothers were unharmed, as was he.

The three of them had begun it together, fighting side by side with the Wallace. But as, one by one, they'd turned aside to staunch the seemingly endless flood of English, they had been torn further and further apart.

By the time the Earl of Surrey and what was left of the English army had turned tail and fled back to the south, Jamie and Ian had been nowhere to be seen.

Graham had ridden some distance from the bridge, and found himself between the Wallace's camp and the ford upriver, when he finally saw Ian.

And what he saw made the blood become ice in his veins.

Ian was alive—but for him, the battle was not yet over!

On foot now, like the wiry Sassenach he was desperately battling, Ian swung his claymore bravely and strongly, yet it was clear to Gray that his strength was steadily waning.

Nearby sprawled several other Sassenachs, all of whom appeared dead. Some were slumped over their shields, others curled on their sides in the grass, still others leaned up against the tree trunks like weary foresters, taking a noonday nap—from which they would never awaken.

With a last wild whoop, Ian dispatched his opponent. The man slumped to the ground and Ian whirled about, victory lending him a last burst of energy.

He spotted Gray as he turned, and whirled his bloody claymore over his head in a wild, triumphant arc, gleeful as any small boy. His cherubic face broke into a broad grin to see Gray alive and unharmed.

"We did it, Gray! They ran for their lives!" he crowed. "A MacKenzie! We shine, not burn! Yeeeehaaaaaa!"

So great was his relief, Gray started to laugh. His laughter was abruptly cut off when, from the corner of his eye, he saw a wounded Sassenach suddenly push himself up off the ground. In his fist was gripped one of the lethal Scottish spears.

Drawing back his arm, the man used the last of his strength to hurl the spear at Ian's chest.

"Nooo!" Graham roared, setting spurs to his horse.

The gray leaped forward, planting its bulk squarely between Ian and the spear in a single stride.

Instead of impaling Ian, the spear buried its metal blade deep in Graham's thigh. The long handle shuddered as it jutted from the wound.

Blood spurted instantly.

"Graaaay!" Graham heard Ian calling his name as if from a long way off as he slipped bonelessly from his horse's back to the hard ground.

"Skyla!" he whispered. *"Skyla!"*

Then everything turned blacker than the bottom of a well.

In the sun-filled solar, its walls hung with colorful tapestries, the four women were trying to finish the section of weaving they had started before the waning light made such work impossible. Suddenly, the odd sensation came again. It struck far more forcefully this time.

"*Aaah!*" With a sudden cry, Skyla sprang to her feet, a fist pressed to her thigh. "Help me!" she whispered. "Aaah, help me! Mary! The pain!"

"What is it, my lady?" Mary cried, letting her shuttle fall and hurrying to her side. "Och, lovie, have you hurt yoursel'?"

"I dinna ken. Ohh, my leg. It burns, it burns like fire!"

She swayed as she attempted to stand, lightheaded and suddenly overwhelmed by weakness. Her eyes fluttered shut.

"You, Ross!" Mary ordered crisply, all bustling efficiency. "Catch our poor lady, before she falls. Hurry now! Carry her up to her chamber."

For once, Skyla did not protest, but allowed the stalwart Ross to pick her up and carry her.

Mary hurried after them, panting from exertion, her plump face flushed and rosy, her brow moist. She motioned Ross to set her mistress down upon the bed, then shooed him from the chamber and closed the door behind him.

"Now. Where are ye hurt, madam? Show me, do!"

"Here," Skyla whispered, pointing to her upper thigh. Her eyes closed, and she caught her lower lip between her teeth as another pain engulfed her. "Aaah!"

Mary pushed up the hem of her kirtle and the gauzy sark beneath, searching for some mark upon the flawless skin. Some wound or swelling to explain her mistress's obvious pain.

But her thigh was firm though slender, the skin as smooth and unmarred as ivory silk. There was no sign of swelling, redness, or poison anywhere.

"Ahh," Skyla sobbed, her face contorted. "It hurts so—! I canna bear it!"

Mary pressed her palm to her mistress's brow. Skyla's skin felt clammy.

"I'll send for Morag straightway," she promised, hastily tucking a woolen coverlet over her mistress. Her lady's hands were like ice. Mary's normally rosy face was pale with worry as she splashed watered wine into a goblet.

"Come, my lady. Drink this down. 'Twill help the pain, whatever its cause, and warm ye, too. I'll have Morag brew ye something stronger."

"Nay. None of your brews. I canna stay here. Don't ye see? I have t'go t'him. He needs me!"

She was still muttering and restlessly tossing her head when Wilda returned with Morag.

"Who, mistress?" Mary asked gently. Her expression said she thought Skyla's wits were addled. "Who needs ye? Where must ye go?"

"To my lord husband. He needs me sorely," she insisted, feeling faint and dizzy. "I fear . . . I fear he has been mortally wounded."

Mary hurried to her side. She took her by the upper arms to press her back down to the bed. "The MacKenzie, wounded? Och, mistress, nay! What makes ye think such a terrible thing, my lady?"

"I—I can feel it! I feel what he feels, Mary! I know 'tis madness, but he is as close to me as— as you are now!" Skyla cried, trying to explain. "I feel him here," she added, touching her breast. "And here." She touched her belly, her thigh. "He's everywhere, in every way! Just as I felt him near me earlier, when we were weaving, remember?"

"I remember. But . . . is it real? Is it his—his fetch—his living ghost—or his real ghost!— come t'tell ye? Or are ye just hoping 'tis he?"

" 'Tis real. I know it! But dinna ask me to explain, for I canna. Oh, Mary! He's been wounded. I know he has. I felt it, even as it happened! The force of the blow . . . the searing pain as it shot through his body. A sensation of falling and then landing with such force, it rat-

287

tled my body. Mark well my words, Mary. At this very moment, he has been struck with dirk or sword!"

She shuddered in horror, a vivid image of Gray's wounding filling her head. She closed her eyes, trying to drive it out.

"I can feel the blood pouring from him, draining his life away," she whispered, eyes closed. "Robbing him of strength. I know it makes no sense but . . . his weakness is my weakness. Oh, Mary, if he dies, I shall know the very hour of his death!"

"Calm yerself, do, mistress," Mary said soothingly. "Morag will fetch ye a draught, t'sooth yer nerves. 'Tis naught but a dreadful daydream, I'm sure, my lady. Fear for your mon is what made it seem real. If ye sleep a wee whi—"

"Sleep! 'Tis not sleep I need, I tell ye!" Skyla insisted harshly, springing off the bed and lunging past Mary and Morag, to the door. "What I need is to go to him. I canna just stay here and mind my spinning, not when my husband needs me!"

She saw Morag and Mary exchange fond yet disbelieving glances. Exasperated, she flung herself past them with an irritable snort and took the stairs down to the great hall with suicidal haste.

"My uncles will know what best to do," she

heard Mary say behind her as she went. "Go after her, Morag, while I find them. I'm afraid of what she might do, poor lamb, with no one to watch her. My lady's not herself today. Not herself at all!"

Skyla did not pause to hear Morag's reply. The sense of urgency inside her, of impending doom, was too urgent for delay. She sped down the stairs and on, through the hall, out into the bailey, then hurried past the women gathered about the well, to the stables.

She plunged inside, squinting in the hay-and-horse-scented gloom after the bright light of outdoors.

The groom, Hamish, was forking hay for one of the remaining horses, crooning nonsense to the great beast as he worked.

"Och, ye're a fine braw laddie, that ye are. A wee bit o' liniment, and that fetlock will be right as rain—"

"Hamish? Hamish!" she hissed.

"My lady!" he exclaimed as he turned and saw her. "What are ye doing here, mistress? This mucky place is—well, 'tis no place for a lady, aye?"

"Never mind that. I need ye to saddle my mare. And please, hurry!"

His grin faded, to be replaced by a worried frown. "Ye—ye want a horse? Mistress, forgive me. I canna do it! Dinna ask me, aye?"

Penelope Neri

"What nonsense is this? 'Canna,' ye say? How so?" she demanded, indignant. "Aren't ye the stable lad? Do as I ask, sirrah—and quickly!"

Despite the sharpness of her tone, the boy refused to yield.

"Right before he left, the MacKenzie told me and the lads t'keep ye safe here at Glenrowan till he returns, madam. He said he'd—he'd whip our arses if we disobeyed him! 'Tis only for your own safety, ye ken, my lady?" Hamish explained hastily.

"Oh, I ken verra well what it's for, my lad!" she growled. Two spots of hectic color burned in her cheeks, evidence of her mounting frustration.

"Mistress. He didna want ye running afoul o' the Sassenachs, aye?" Hamish explained.

"Hrrrmph." Had that truly been Gray's reason for setting even the stable boys to watch over her and keep her here? She wondered, her lips tightening in fury. Or . . . had he feared despite their unforgettable wedding night, that she might yet run back to Skye and her family the moment his back was turned?

Either way, his last-minute orders could well prove the death of him, unless—

"Then must I saddle my own horse," she decided, shooting the stable lad a withering glare. "For will he or nill he, I shall go!"

"That's where ye're wrong, my lass. Ye'll go

290

nowhere, for with yer husband gone, *I* forbid ye!" came a quavery yet authoritative voice.

Turning, she saw Graham's ancient uncles in the doorway, their beaky profiles and wild grizzled hair silhouetted against the daylight outside.

Mary and Morag hovered behind them, looking anxious.

"He means, *we* forbid ye," Archie corrected his brother.

"Aye," Kenneth agreed. "We promised the laddie we'd see t'the safety of Glenrowan's women. Ye'll remain here and wait upon your laird's return, my lass, like the other women! The MacKenzie willna thank us, should we let ye ride hither and yon, with Sassenachs bristlin' from every bank and brae!"

She opened her mouth to argue, then thought better of it and abruptly clamped her lips together. "Very well, then, sirs. If you insist."

Inclining her head, she turned on her heel and marched back to the keep proper, her nose in the air, her color high, quite ignoring the two elderly gentlemen.

Her very docility would have warned them, had they known her better.

Morag and Mary hurried after her, like ducklings chasing their mother.

"Ye said the MacLeod woman would prove a shrew as our laddie's wife," Kenneth declared, grinning in triumph at his twin brother. "But ye were wrong! The lassie's as biddable as any lamb! Ye're nooo judge of character, Archie, male *or* female. I've said it before, and I'll say it again, ye—"

"That's the trouble wi' you, laddie. Ye're *always* saying!" Archie grumbled without true rancor.

She waited until everyone was at supper to slip away from the high table, making the excuse that the weaving had given her a throbbing headache.

"I'll come with ye, my lady," Mary Jean offered quickly, giving her a sharp look.

"Nay, nay, Mary. Finish your supper. I can manage," she insisted, adding, "A very good night to ye all."

Once in her chamber, she closed the door behind her and hurried to kneel before the heavily carved chest in which Gray stored those garments he was not wearing.

She selected a tunic and breeks, removed her own clothing, and quickly donned her selections, belting both breeks and tunic about the middle to disguise the bagginess of the garments.

Throwing a plaid over everything, she

pinned it at the right shoulder with one of her own brooches, then tucked her hair up beneath one of Gray's feathered bonnets. Dipping her fingers in the ashes on the hearth, she smeared a little soot over her fair cheeks to imitate beard shadow.

Good enough, she decided, turning her head this way and that to inspect her reflection in the looking glass of polished metal. She would look like a lad under all but the closest scrutiny. Now all that remained was to stuff her bolster beneath her coverlet, so that her bed appeared occupied for the night, then steal some food and a horse and make good her escape.

Please God, Hamish would be at his own supper by now, and her mare left unguarded.

Her plan worked like a charm until she was leading her palfrey from the stable.

Hearing the stable door creak, she hastily ducked back into the shadows and put her hand over her mare's velvety nose to quiet her.

"My lady! My lady!" hissed a voice from the shadows. "Where are ye?"

Skyla groaned silently. Mary Jean. The lassie was like a hound for scenting mischief afoot.

"My lady Skyla? I know you're in here. Take me with ye! I would know how Angus is fairing, aye?"

"*Angus?*" The word burst from her, so great

was her surprise. "Not Angus MacLean?" She straightened up and stepped out into the broad bar of moonlight that spilled into the stable. "Whatever for?"

"Me and Angus, we're . . . sweethearts, aye?"

"You are?"

"Aye. It happened the night . . . the night before all the men left for Stirling. He asked me t'wait for him."

"He did?" Skyla's voice squeaked with incredulity. "Mary Jean? Ye didna—?"

"Aye, I did!" Mary confessed, and even in the bleaching light, Skyla could see the young woman's cheeks turn scarlet. "I couldna help mysel'. I love him, ye ken, madam, and besides, he was going off t'fight, and he said I was bonny, and so . . . Well, I couldna tell him nay, could I, the poor lad? Besides, we're to be wed when he comes back, with our laird's permission."

"I see," Skyla exclaimed, thunderstruck. "And I understand. But . . . ye canna come with me now."

"Oh? And why not?"

"Well, do ye know how to ride?"

"Nay. But I'll learn," Mary Jean persisted, her chin jutting now. "I'm very quick."

"Nay. You'll slow me down."

"I will not."

"You'll starve. I stole only enough food for mysel'"

"Aye, but I stole enough for *two*." She held up her shawl, lumpy with whatever she'd tucked into it. "There's bread. Cheese. Even a skin of wine."

"Cheese? *And* wine? Hmm." Skyla considered, then caught herself. What was she thinking? "Nay, nay. You must stay here. It—it could be dangerous."

"Aye, it could. But . . . oh, my lady, I'll take that chance, if ye'll let me go with ye. That great bear, he means that much to me, ye ken, mistress?"

Her heartfelt plea tore at Skyla's heart. How could she fault the girl, or refuse her, when Mary Jean wanted only what she wanted for herself? To reassure herself that the man she loved was safe, or to be there if—God help Gray and Angus!—he needed her.

"Och, very well, then. But ye canna go dressed like that."

"Aye. I know. When I saw the boltster and the garb peeking out from his lairdship's chest, I knew ye were planning something like this, my lady. So, I brought these." She giggled and held up another lumpy bundle. "These belong to ma Cousin Ian. We're the same height, aye? He'll no' be too happy when he gets back!"

"We'll worry about that later. Get changed. I'll saddle a horse for ye."

The horse she selected for her maid was

actually a pony. It was a docile yet game little beast, well suited to Mary Jean's unskilled seat.

Moments later, they were leading their mounts across the causeway. The guards there, all old men, either too ancient or otherwise unfitted for war, were gathered around a small fire, playing at dice and laughing.

"Who goes?" one of them called out.

" 'Tis I, Ranald, and my wee brother, Lachlann," Skyla called back in a thick, gruff voice completely unlike her own.

Her heart was in her mouth for a second, before the old man waved them on.

Moments later, their mounts' hooves struck the turf of the lake's far side, and they were free, and riding forth into the moonlit glen.

"We'll ride until 'tis too dark t'see our way, then find a broch or a hollow where we can sleep till it gets light," Skyla told Mary.

"Aye, my lady," Mary eagerly agreed.

Skyla grinned, enjoying the adventure. "If we're t'be 'brothers,' Mary, 'twould be better if ye called me by my name!"

"Very well, Skyla."

"*Skyla?* The name's *Ranald*, laddie." She grinned. "How is it ye dinna ken your brother's name?"

Eighteen

Two days had come and gone since Gray and Jamie had left Ian at Stirling with the other Glenrowan men to celebrate their triumph over the English. The victorious Scottish army was tending to its wounded, including Sir Andrew de Mornay, who had been badly hurt. It was unknown whether he would survive to fight again.

The two brothers headed north, drawn by an urgency Gray felt, but was at a loss to explain, following the Forth north and west.

They had come most of the way home, sharing a horse, and were moving through a shallow wooded glen where ferns and mosses formed a living tapestry of leafy green between the trees. Graham was riding when their gallant horse's heart burst.

It fell dead in its tracks with barely a snort.

Gray toppled over its bowed head like a sack of oats. He cursed and yelped as the fall jarred his injured thigh.

"Ha! Sound in wind and limb, ye said!" Jamie teased. " 'Sound' my arse."

"I was talking about mysel', ye miserable bastard," Gray grumbled, wincing as he pulled himself up. "Not the bluidy horse!"

A quick check confirmed his fears. The fall had reopened his wound. He was bleeding again. Not as hard as before, but too steadily for comfort.

"Wrong on both counts," Jamie added.

"What?"

"The horse or yersel'. Neither one of ye are sound!"

"Ye're right about that. The leg's bleeding again. Can ye hel—"

He abruptly fell silent, twisting in the other direction with his head cocked to one side to listen.

Jamie's brows lifted as he, too, heard the drumming of hooves.

"Riders coming!"

"Aye. And in a hurry t'get wherever it is they're going, too!"

Eyes narrowed against the light, Gray saw two horses thundering toward them down the glen, growing larger and closer by the second. In a few moments, they'd be on them.

"Deserters, ye think?" Jamie asked, squinting against the light.

"Aye. And Sassenachs, at that! They must be! God knows, we Scots had few enough horses t'begin with. Come on!"

They had to hide—and quickly.

"Where?"

In the height of summer, they might have climbed a tree and sought refuge within in its leafy foliage. But this was the month of September. The trees had already shed most of their leaves for the winter. What remained offered a man little by way of concealment.

"Somewhere close. Ye canna walk on that leg," Jamie panted. His chest heaved with exertion as he hooked Gray's arm over his shoulder and pulled him to his feet. "Here. Lean on me. The ferns . . ."

"Not the ferns. There's no' enough cover. Up there!"

Gray pointed to the dance of blighted standing stones that reached skyward from the wall of the glen, like grasping black fingers. The cairn of stones at its heart would hide them.

Jamie grinned. "Let's go!"

It was the perfect hiding place, Gray thought

299

as, dragging his right leg, he hooked his arm over Jamie's shoulders. The English were wary of Scottish holy places, however ancient. They gave them wide berth, believing them haunted.

With Gray leaning heavily on Jamie, they reached the top of the slope just as the first rider came into view.

Once a Druid burial place, the cairn had been built centuries ago in the center of a grove of sacred trees.

The leaves had turned scarlet with the season, and were now as red as the blood that had once been spilled on the altar stone nearby.

At the heart of the stone circle, a shaft led deep into the musty bowels of the earth, to the burial mound where the remains of a Celtic chieftain lay buried. The tunnel was littered with shards of pottery, left behind by the family and friends who had brought food offerings for the souls now housed within.

Giving the cairn's ghostly occupants not a second thought, both men dived headfirst into the opening, then turned and peered from their bolt-hole, like foxes gone to earth.

Their hiding place afforded them a fine view of the glen below, and of the riders they'd heard. Men who were not Sassenachs, at all, it appeared, but desperate fugitives—Scots, like themselves.

The pair—just lads, judging by the size of

them—were fleeing a half-dozen English soldiers, led by an older man of higher rank. A sheriff, perhaps, or a constable.

The lad in front, who was mounted upon a showy white palfrey, lay along his galloping horse's neck. Rider and beast flew like the wind as he urged his mount on with wild Gaelic shouts that challenged the Sassenachs' manhood.

"That's the way, laddie!" Graham muttered under his breath, his heart racing with excitement—and with fear for the lads' safety. "Outride the bluidy bastards! Show them what ye're made of!"

Unlike the first, the second boy was no rider. Nor was his pony as swift as the other mount.

The pudgy lad grimly clung to the saddle like a limpet to a seawall, flung this way and that by the pony's desperate rattling gallop. Pure terror locked his fingers over the reins and gave his knees their viselike grip on his pony's sides as they fled.

It was a race he could not hope to win.

The Sassenachs overtook the second lad in less than a minute. From where they crouched, he and Jamie could hear the lad's frightened cries as the riders hauled his screaming pony to a halt and dragged him down off its back. The terror in his desperate pleas struck to the heart.

The first rider could have made good his escape while his pursuers surrounded his companion. But, to his credit, he did not.

Instead, he reined in his fleet mount and rode slowly back to meet the English.

Admiration swelled Gray's chest. By God, what a lad he was! Some day, Lord willing, Gray would have a son just like him! A lad of valor and honor who did not abandon his friends, not even when his loyalty planted him square in the hands of his enemies.

Perhaps even now, such a son was growing beneath Skyla's heart, he thought briefly, tenderness flooding through him—and with it, fresh fear for the two young captives below.

In light of their recent defeat, the English would not deal kindly with any Scots they stumbled upon. The two laddies were as good as dead, without help of some kind.

"Move yer great head, mon. Yer blocking ma view!" Graham growled as Jamie, for no apparent reason, abruptly shifted his position. Sweet Jesu, what ailed him? he wondered, shivering. His wound throbbed and burned like the devil, yet his toes were cold as ice. Would he lose the limb?

He forced the fear down and instead asked, "What's going on down there?"

When Jamie didn't answer, he cursed under his breath and crawled forward on his elbows, dragging his useless leg behind him, until he lay on his belly alongside his brother.

"I said, what's happening?" he asked a second time.

"Keep yer daft head down, ye lummox!" Jamie growled. "Do ye want them to see ye, is that it?"

He planted a heavy hand on Gray's head and tried to force it down, but Gray evaded it.

Wriggling forward, he peered around a crumbling monolith that bore the ancient symbol of cup and ring, chiseled deep into the pitted stone.

The Sassenachs had surrounded their terrified quarry, he saw. A brace of braw Scottish lads, just as he'd thought, their breachans too worn and faded to know which clan had bred them.

The soldiers were laughing and jeering as they roughly dragged the first rider down from his saddle.

"Well, well, lads. What have we here, eh?" Graham heard one of the beefy louts ask. "A fine pair of barbarians, if ever I've seen one! Ho, Godfrey? Will ye look at this un's cheek? Beardless as a milkmaid's, it is!"

"Why, so it is. Smooth as a virgin's arse!" One—obviously Godfrey—stroked the lad's cheek. "An' he's pretty enough t'give me a cockstand! Come, on, pretty boy. Don't be shy! Bend over and drop yer breeks. Lad or nay, you're more comely than the whores I've plowed this twelvemonth! Ugly as sin, your Scottish drabs are. Are they not, Simon?"

Enjoying their sport, the soldiers jostled the frightened pair about, crudely taunting and shoving the lads from one to the other, pulling at their clothes, and handling them roughly, lewdly, until one of the boys—the taller of the pair—exploded in anger.

"Take your clarty paws off me, ye bastard!" he demanded, lashing out. "Dinna touch us, ye filthy swine!"

His bunched fist connected with the soldier's beaky nose and the laughter abruptly died.

From his hiding place, Gray saw the sudden spurt of blood that splashed from the Sassenach's broken nose. Heard the crunch of broken bone, the man's yelp of pain.

"For God's sake, *run*, laddie!" he urged under his breath.

But it was already too late for running.

Livid and hurting, the injured man quickly retaliated.

His hand snaked out. Grasping the youth by the throat, he lifted him up off the grass in one meaty hand, then slammed him up against the nearest tree trunk.

The boy's feet dangled, frantically kicking air. His heels drummed the rough bark behind him as he fought for breath, for his very life.

The gurgling sounds were followed by deafening silence. His fair complexion turned crimson, then purple as his face engorged with blood.

Without air, he would be dead in seconds, Gray realized, his own muscles tensing as he prepared to attack. They had to do something!

"Keep down, damn ye!" Jamie hissed, sensing what Gray was about to do.

But Gray flung aside his restraining hand.

In that same moment, the Sasseneach released the lad and his feathered bonnet tumbled from his head.

Gray's eyes widened in shock as long auburn hair tumbled down about the "lad's" shoulders, spilling halfway to his waist. Hair too long, too bonny for any lad—

"*Nooooooo!*" The roar of denial started, deep in his bowels, like the distant rumble of a volcano.

No lad at all, by God, but his own sweet bride!

With a sob of fury, of despair, of sheer desperation, he dragged himself up onto his knees, ready to charge headlong to his beloved's rescue, and devil take the consequences.

Jamie cursed bitterly under his breath as he saw Gray's eyes narrow in rage. His efforts to hide Skyla and Mary Jean's true identities had failed. Gray had recognized his lovely young wife.

And yet—unarmed and badly wounded as they were—there was nothing they could do to help her or Mary Jean escape their captors. *Nothing*.

Clamping a hand over his brother's mouth, Jamie wrestled Gray down to the frosty turf. Though by far the lighter man, he pinned him there with the weight of his own body.

"Easy, mon! Easy!" Jamie hissed as he struggled to escape. "Give yer word ye'll stay put, and I'll let ye up!"

"The devil, ye say! Get off me, damn ye!" Gray snarled, straining to break free. *"They have my woman!* I'll kill them all, the bluidy bastards! I'll cut out their eyes—I'll cut off their bluidy balls!"

"Stay down, damn ye! There's nothing ye can do, mon, don't ye see? If they catch us, 'twill be worse for *them*! No one will know where they are!"

"What?"

"I said, if we die trying t'save them, no one will ever know what happened t'them. We have to get help. Use your head, mon, not your heart. We've no horses nor blades t'our names. Not sae much as a broken dirk between us! Lie low, I tell ye. Bide your time. Dinna let the bastards get you, too!"

"You mean, watch? Let them ride off wi' her, wi'out lifting a hand?" Gray jeered. "Maybe you can crawl on your belly and do nothing, brother, but I canna. I have t'try!"

Knotting his fist in Jamie's bloodstained breachan, he shook him like a terrier to add weight to his words. "I love her, Jamie! Wi' out her, I'm already dead!"

"I ken, laddie, I ken," Jamie crooned. "But . . . who'll lead the clan if yer gone?"

"Dinna fret, brother," he said witheringly. "Ye can be laird in my stead. I havena forgotten my duty t'ma people. . . ."

Vivid blue eyes blazed fleetingly in his haggard face. Cracked lips parted in a mirthless smile.

"Any more than I've forgotten my bonny bride. So. Unhand me, little brother. Dinna make me break your fingers, aye?"

Though low, his voice was menacing. Deadly.

With what appeared to be a resigned nod, Jamie rocked back on his heels. "So be it, then, ye hotheaded fool."

Gray dragged himself to his knees. He knelt there, hugging a pitted stone slab, his grip so fierce his fingers bled and his arms shuddered. He had to force his gritty eyes to focus, for weakness engulfed him again as fresh blood seeped from the thigh wound.

Bright lights danced like corpse-candles in his vision, the flames sharp, then blurred.

"I canna . . . I canna let Hartford take her, ye

ken, Jamie?" he whispered earnestly, patting his brother's face.

Tears made tracks in the dirt and blood that coated his cheeks.

"She's sae sweet and fair. My bonny angel, aye? I ken full well what Hartford will do t'her! Let gooo, mon . . . let meee . . . lemme . . . *aaah*."

Gray never saw the blow that sent him gently into oblivion. His bright blue eyes rolled back in his head as he fainted away.

Jamie lowered Gray to the ground, alarmed by his brother's waxen pallor.

"Please God, I didna kill ye, laddie," he prayed under his breath, letting the stone he'd used fall to the ground. "Dinna die on me, ye great lummox."

Seconds later, he watched, unarmed and helpless, his heart in his mouth for fear of discovery, as Hartford's men-at-arms found their dead horse.

Swords drawn, they hunted about, raking the ferns with their blades and swatting the bushes, searching for the horse's missing rider. He saw them point directly at their hiding place once, before their leader vehemently shook his head. Clearly, he was not of the mind to disturb the spirits of ancient Scottish chieftains, any fugitive notwithstanding.

Moments later, they abandoned the search and rode off.

The Lady Skyla and little Mary Jean, their hands bound, rode between them on their own mounts, under close guard.

"God be with ye, lassies," Jamie murmured fervently, crossing himself, "until we can."

With that, he grasped Gray's feet and dragged him, inch by inch, back down into the cairn.

Soon after, the rain began.

It had been raining steadily for two hours and the light was fast fading when the moated keep of Fort Edward loomed into view. Seen through the vapors of evening mist that curled up from the ground, Hartford's garrison possessed a nightmarish aspect—looking much as Skyla imagined the gateway to hell itself.

Her belly was filled with dread as they rode beneath the keep's raised portcullis and into the bowels of the somber keep. She had a horrible sensation of being swallowed alive by a huge grey monster's wide-open maw.

Even worse was the knowledge that no one who loved them knew where they were. And those that did, of a certainty, had no care for their comfort—or even for their lives, she thought as grinning English soldiers stopped whatever they were about to ogle and stare and make lewd remarks about the two of them.

The English could kill them slowly, if they chose, or swiftly, or keep them locked up forever. Whatever their fate, Gray—if he yet lived—would be none the wiser.

What had she talked Mary into? What had she talked herself into?

"Forgive me," she whispered, her mouth dry with fear.

"I do, madam," Mary quavered, her own voice husky. "Dinna blame yersel'. I made ye take me with ye. I—I so wanted t'see Angus again."

Her maid's lower lip quivered.

"And so ye shall," Skyla promised firmly. Despite her efforts to sound brave, poor Mary sounded terrified. Still, Skyla did not feel so brave herself right now.

Within moments of their arrival, they were dragged from their horses, their hands still tied, and ushered into a large square chamber. Hartford sat before a massive table on which lay several parchments, a quill, and inks in horn bottles.

"And so we meet again, Skyla MacLeod. Or is it MacKenzie? This slut tells me you are the MacKenzie's bride?" Hartford scowled at a black-haired serving wench who cowered in one corner, almost lost in the deep shadows.

It was Fionna MacRae, Skyla realized. Despite her fear, she could not resist stealing a glance at the woman who had been her uncle's leman, and who—quite unknown to him—had borne his only child.

A handsome woman at one time, Fionna was not handsome any longer.

Her figure had gone slack beneath the ragged homespun she wore. Her dirty feet were bare, despite the chill in the air. There were both new and old bruises on her cheeks and ringing her dull eyes. Her long black hair was wild and unkempt. A mare's nest that had not seen water or comb for many a day—perhaps weeks—and was liberally streaked with gray. Moreover, she moved stiffly, as if in pain, then flinched and cowered when Hartford raised his hand to scratch his head, like a dog that was accustomed to being beaten.

Skyla felt an unexpected surge of pity for the woman. Whatever her sins, Hartford and his men had not dealt kindly with her since they'd taken her from the cottage she'd shared with her son.

"Mistress MacRae," Skyla said softly, tentatively in Gaelic. "Wee Dougie said if I saw ye, to tell ye he misses ye."

"Ye've seen him? He is well?" Fionna replied in the same tongue.

"I have. My lord husband has taken him into

his safekeeping. To Glenrowan, ye ken? The lad was starving."

Fionna caught her lower lip between her teeth. Tears sprang into her eyes. "Pray tell him that I am grateful, when next you see him?"

"I will," she promised.

"Enough of that heathen jabbering!" Hartford growled. "Get out of here, slut!"

Waving Fionna from the chamber with obvious contempt, Hartford rose from his carved chair. He came around the table to stand before Skyla, a hateful sneer plastered across his pox-marked face.

"I must confess, my lady Skyla, it came as something of a shock to learn that you had wed the man who slew your uncle, then kidnapped you. Surely it cannot be true?"

"Indeed it is, I'm proud t'say," she admitted, her chin coming up, her gray eyes flashing.

"How so, my dear? Did that . . . *barbarian* ravish you? Does your belly swell with his bastard, hmmm?" he asked silkily.

Quick as a striking snake, his hand came out. The palm flattened against her stomach, pressed against her belly. His almost colorless eyes lanced deep into hers as he did so. Her flesh crawled in revulsion. He would have slid his paw lower in a lewd caress, had she not grabbed his wrist to halt him.

"Don't!" she hissed. It was a command, not a plea. Her eyes bored into his like shards of silvery ice, unblinking. Her nails stabbed deep into the back of his hand and she saw the blood drain from his face in pain, before she flung his hand off with a contemptuous snort and a Gaelic curse, as if his touch was verminous.

"Your spies were correct, Sir Roger. I *am* Glenrowan's bride, before God and under the laws of Scotland! And, since I have done no wrong, I demand to know why my servant and I were brought here under guard?"

"Done no wrong, you say?" Hartford chuckled nastily and shook his fair head. "I beg to differ, my lady. Your clan makes war upon the English army. The MacKenzies are, in effect, part of a rebel faction of clans that must be put down, in order for there to be peace in Scotland. You and your servant are spies for that rebel faction!"

"Spies!" she exclaimed. "What nonsense is this, Constable?"

"Not nonsense at all, my lady, but fact. You were arrested by my men shortly after the battle for Stirling Bridge, disguised as men. What else am I to believe, but that you are Scottish spies? Spies fleeing a battle, I might add, that the English won!"

He smiled nastily. "The Scots were slaughtered, to the last man! Whether you know it or not, my lady, you are no longer a bride, but a widow. One who is, moreover, guilty of treason."

If he was hoping for some response, he was sorely disappointed, for she did not betray her feelings by so much as the flicker of an eyelash.

"However, I might be persuaded to overlook your activities in this regard, should you prove . . . accommodating, shall we say?"

"Devil take ye, Constable," she said softly. "I'd sooner 'accommodate' a crippled goat."

"As you will, then," he ground out angrily, his jaw hard. "I wager you will have changed your mind when next we meet. You, there. Take her below." He nodded at the men-at-arms. "Leave the other one here. With me."

"My lady!" Mary whispered, the blood draining from her face.

"Nay!" Skyla exclaimed, throwing off the guards' hold on her. "I will stay! Leave my serving maid alone. Unhand me, I say!"

She tried desperately to wriggle free of the two men-at-arms, but could not escape them.

They half-carried, half-dragged her from the chamber and down some stairs, to the damp cells below the sombre keep.

And there, mercifully, they left her. Mercifully, because she quickly decided she much preferred both the rats and the damp that ran down her cell's clammy walls to the company of Hartford and his ilk.

There were rats, and then there were men who were worse than any rat could ever be. Hartford was one of them.

Dropping to her knees, she closed her eyes and offered up a fervent prayer for Mary's safety.

Nineteen

Angus McLean staggered outside to make water soon after sunrise, still bleary-eyed from sleep.

He had returned to Glenrowan with the victorious Clan MacKenzie, following the battle for Stirling Brig.

Arriving late the day before, he had expected his wee pigeon, Mary Jean, to be waiting for him with a hero's welcome in her bed, followed by a victory feast.

Instead, he had found the injured laird and his brother Jamie butting heads like stags in a violent argument that threatened to end in bloodshed, if one of them did not yield.

He had also learned that the laird's bride and his own bonny lass had been taken captive by the English!

A man who favored taking immediate—and often physical—action, he had given the Mac-Kenzies until this morning to go after their women.

If they were still against it . . . well, then, a pox on them all! *He* would go after the lassies, alone, if he had to.

Positioning himself comfortably some distance from the wall of the armorer's shop, he sighed and let loose a powerful stream of urine, grunting with the pleasure that only emptying a full bladder can give a man.

He was still pissing when he spotted her, sitting astride a weary pony in the middle of the bailey.

His jaw dropped in shock.

Her pretty brown hair was a mare's nest now, and stuck up in every direction. Its softness was snarled with twigs and leaves.

Her clothing—men's clothing, he noticed belatedly—was torn and dirty, the tunic gaping in a way that bared most of one lush pink breast.

Normally, he would have found the forbidden glimpse of a lassie's teat a rare treat.

Instead, something in Mary's eyes filled him with shame that he was a man.

Adjusting himself, he dropped his kilt, then strode slowly toward her.

He moved quietly despite his great bulk, crooning to her all the while, as if she was a wild creature he feared to startle. A doe, perhaps, or a newborn foal.

"Mary? Aaaah, Mary, lass. Here ye are. I've been waiting for ye. What are ye doing out in the cold, hinnie? Won't ye come in?"

She stared past him with no reply. Nor did she give any sign that she'd heard him.

"Lassie? 'Tis me. Angus. I've come home to ye, dearling, as I promised. Were ye waitin' for me?"

"Angus?"

Her small frightened voice made his throat ache. She sounded like a wee bairn, waking from a nightmare.

Her lower lip began to wobble uncontrollably. Tears filled her eyes, and then recognition, thank the Good Lord, replaced the blankness in their depths.

"Oh, Angus!" she murmured. "It really is you!"

"Aye, lassie, aye."

"Please, Angus! Hold me. Dinna let me fall!"

"I'll not, sweet Mary. Ye're safe wi' me."

Lifting her from the pony's back, he carried her inside the great hall.

"Where's your mistress, lovie?" he asked gently as they went in. "Can ye tell me? Where and when did ye see her last?"

Hesitantly, and with a great many tears, Mary told him, along with the terms for her lady's release.

"In the name of Edward Plantaganet, by the Grace of God, King of England, Wales, and Scotland, who goes there?"

The voice, with its flat, nasal tones, rang out in challenge as Gray rode up to the gates of Fort Edward.

" 'Tis Graham, by the Grace of God, the Mackenzie of the Glenrowan Mackenzies," he shouted back with no little sarcasm. "Open yer damned gates!"

"Not bloody likely! No one gets in 'ere unless they're on foot and unarmed, ye heathen lout," scoffed the guard. "Including your Robert the Brute!"

Both guards chortled, thinking themselves great wits for their silly substitution.

Scowling, Graham swung himself down from his horse, wincing as he put weight on his right leg.

He was in a foul temper, for he had left Glenrowan without mending his quarrel with Jamie. The one begun when he came to, and learned what his brother had done.

The harsh words they had exchanged could

well prove the last words they ever said to each other in this lifetime.

But he'd had no choice, if he was to meet Hartford's conditions for Skyla's release: the exchange of his own freedom for his bride's.

"Have ye gone mad, mon? Have ye lost yer wits?" Jamie had demanded. "Ye must have, t'consider such a trade!"

"Hartford is not like you, Gray," Ian had added. "He has no honor t'speak of! He'll not let Skyla go, once ye surrender—you do know that?"

"He's right," Jamie had agreed. "Ye canna trust the man to keep his terms! Once he has you, he'll keep ye both—although 'tis you he really wants."

"Me? Why me?"

"You're the Wallace's friend and ally, aye?" Ian had explained, to Graham's surprise. "He can use ye t'gain favor for himself."

He sometimes forgot that Ian was no longer a boy.

"Everyone knows the Wallace trusts ye. That he counts ye among his closest friends," Ian continued. "That ye fought at his right hand at Stirling. Ye share his hatred of the English, too, because of your fathers."

"Ian's right. You're closer than most brothers!"

"Aye. And the Sassenachs will think your friendship can be used to catch him! Leverage, t'bend the Wallace to their will."

"Your surrender would be a feather in Hartford's cap, and no mistake!" Jamie finished. "Enough, perhaps, to put the constable permanently in Longshanks' favor."

Graham grunted noncommittally. Let his brothers think what they would.

Although much of what they said was true, he knew that the Wallace put no man before Scotland's freedom and his hatred of the English—not even someone he considered his closest friend.

Should it ever come to the test, Graham had no illusions. The Wallace would choose Scotland over their friendship.

Gray had no choice.

"Nevertheless, 'tis a chance I must take," he said at length. "You heard what Mary said. If Fort Edward is attacked, Hartford will have Skyla's throat cut before the second arrow is fired!"

"He canna, not if we have enough men!" Jamie reasoned. "Think on it, Gray! With more men, we could surround the keep, then storm its walls from all directions at once!

"By the time the constable realized what was happening, we'd be inside the fort! Hartford wouldna have time t'harm her."

"Nay? How long does it take t'kill a lass? Five seconds? Ten?"

"I tell ye, he'll not kill her—he's too clever for

that. Killing her would deprive him of a valuable pawn. If you're the leverage for Wallace's capture, then she is the key to yours! Without her, he would no longer be able to bring you to your knees. Your lady is worth far more to him alive than she is dead. Think, man!"

"I have, Jamie. And there are too many holes in your plan—and no' enough men to carry it out."

"But I know where we can get the men. I have sent—"

"Nay. 'Tis too late, I said," Gray declared, cutting off whatever Jamie intended to say. "My mind's made up, laddie. I'm going, and there's naught ye can do t'stop me. Not this time."

He clamped a hand over Jamie's shoulder. "I leave the clan to you. If I dinna come back, take my place. 'Tis what Father would have wanted, aye? Farewell, brothers."

"Ye bluidy pigheaded obstinate misbegotten whoreson . . ." he'd heard Jamie muttering as he left.

Ian had added some surprisingly imaginative insults of his own.

Gray grimaced. As farewells went, he'd had fonder!

Then again, he'd had warmer welcomes than this one, too, he thought, eyeing the sentries with suspicion.

Despite what he'd told Jamie, he had no illusions that the English constable would prove honorable. Far from it.

However, he could think of no other way to get inside Fort Edward, other than the obvious: meeting the terms Hartford had set for Skyla's release.

In other words, offering himself as hostage in her place.

"We're waitin', Scot!" the guard reminded him.

"And we don't have all day, neither," the other added.

"Aye, aye. Dinna get your bollocks in a twist, laddies. I'm coming," he flung back at them.

Unbuckling his claymore and the scabbard that hung from his belt, he let them fall, then strode through the open gates and into the grim fortress. His black hair furled on the wind like a banner of ebony silk.

Though weaponless and on foot, he carried himself with Highland pride, shoulders thrown back, head held high, his stride long and powerful, with no trace of a limp.

Hold Fast, ma doo, he prayed silently as the shadow of the gates fell across his face, like the shadow of the gallows.

He willed her to hear his silent plea, wherever she might be. *Remember your clan's battle cry! Hold fast, for just a wee while longer! I'm coming for ye!"*

* * *

The first bloodcurdling skirl of the pipes froze the marrow in Hartford's bones early the following morning.

Shoving aside the weeping serving girl he had bedded the night before, he sent another servant to discover the source of those ungodly sounds.

"Sir Roger! There's an army of Scots outside the gates, sir! The MacLeods and the MacKenzies! They're using a—a tree as a battering ram! Once they get in, they'll slaughter us all!"

The girl's hysterical screams doubled as the first gate gave with a splintering crash. It served to convince the constable it was past time he rode south, and devil take his two prisoners.

Clearly, a prolonged visit to his wretched wife across the Borders was in order, he decided as he hastily pulled on his clothes.

Grabbing what valuables he could readily lay hand to, he tossed candlesticks, coins, jewels, and such into a sack and hurried from his chamber.

"Please, sir! Help me!" the girl cried, but he hurled her aside and raced from the chamber, intent only on saving his own skin.

From the fortress's upper gallery, he raced down the stairs and across the great hall, bound for the stables. He was breathing heavily as he skirted the bailey, headed for the stables and a horse. All around him, the men of his garrison were fighting for their lives.

Leaderless and taken unaware by the Scottish attack as they slept, they had stumbled from their blankets and been plunged headfirst into a bloody fight for their very lives.

Devil take the lot of them! Hartford thought. He'd had enough of Scotland and of the Scots. Let his men fend for themselves!

Some of his garrison had been enticed through the fallen gates. Others crossed swords in the fortress's bailey. The sound of metal clashing against metal rang out on the dewy morning air, along with grunts and cries as men fell or were wounded.

Some of his men-at-arms grappled their enormous, kilted foes up and down the staircases. Others defended themselves far above him, coming perilously close to toppling over the battlements.

No sooner had the thought entered his head than a sound jerked his head back. He looked up just as his ever-faithful Godfrey toppled over the crenellations with a high-pitched scream.

The man landed on the flagstoned bailey with a sickening thud, only a few yards from where Hartford hovered, crippled by indecision.

A pool of dark blood quickly spread out under Godfrey's cracked skull.

Hartford was still wondering how to escape without having to pass through the flattened gates—which were in the very thick of the ferocious battle—when an idea struck him.

If his men failed to repel this Scottish rabble—as well they might—he would need some guarantee of safe passage to get out of the fortress.

What form should that guarantee take? he wondered desperately. A bribe of some sort? Gold? Silver? The booty that he had, with great presence of mind, tossed into the sack?

Nay, nay, surely there was another, better way to save his skin.

He smiled thinly. Of course! What—or rather, who—were these barbarians fighting to protect, after all? He had the perfect hostage—nay, *two* perfect hostages. Of the two, the woman would be easier to control. He turned away from the stables and stumbled down the steep staircase to the fortress's dungeons.

He would use Glenrowan's bride to escape the Scots, he decided. What splendid irony. With her as a human shield, he would be safe from attack by either MacKenzies or MacLeods. They would be much too afraid of hurting his hostage to harm him.

And later, once Fort Edward lay far behind him, and he was headed south to safety, he would find another use for the MacKenzie's lovely bride.

Skyla sighed as she caught a glimpse of the lightening sky through the barred window of her cell.

By falling into a fitful sleep, she had missed it. The evening star had already faded. Sunrise was breaking, splashing the dark sky with saffron, rose, and flame.

Its beauty brought tears to her eyes.

Had Gray been staring up at their special star and thinking of her as the day dawned? Was that why she had awoken, with such a start, to the sensation that he was close by?

Or had the pain she'd felt at Glenrowan been Graham's mortal wounding?

He could be dead, herself a widow, and she would never know it.

Hearing the chinking of metal against metal, she glanced up, thinking one of the rough guards had come to take her to Hartford again. The constable enjoyed the power he wielded over others.

Instead, she saw Hartford himself, fitting the key in the lock of her cell door.

Her belly churned with dread. That he had come here, alone, boded only ill for her.

"I bring you good news, my lady!" he began, his expression unreadable. "Your release has been negotiated. If you will come with me, I will take you to your lord husband."

She appeared somewhat dispirited this morning as he entered her cell. Yet three days of captivity had done very little to dim her vivid beauty.

Her pale skin was like the finest vellum. Flawless. Her dark red hair was a wonder of creation, spiraling halfway to her waist in glorious ringlets.

Was the fleece at her quim that same rare hue? he wondered suddenly, hardening. It would be in fiery contrast to those tranquil eyes, he thought with a rare poetic turn. Their color put him in mind of sea mists, smoke, and cobwebs strung with dew.

The dirty Scot rebel she had wed was no better than that dog Wallace! MacKenzie did not deserve such a woman in his bed.

The pleasant prospect of taming her almost made up for the need to go back to his ugly wife and his litter of whining brats, he told himself.

But first, he must make good his escape. And to do that, he would need the lady's cooperation.

Unlocking the door to the cell, he smiled down at her.

329

The joy that leaped into her eyes was almost laughable.

Like a lamb to the slaughter, she stood and followed him without question.

Twenty

Gray awoke from an uneasy dream of Skyla to hear an odd scratching sound.

He had just decided he must have been imagining things when the heavy door to his prison opened a crack. Fionna MacRae, aged a dozen years since last he'd seen her, slipped through it.

She was carrying a shabby brown mantle in one hand and something long, wrapped in a white cloth, in the other.

Bread, he decided.

"Quickly, sir! I've come t'help ye get away. Throw this on! The constable's still abed, but he'll be up and about soon enough. Oh, hurry, do!" she whispered urgently, draping a coarse mantle about his shoulders to hide his tartan.

"Do ye know where they're holding my wife?" he demanded.

"Below. In the dungeons." Fionna had shuddered. " 'Tis a wretched place."

"Have they hurt her?" he demanded, grasping Fionna's arm.

"Nay. She is cold and hungry, but unharmed."

"Thanks be! Can ye guide me to her?"

"I dare not. Sir Roger would kill me. For *this*, he will kill me," she added, indicating the mantle and the other bundle, "should he ever learn of it. My laird?" she said quickly as he hurried to the door. "Your lady said . . . she told me ye made a place fer my boy at Glenrowan?"

Gray shrugged. "What of it? He was starving."

"Ye didna have to help him," she whispered, "not after . . . not after what I did." She blinked several times. "Here. I brought this for ye, too. Take it and go!" she urged.

What he'd thought was a loaf of bread was a sword, he saw. An English sword, wrapped in a linen cloth.

He took it from her by the hilt with a curt nod of thanks. It was a fine weapon, well balanced and keen as any razor.

Fionna wetted her lips. "I thought, if her clan

blamed ye for her uncle's murder, she'd never wed ye," she told him, answering the unspoken question in his eyes.

"Ye killed an innocent man t'keep us apart?" A bitter smile played about his lips. "Then you underestimated the power of love, lassie. True love—our love!—is much stronger than that."

"I know that now." Fionna swallowed. "Tell Dougie I loved him, will ye, sir?" she whispered. "For I'll never see him again."

With those ominous words, she quickly left the small chamber, tears blurring her eyes.

"Fionna?" he called after her, following her out.

She paused.

"Whatever I did, 'twas never done t'hurt ye. Not intentionally. I hardly knew ye existed."

She nodded sadly. He would never understand.

"I know ye didna. 'Tis all right. Go now, sir. Go find yer bride, before Hartford misses his sword."

So it was that he found himself making his cautious way down some stairs to the great hall when he heard the wild song of the pipes. Gaelic war cries. A bloodcurdling scream, abruptly cut off. The sudden shuffle of booted feet.

Something was up!

Tossing caution to the winds, he raced down the stairs and out, into the bailey.

Sweet lord! There were Scots everywhere! Fort Edward was under attack—and not all her attackers wore the blue-and-green plaid of the MacKenzies, either, he noticed.

Some wore the faded plaids of their septs, the MacRaes among them. Still others wore green-and-red tartans—the colors and sett of the MacLeods, Lords of the Isles!

But how could that be? How could they have known? he wondered, confounded.

For as long as anyone could recall, their two clans had been bitter enemies, locked in a feud with no end in sight. Unless—?

Jamie.

Aye, by God! This was all Jamie's doing. His way to "increase their numbers."

"You, there! Dinna just stand there, gawking, MacKenzie!" yelled a strapping young man who looked somehow familiar. "Find my sister—if ye ken what's good for ye!"

Alexander MacLeod. Skyla's brother was fighting side by side with the MacKenzies. And there was John MacLeod of Dunvegan, her father, and her cousins, Gil and Rory McLeod.

Just a few yards away, Angus MacLean battled the English like some Viking berserker of old.

His wild red hair sprayed about him as, roaring like a bull-seal, he grabbed two of the Sassenachs by their hair and swung them in a wide arc, toward each other.

"For Mary!" he howled.

Their skulls slammed together with an audible crack.

As their eyes rolled back, he released them, then moved on to his next two victims.

Some of the Sassenachs took one horrified look at him, turned tail, and fled for their lives, spilling out into the nearby forest to hide.

Others climbed over the walls and jumped into the broad moat that surrounded the fortress, where many of them drowned, rather than face the giant Scot.

The English garrisoned at Fort Edward had numbered over a thousand before the battle for Stirling Bridge.

But now, their number had dwindled to half as many. Some had been lost to desertion, others slain. He estimated their number at approximately equal to those of his clan and the MacLeods combined.

Jamie had done the impossible, Gray thought, swallowing hard as he crossed the bailey, his weapon raised before him.

He had brought the Clans MacLeod and MacKenzie together under a common cause: Gray's and Skyla's lives!

Now it was up to him to get her out of harm's way, so that the risks their kinsmen had taken in coming here would not be in vain.

"My laird?"

"Angus." MacLean had followed him, he realized.

"The constable. Have ye found him yet, sir?"

He shook his head. "I didna try. My lady's safety comes first. Hartford can wait."

Angus grinned, wheezing like a blacksmith's bellows as he hurried after Gray.

"I'll help ye t'find her, sir! And when the lassie is safely away, I'll tend t'the constable, aye? I promised ma Mary, ye ken?"

Graham nodded. He would not want to be Hartford when Angus "tended" to him, he thought, rounding a murky corner . . .

. . . and almost slamming into the man.

"Gray!" Skyla cried out.

The constable grabbed her wrist and hauled her in front of him, his dagger pressed to her throat.

"Back away, Scot, or she dies—right before your eyes!"

"The devil ye say!" Skyla yelled.

Drawing back her elbow, she cracked the constable squarely on the nose!

As a former recipient of her blows, Gray could almost sympathize as bone crunched and blood poured.

As Hartford doubled over, Gray grabbed Skyla's wrist and growled, "Come on!"

"But . . . he'll get away!" Skyla panted, hanging back. "He canna go free, not after what he's done—"

Gray risked a glance over his shoulder, just as Angus cupped the Sassenach by the stones and gave them a none-too-gentle squeeze.

Hartford screamed.

"Och. Somehow, I dinna think he'll go free, lassie. Angus wants t'play wi' him first, aye? Now, come on—!"

Twenty-one

The awareness of how close they had come to losing each other gave their lovemaking an urgent edge that night, though they were safe in their chamber at Glenrowan. It was in sharp contrast to the dreamy tenderness that had followed their wedding.

"At last!" Graham breathed, leaning on the door the moment it had closed behind Mary and Angus and the MacLeod menfolk, which included Skyla's father. "I didna think they'd ever leave!"

"Nor I!"

Hauling her into his arms, he simply held

her to his chest, saying nothing for several seconds as he drank in the beloved sight, scent, and feel of her.

After coming so very close to losing her, he thought nothing had ever felt so precious.

His breathing was ragged, his hands unsteady with the force of his emotions as he dipped his head and crushed his mouth over hers.

He kissed her gently, tenderly at first, then with greater ardor.

No less eager, Skyla melted into his arms, molding her body to his. Yielding her lips, she gave back his kisses, measure for measure.

"I missed ye so, sweetheart," he told her after he tore his mouth from hers. "I feared I would never see nor hold ye again, and I couldna bear it."

"No more could I, my dearest love!" she confessed, unable to keep from smiling as she slipped her arms around him.

He kissed her again, this time thrusting his hand up her skirts and reaching between her thighs without breaking the kiss.

She moaned against his mouth.

"Aaah, lassie. Ye're sae sleek and hot," he whispered thickly. "Open your legs, ma doo. Let me feel ye, aye, sweet?"

His fingers slid deep inside her as he stroked her intimately, moving his hand in, then out, as if he were making love to her, until she could hardly breathe, let alone remain standing.

Her legs threatened to buckle, she was so aroused.

"Take me!" she pleaded. "Now! I canna wait. Ohhh, take me, do!"

The breath caught in her throat as he pushed the neck of her kirtle down, off her shoulders, with impatient hands.

She wore only her under-chemise beneath it.

Hooking his hand over the neck of it, he tugged.

The gauzy cloth ripped clear to the waist, baring her body.

Uttering a strangled oath, he filled his eyes, then his hands with her treasures, before leading her to their bed. Gently pushing her down, he followed her.

His hungry lips roamed everywhere, tasting each part of her. Eager hands caressed each curve and plane.

She surrendered utterly, writhing as his tongue danced over her burning skin. Clawing at the pallet beneath her as he ducked his head and loved her with tongue and lips.

Her smoky eyes were heavy-lidded, smoldering with desire as she knotted her fingers in his thick black hair.

"Now!" she urged as he rose to loom over her.

She bit his ear lobe, his throat, before darting her wet tongue deep into his ear. "My dear laird! *Hurry!*"

She embraced him, running her hands over the warm skin of his broad back. Gooseflesh prickled at her feather-light touch; then a muscle jumped in response as her fingers trailed lower.

Boldly, she reached beneath the heavy plaid of his breachan, to squeeze his buttocks. To stroke his powerful thighs—and that part of him that gave her greatest pleasure.

He sucked in a breath, his vivid blue eyes dark now with lust.

"Och, but ye're a wicked lass," he murmured thickly, nipping her ear as her fingers gently squeezed his manhood. "T'make so bold and free with yer father and brothers under the same roof as yersel'! But I wouldna change ye for the world!"

"If I'm wicked, my laird," she murmured demurely, her voice as low and throaty as a purring cat's, her smoky eyes slitted with desire, "then so are you. Are ye not?"

"How so?" he demanded playfully, grinning.

She eyed him archly. "Because *this* has nothing t'do with creation, since I already carry your bairn in my belly. So, it must be what the priests are always calling the 'sins of the flesh'—and ye ken full well what they say about that!"

He looked startled for a moment at her news, then kissed her thoroughly. "I do. But ... I willna tell if you dinna."

"For shame, sir! Ye must certainly confess tonight's wickedness at your next confession," she told him in a stern tone. "Along with your other many transgressions."

He chuckled and reached between her legs, grinning at the honeyed welcome he found there. Her flesh was more than ready for sinning, by his reckoning.

"And what about this, ma wee wanton? Shall I confess this, too? Or shall you?"

She giggled. "One of us must, I suppose, though I wager smoke will pour from Father Andrew's ears when we tell him!"

They both laughed.

"Now. Lie back, husband," she urged softly. Her body was pale-pink perfection in the shadows as she knelt alongside him. "I've a mind to welcome my laird home in ma own special fashion," she added huskily.

"Aye? And what special fashion is that, ma doo?"

"Ye'll see, sir, soon enough."

And see he did.

Desire. It was as potent as mead, as heady as

343

wine, she thought as she pressed her lips to his chest, his belly, and then to the ropy, newly formed ridge of scar where his powerful thigh met his torso.

She rested her head there, her fingers tracing the long angry wound.

"A wee bit more t'the left, and there would have been no homecoming, not for me. And certainly none of this kind," he said, gazing deep into her eyes.

He sucked in a shuddery breath as her mouth traveled lower.

" 'Twas my—aaah!—'twas my good fortune the narwhal's—aah!—horn deflected the lance the Sassenach threw at me."

"Aye. And 'twas *our* good fortune," she murmured seductively, "that ye didna lose *this* lance completely."

He gritted his teeth and groaned in sheer pleasure as she took him in her mouth, sheathing him in velvety heat and pleasure.

He was still reeling when, only moments later, she knelt astride his flanks.

His manhood vanished, sheathed to the hilt in her loveliness.

Lifting her hair up over her head, so that ringlets spilled in wanton strands between her fingers, she began to undulate her hips, rising and falling in an ancient erotic rhythm that made the sweat spring out on his brow in glistening beads.

Her rosy breasts quivered as she rode him. Both puckered nipples grew ruby hard and acutely sensitive.

No longer content to simply lie there without touching her, he placed a hand over each firm mound and rolled the rosy peaks between his fingers. Then he strummed the tiny nubbin between her thighs.

"Aaah!" Her head fell back. Her eyes closed. Her lips parted on a blissful moan of delight.

Another heartbeat, and he felt fluttery pulses squeezing his shaft as she reached her release.

"My turn, lassie," he rasped thickly. Rising from the pallet, he bore her down beneath him.

Anchoring her legs about his waist, he pinned her hands above her head and covered her softly curved body with his own.

He drove into her, until the powerful thrusts of his flanks pushed them both over the edge.

With a roar of triumph, he spent himself deep inside her. Aftershocks rippled through him like tiny explosions.

He was shuddering as he fell to the bed beside her. His heart still hammered as drew her tenderly into his arms and kissed her.

"Look, out there!" he murmured. "Do ye see what I see?"

She looked in the direction he was pointing and saw, through the narrow latchet, the lovely evening star.

It shone as bright as any diamond against the midnight sky.

A sleepy, contented smile curved her lips as she snuggled up to him, her hand pressed lightly to her belly, protecting its promise of new life to come.

God willing, this was only the first in a lifetime of such times. Drowsy· moments after making love when they would see *their* evening star as they had seen it the very first time from the battlements of Glenrowan:

Together.

"So joined by love are we, now joined forevermore shall be." She whispered the words, linking her fingers through his.

"It's supposed to be 'joined by blood are we,' " he murmured.

"I know," she said with a sigh. "Does it matter?"

"I dinna think so."

Twenty-two

Spring came early to the highlands in the Year of Our Lord 1298.

Everywhere she turned, Skyla saw evidence of the wonder of creation, and the beauty of new life. It was not surprising to her that in earlier times, the pagan feast of Beltane—the feast of new birth and fertility—had been celebrated in the month of May.

She saw evidence of that fertility everywhere. In the woolly lambs that gamboled after their mothers up on the shielings. In the new calves and colts who tottered about on stiff legs, whisking their tails.

She saw it in the baby rabbits that appeared from their warrens after sunset, and heard it in the chirps of fluffy chicks tucked in their hedgerow nests.

But by far the greatest evidence of the season's fecundity, to her thinking, was her own burgeoning belly! She had grown enormous, for all that she had yet another month before her babe was born.

And that month might well pass like a lifetime, Skyla thought wearily, kneading the small of her back and wincing over yet another nagging pain.

She and Gray had gone to the Isle of Skye to visit her family and share the Beltane festivities with them there.

A brace of servants had accompanied them, as had Morag, the midwife.

However, unsettled by rumors that Edward of England was planning to march north into Scotland in the spring or summer of the year, burning towns and villages as he came, Gray had decided they would cut short their stay and return to Glenrowan a little earlier than planned, to prepare the keep and the clan for that possibility.

Gray was concerned, too, by the occasional pangs Skyla was having, despite Morag's assurances that this was common in the last weeks of childbearing, especially for women carrying their first bairns.

Uncomfortable with her enormous belly and eager to be back home at Glenrowan, in her own chambers, Skyla had been unusually quick to agree.

They had made their farewells to her lady mother, her father, her sisters, and her brother, then set off soon after matins in Dunvegan's chapel. Everyone had gone down to the water gate to bid them good-bye and wave farewell as they piled into dories for the brief sail across the glassy strait to Lochalsh.

From there, they had continued their home-ward journey with Skyla perched sidesaddle upon the broad back of an ancient gelding, led at a sedate walk by young Hamish, the groom.

Gray rode at her side, while her old nurse Moira—grumbling all the while—followed after them, mounted on a donkey.

Morag, the midwife, had elected to walk. She did so, using a knobbly staff to help her along.

As the leagues fell away behind them, and Glenrowan grew closer, the little party made frequent halts for Skyla to stretch her legs and aching back and to relieve herself—something she had to do more and more often of late.

It was a glorious spring day. A haze of purple heather broke the green of the rolling moors.

Between outcroppings of somber black granite, vivid harebells made gay splashes of bonny blue. Bright yellow blossoms showed, even from a distance, where the gorse and broom were in full flower, filling the air with musky scents.

On the Isle of Skye, and even here, in the Highlands, there were those who still kept the old ways, and followed the Wheel of Life as it spun, from Beltane to Samhaim, as had their ancestors.

At Dunvegan, from her chamber window slit, she had seen orange bonfires blazing from the highest hills on Beltane Eve, and had known that those who celebrated the spring solstice were leaping through it, naked, as was the custom.

She knew, too, that many of the young men and women from the croft houses had gone a-Maying in the woods that same evening, for she had seen the flower garlands they had gathered by moonlight, adorning Dunvegan's great hall the following morn.

Had she not been so heavily with child, she'd thought that morn, eyeing Graham over the heads of the others, she and her husband might have gone into the woods together, and done as so many other couples did, whether married or nay, by the Goddess's silvery light!

Gray's sensual grin, a certain kindling in his

eyes, had betrayed that he was thinking the same thing.

And so, blushing, she had quickly looked elsewhere.

Moira, her old nurse, had herself confessed to going out into the May dawn and washing her face in the morning dew, for it was said that by doing so, any woman could recapture her youthful beauty. It could only help her efforts to attract a husband, she'd said.

"After all, you and yer sisters dinna need yer old nurse anymore, do ye, hinnie?" she had said pointedly, eyeing Skyla's belly.

Not surprisingly, it had taken little persuading to convince Moira to return with them to Glenrowan, to become nurse to their child.

It was midday, and they had crossed the borders onto Glenrowan land, when Skyla realized that the flickering pains in her back had grown steadily stronger, rather than weakening.

She could not go on—and nor could she perch upon this horse another moment!

When she whispered as much to Morag, the old woman was quick to call a halt.

"The auld broch is nearby," Graham suggested, his expression concerned. "We'll take her there. At least ye will be dry and out of the wind and the rain, if the weather should turn," he promised his wife.

"You, Hamish. Go ahead to Glenrowan," he

told the groom, handing him the reins of Skyla's horse. "Bring back a cart, blankets, fresh straw—whatever is needed. Mistress Mary will know what t'send with ye. And laddie?"

"Sir?"

"*Hurry!*"

The broch was a tall stone tower, built long before any man or woman living at Glenrowan, or even their mothers, grandmothers, or great-grandmothers could remember.

Its double walls held small cells, like a honeycomb, Skyla thought, though for what purpose such a place had been built, she could only imagine.

There was a well at its heart that still provided sweet water, Gray claimed.

He said the broch's original purpose had been as a lookout point. A high spot from which the local chieftains could see an enemy advancing on them from a considerable distance. And, thanks to its ready supply of drinking water, a number of men could withstand even a lengthy siege within its walls.

Bidding the women wait, Graham strode inside, disturbing a number of bats that hung there, their leathery wings folded.

They flapped blindly out into the daylight to escape him.

There was a barn owl, too. Its round, unblinking golden eyes followed his movements from, one of the upper galleries, its white body and white wings ghostly in the shadows.

Once his eyes had adjusted to the gloom, he spread his plaid over the hard-packed earthen floor. His breachan would do for his wife to lie upon, until Hamish returned with the soft straw he'd requested. He looked about him, but there was nothing he could use to soften her bed.

He shook his head. This humble, ancient broch was not where he would have chosen for his beloved to give birth to their bairn, but the babe's imminent arrival left them without choices. His lassie could not go on. She was exhausted.

The pains continued off and on for the remainder of that day, and on throughout the night, increasing in severity and duration as night crawled slowly into dawn of the second day.

Shortly after sunrise, her water broke with a great splash, soaking the breachan, which was quickly replaced by a thick layer of the soft, fresh straw Hamish had returned with.

There seemed more purpose to her pangs after that. She sensed that the child was eager to be born. Determined.

Her enormous belly surged beneath her palms, rising almost to a peak with every pang.

The pain was so intense now, and of such duration, it seemed she must surely burst in two—like a ripe pumpkin left too long on the earth, she thought.

At Morag's urging, she twisted her hands in the leather thongs the midwife had hastily fashioned and looped around a wooden pillar.

"Did ye slip a blade beneath the straw?" Skyla asked anxiously, sweat beading her face as another pang stabbed through her. "Is it there t'cut the pain?"

"Aye, lovie, aye," Morag crooned, brushing damp hair off her brow. "Never fear. 'Twill not be long now. When the next pang comes, bear down as hard as ye can, aye?"

It was no longer a matter of choice, Skyla thought grimly as the next pang hit, hard and long. Her entire being strained to bring forth the child inside her. To push it out into the world, and have an end to the relentless waves of pain that seemed to build, one upon the other.

But although her face turned crimson with the effort, the bairn would not leave his warm, dark nest and slip easily into the world.

"Get up, lassie. Walk about," Morag encouraged her.

"Walking will help it," Moira agreed. "Come along, now, my wee chick. I ken ye're weary,

354

but ye've work t'do yet. On your feet. Aye, that's the way, my good brave lass."

Kneading her lower back, Skyla rose clumsily to her feet and waddled the length of the chamber like some huge, ungainly goose, holding her back and moaning softly.

She was exhausted. From where would she draw the necessary strength to push their son out?

All last night and most of the previous day she had labored, and there was still no end to it in sight, despite Morag and Moira's insistence that it would soon be over.

Perhaps they were but trying to comfort her? Perhaps her child would never be delivered?

No sooner had that frightening prospect entered her mind than a searing pain sliced through her, centering between her thighs.

She cried out and clutched her belly, cradling it as if she cradled the child itself.

"Where is my husband?" she whispered through cracked lips.

"Where else should the puir mon be, but outside, and pacing?" Morag replied, shaking her head.

"Please. I would see him."

"Better ye wait a wee bit, my lady. Men have no stomach for birthing."

"Nevertheless, fetch him. Please."

"As ye will, my lady."

There was both love and fear in Gray's eyes when he came in to her. Great fear that he would lose her to this difficult birthing. Great love that she would endure all this to give his child—their child—life.

For his sake, she forced a wan smile.

"Your son is not impulsive like his mother and father. He chooses t'bide his time," she explained breathlessly, trying to smile and reassure him between her pains.

Gray nodded as he knelt on the straw beside her.

"My son takes after his Uncle Jamie, no doubt. A shrewd and cautious fellow, if ever I've seen one! How are ye fairing, ma doo?" he murmured, tenderly swabbing her face with a damp cloth he took from Morag.

Pressing an earthenware mug of watered wine to her cracked lips, he held it while she sipped.

"I would be better were this over and done with," she admitted frankly, licking her dry lips when she was done drinking her fill. "And our babe at my breast."

"Is all as it should be?" he asked the midwife in a low aside.

"Och, aye. 'Tis slow but sure, my laird, as are most first birthings, aye? The oldest child is always the slowest being born. Go back t'yer fire, sir, where ye belong," Morag urged, her dark eyes twinkling.

Gray shook his head.

"Nay. I will stay, and see my son come into this world," he murmured, lifting Skyla's hand to his lips and kissing it.

They both started as Skyla made a sudden tremendous grunting sound. Releasing Gray's hand, she grasped the thongs with all her might, and bore down. Her face contorted, turning almost livid with effort.

Morag hurried to kneel at her feet. Moira hovered at her side, holding linen swaddling cloths in readiness for the impatient little one who had decided to make an early entrance into the world—and was now taking his time in doing so.

"Ahh! He comes!" Skyla panted.

"Push, lovie. Aye, and again—yea! Another breath—bear down—that's it, that's the way! That's my lassie! Och, there's his wee head. I see it, dark as his sire's! Another push will do it!"

A small shriek escaped Skyla as the baby's head finally emerged from her body. The rest of its body soon followed, sliding smoothly into Morag's waiting hands like a slippery, bloody salmon sliding into the net.

"A bonny daughter, my laird!" Morag declared, wiping the baby's face and beaming. " 'Tis a girl."

"Ho! A lassie!" Graham crowed with a glad shout and a broad grin as his red-faced little daughter's first wails filled the galleries of the ancient broch, growing steadily more strident.

"Shoo, shoo, ma wee lassie! Yer da's here. Och, listen to her sing, ma doo! Ye've yer mother's temper, dearling!" he murmured. Taking the tiny red-faced infant from the midwife, he planted a kiss upon her brow and on her tiny rosebud lips.

She squealed like a piglet in protest and screwed up her face, squirming about.

Graham laughed, plainly delighted, unable to take his eyes off his "wee lassie."

"A girl!" Skyla exclaimed. "Has she all her toes and fingers? Is she perfect? Is she bonny? Oh, let me see her, do!"

Laughing, Gray carried the bairn over to her weary mother, and placed their little daughter on Skyla's breast. "As sonsy as the morning, and every inch as perfect as her mam. Here she is, my love. Our daughter."

Never had Skyla looked more beautiful to him than she did right then, with their first bairn nestled in the crook of her arm, one breast bared for their wee daughter's first suckling.

"You're not disappointed? That we have a daughter, instead of a son, I mean?" Skyla asked anxiously, looking up at him.

But before her husband could answer her, she suddenly doubled over, gasping as her belly clenched in yet another pain.

"Morag? What is it? What's happening to me?"

" 'Tis but the afterbirth coming, my lovie. Your body must expel it. 'Twill soon be done with. A few wee pains—"

"*Wee?*" Skyla blew out a breath, shaking her head as she panted. "Pheeew! That last was as strong as the birth pains!" she exclaimed with a questioning glance at Morag, who frowned.

"Nurse, take the bairn, will ye?" the midwife urged suddenly.

She was not a moment too soon, for even as the nurse swept the babe from her mother's arms, Skyla gave another great shout.

In only a moment or two, a second dark head appeared between her bloody thighs.

"Dear Lord in Heaven, 'tis *twins*!" Moira exclaimed, taken aback.

"Another lassie?" Gray asked.

The midwife grasped the infant by both ankles and held it up in one hand, slapping its wee buttocks with the other.

"Nay, my laird. 'Tis no lassie, this time—not with those stones between his legs! Ye have a fine lad!" she declared, beaming.

The baby sputtered, then began to cry just as lustily as his sister had done moments before.

"Well!" Skyla declared, falling back, exhausted,

359

to the straw to await the delivery of the after-births as Morag cut their son's cord.

Skyla was wearing a smug smile.

"What is it?" Graham asked. "Ye look like the wee kit that swallowed the cream!"

"Your uncles can have no complaints this time. They wanted an heir for Glenrowan from me in the first year of our marriage, and an heir they have.

"How's that for a 'shrewish MacLeod,' hmm?" She smiled up at him. "I've given ye not one, but *two* bairns, my laird. A tom *and* a betty!"

Graham nodded, his expression fond as he stroked her damp hair.

"That ye have, my lass—and so much more! Though I've a mind t'christen the wee laddie Adam after my father, rather than Thomas. And what say ye t'Elise for our wee lass, instead of Betty?"

Glenrowan was ablaze with the light of torches and candles when the cart bearing Skyla and their bairns rattled across the causeway and into the bailey.

Yet despite the lateness of the hour, the people of Glenrowan had come from far and wide to welcome their lady home.

Love for the Clan Mackenzie swelled Skyla's heart as Gray lifted her into his arms amidst their people's cheers and good wishes for her health, and exclamations of delight over the twins.

"My thanks to all of you, good people of Glenrowan! God bless you all!" she called to them over her husband's shoulder as he carried her inside. Morag and Moira followed, each bearing a swaddled infant.

"Slainte!" cried one fellow, raising his mug. "Good health, long life, and happiness to our laird and lady, and t'their bonny bairns. God bless 'em all!"

And so, the Wheel of Life spun on, she thought as Gray bore her up to her chamber, where she would spend the weeks of the lying-in.

Only a few months ago, she had faced death, and imprisonment, and losing Gray. But now, against all odds, they were together again, their family enriched by the birth of two precious babes, Adam and Elise.

Who knew what the future might bring them tomorrow, or the day after? No one knew how the Wheel of Life would spin, or where it would stop.

There was only one thing of which she was certain. That whatever the future might hold for them, she and Gray would stand side by side, and meet it together. Man and woman. Husband and wife. Laird and lady.

Graham and Skyla!

Theirs was a love that would withstand the tests of time and the trials of adversity.

A love that, like the sweetest ballad, would endure forever.

For, like a beautiful Highland song, it lived on in Highland hearts.

KEEPER OF MY Heart

PENELOPE NERI

Morgan St. James is by far the most virile man Miranda Tallant has ever seen and she realizes at once that this man is no ordinary lighthouse keeper. But while she does not know if he has come to investigate her family's smuggling or if he truly has been disinherited, one glance at his emerald-dark eyes promises her untold nights of desire. Bent on discovering the blackguards responsible for his friend's death, Morgan doesn't expect to be caught up in the stormy sea of Miranda Tallant's turquoise eyes. The lovely widow consumes his every waking thought and his every dream with an all-encompassing passion. For while he cannot abandon his duty to his friend and his family, he knows that he can not rest until Miranda's heart is his.

___4647-4 $5.99 US/$6.99 CAN

Dorchester Publishing Co., Inc.
P.O. Box 6640
Wayne, PA 19087-8640

Please add $1.75 for shipping and handling for the first book and $.50 for each book thereafter. NY, NYC, and PA residents, please add appropriate sales tax. No cash, stamps, or C.O.D.s. All orders shipped within 6 weeks via postal service book rate. Canadian orders require $2.00 extra postage and must be paid in U.S. dollars through a U.S. banking facility.

Name_____

Address_____

City_____ State_____ Zip_____

I have enclosed $_____ in payment for the checked book(s).

Payment <u>must</u> accompany all orders. ❑ Please send a free catalog.

CHECK OUT OUR WEBSITE! www.dorchesterpub.com

The Sorcerer's Lady

DEBRA DIER

Victorian debutante Laura Sullivan can't believe her eyes. Aunt Sophie's ancient spell has conjured up the man of Laura's dreams—and deposited a half-naked barbarian in the library of her Boston home. With his bare chest and sheathed broadsword, the golden giant is a tempting study in Viking maleness, but hardly the proper blue blood Laura is supposed to marry. An accomplished sorcerer, Connor has traveled through the ages to reach his soul mate, the bewitching woman who captured his heart. But Beacon Hill isn't ninth-century Ireland, and Connor's powers are useless if he can't convince Laura that love is stronger than magic and that she is destined to become the sorcerer's lady.

___52305-1 $5.50 US/$6.50 CAN

Dorchester Publishing Co., Inc.
P.O. Box 6640
Wayne, PA 19087-8640

Please add $1.75 for shipping and handling for the first book and $.50 for each book thereafter. NY, NYC, and PA residents, please add appropriate sales tax. No cash, stamps, or C.O.D.s. All orders shipped within 6 weeks via postal service book rate. Canadian orders require $2.00 extra postage and must be paid in U.S. dollars through a U.S. banking facility.

Name_____
Address_____
City_____State_____Zip_____
I have enclosed $_____ in payment for the checked book(s).
Payment <u>must</u> accompany all orders. ❑ Please send a free catalog.
CHECK OUT OUR WEBSITE! www.dorchesterpub.com

DEBRA DIER

SHADOW OF THE STORM

He is her dashing childhood hero, the man to whom she will willingly surrender her innocence in a night of blazing ecstasy. But when Ian Tremayne cruelly abandons her after a bitter misunderstanding, Sabrina O'Neill vows to have revenge on the handsome Yankee. But the virile Tremayne is more than ready for the challenge. Together, they will enter a high-stakes game of deadly illusion and sizzling desire that will shatter Sabrina's well-crafted facade.

___4397-1 $5.99 US/$6.99 CAN

Dorchester Publishing Co., Inc.
P.O. Box 6640
Wayne, PA 19087-8640

Please add $1.75 for shipping and handling for the first book and $.50 for each book thereafter. NY, NYC, and PA residents, please add appropriate sales tax. No cash, stamps, or C.O.D.s. All orders shipped within 6 weeks via postal service book rate. Canadian orders require $2.00 extra postage and must be paid in U.S. dollars through a U.S. banking facility.

Name_____
Address_____
City_____ State_____ Zip_____
I have enclosed $_____ in payment for the checked book(s).
Payment <u>must</u> accompany all orders. ❑ Please send a free catalog.
CHECK OUT OUR WEBSITE! www.dorchesterpub.com